"Are you Married?"

"You certainly get right to the point, don't you?" Vanessa said.

"I think it's a good idea to get preliminaries out of the way. Wouldn't want to stagger into any big obstacles later on."

"Later on?" Vanessa's eyes filled with question.

"I know what I like right off the bat. I think most men do. When we're beating around the bush and talking about how uncertain we are . . . it's just that. Talk."

"Really," Vanessa replied.

"Yes." Xavier looked into her eyes. "I have the feeling you're the kind of woman I've been looking for all my life."

The air around them suddenly felt warmer. "Now that's quite a line," Vanessa replied.

"I'm too old and busy for lines, Vanessa."

"So you're serious?"

"Very. I can't remember a time when I've been so certain."

Other Avon Books by
Eboni Snoe

WISHIN' ON A STAR
CHANCE ON LOVIN' YOU
TELL ME I'M DREAMIN'

EBONI SNOE

Followin' A Dream

AVON BOOKS

An Imprint of HarperCollinsPublishers

AVON BOOKS
An Imprint of HarperCollins*Publishers*
10 East 53rd Street
New York, New York 10022-5299

Copyright © 2001 by Eboni Snoe
ISBN: 0-380-81396-3
www.avonromance.com

First Avon Books paperback printing: July 2001

Avon Trademark Reg. U.S. Pat. Off. and in Other Countries, Marca Registrada, Hecho en U.S.A.
HarperCollins ® is a trademark of HarperCollins Publishers Inc.

Printed in the U.S.A.

10 9 8 7 6 5 4 3 2 1

For all parents and children
who have weathered the storm
of a difficult relationship and found
unconditional love

prologue

Columbus, Georgia
July, 2000

The folding chair cut into Vanessa Bradley's shoulder blades as she scanned the bare room. Her gaze lingered at the door. It wasn't too late to change her mind. She could get up, walk out . . . but Vanessa knew that was no solution. Her life had been so empty she wanted to know if the emptiness was permanent.

Vanessa's long skirt tightened about her legs as she crossed her feet beneath the card table. Maybe empty was too drastic a word. Life in general was a steady status quo sprinkled with work, volunteering, and the daily human dramas in the neighborhood where she grew up. There had been nothing to truly move her since the day her father died two years ago. Vanessa longed for excitement, that special spark that made life wondrous. Anything that could reassure her that at thirty-three she had not crossed over but hadn't been told.

"I'm ready when you are." The palm reader's voice cut into her self-examination.

Vanessa looked at the woman's palm, which rested on the table. Slowly she placed her hand within it. It was only a game, Vanessa told herself. One that she had launched on an emotional whim. This woman, Dellia, could not really tell her future by looking at the curves and lines of her hand. Or could she? Vanessa studied the woman's mole-splattered features as if she were the visionary, as a distant memory of her parents returning from China surfaced. Her mother had once told her that some Chinese fortune-tellers read the moles on a person's face like a palm reader reads the human hand.

"You have a very nice hand." Dellia slid her palm across Vanessa's as if to wipe away any ambiguity. "The lines are very clear."

"I guess that's good." Vanessa waited for a schmoozing affirmation.

"Perhaps," Dellia said slowly. "Your life line is very long." She followed the groove with the tip of her finger until it joined another that wrapped around Vanessa's wrist.

"You had a rather solitary childhood." Dellia analyzed the lines and the mounds of Vanessa's palm. "It's not something you would have preferred, but you dealt with it well. You found solace in the world of books."

Vanessa suddenly stiffened. She looked at the

top of Dellia's head as the woman leaned over the table. Vanessa wanted to say, *Yes I did have a lonely childhood, and I loved to read*, but she decided against it. She wanted to find out if Dellia's remark was simply a lucky guess.

Silence filled the room, as if Dellia was waiting for feedback, but Vanessa had predetermined she wouldn't give up any information. She would allow the psychic to do her job. Nevertheless she found herself looking at her own palm with renewed interest.

"Were you close to your father?" Dellia looked deep into Vanessa's eyes.

Vanessa looked down. "Close enough."

"He really liked his work." Dellia drew out the sentence, as if she was reaching for something. "You're the creative type. Did you pursue a career that would nourish that part of you?"

"Ha! I don't think my mother would agree with you there." Vanessa almost laughed. "I create all right. I write computer code. My mother writes poetry." The comparison was obvious in her tone. "But my job keeps me stationary."

"That's a rather interesting thing to say," Dellia replied.

"But it does. I know what I'm going to do today, tomorrow, the next day. I know *where* I'm going to be."

"Unlike your father?" Dellia asked.

Vanessa looked her straight in the eye and nodded. Dellia had unknowingly pushed one of her buttons. Or had it been done on purpose?

Dellia paused before she spoke again. "There's some unresolved issues between the two of you. Your mother was, and somehow still is, caught in between." Dellia squeezed Vanessa's hand. "Your father has made his transition, hasn't he?"

"Transition?" Vanessa was confused.

"Your father has passed away," Dellia replied softly.

Vanessa's eyes widened. She could feel her heartbeat speed up. *How did this woman know that?* "He died two years ago. That's when I moved back home with my mother. She asked me to."

"Your life changed quite drastically after that move." Dellia cocked her head as she repositioned Vanessa's palm.

"Yes, it did. I had been living in Atlanta until then." Vanessa forgot her decision to let Dellia do the talking. "I had a few friends. Women and men. But I was a late bloomer when it came to guys, so . . . there had been a few relationships but nothing serious." Vanessa's brows furrowed. "I always had the need to stand up to them, to make sure my point was taken seriously. And I found out most men don't want to deal with that." She gave a perfunctory smile. "But I can tell you that was something I should have known, growing up with my mother and father." Vanessa's face saddened.

Dellia waited for her to continue.

"I don't know." Vanessa shook her head to find the right words. "My dad always appeared to be so invincible. I guess I expected him to live forever. But when he died and I saw how bad my mom was taking it, I kind of stuck close to home once I moved back." Vanessa sighed. "Then before I knew it, one week had turned into half a year, and then it's a year and a half. All this time I'm gaining weight eating my mother's cooking. But life is kind of a blob," Vanessa stated comfortably, now that she was almost convinced there was something to the art of palmistry.

"The man in your life keeps things pretty exciting," Dellia said. "As a matter of fact he confuses you. But don't worry, it's early in the relationship." Dellia pressed her thumb into the center of Vanessa's hand. "Everything will clear up with time."

"I don't have a man in my life." So much for the art of palmistry.

"You don't?" Dellia said with disbelief.

"No."

"Well he must be very near." Dellia tapped the center of Vanessa's hand. "His influence is very clear at this stage of your life. He will be instrumental in the healing of a long-term wound that you have suppressed." Dellia paused. "But there will also be love. A deep, tempestuous love."

Wound? What kind of wound? Vanessa felt a tinge of apprehension. "Well . . . like I said, there is no man in my life and there haven't been any prospects for at least two years."

"These things happen suddenly," Dellia persisted.

"I don't trust big bang relationships," Vanessa announced, her trust in Dellia gone.

" 'Big bang'?" Dellia repeated.

"Yes. The big bang. You meet someone and all of a sudden you can't drink, eat, sleep . . . nothing. You end up trying to function out of deprivation. Which is impossible. So when all the red flags start waving, telling you the man of your dreams is a jerk, your perspective is so screwed up you don't even acknowledge them."

"Obviously, this has happened to you," Dellia stated.

"Now you're putting words in my mouth. I didn't say that." Vanessa shook her head. "I've seen others go through it and I know it's not for me."

"I understand." Dellia traced another line. "You do have an issue with control."

"I've got what?" Vanessa looked at the palmist beneath furrowed brows. "I think *you* may have. You're the psychic, and you obviously have the whole thing about a man and a relationship wrong."

"I'm not looking for a confrontation," Dellia replied. "But it's okay." She patted Vanessa's hand. "You've got so much penned up inside of you, you can't help but explode from time to time."

Vanessa's mouth dropped open. "I think I've heard enough. Thank you." She withdrew her hand and stood up. "How much do I owe you?"

Dellia sat back and eyed Vanessa quietly. "You

do have an issue with control, Ms. Bradley. I don't know exactly why, but it has something to do with your childhood. There was something you wanted to control but you couldn't. Your parents are involved somehow. Your father in particular. And the man I spoke of, if he is not in your life now, he *will* come. He will stir up all the feelings and issues that you need to address in your life." Dellia made circular motions with her hands, then held her fingertips together. "Somehow the two of you will aid each other in the healing of deep wounds." Her eyes filled with compassion. "It is because of these wounds that you will be drawn together. Like two opposing magnets." Dellia placed her palms together. "Your paths will cross in what appear to be uncanny ways, but it will simply be what was destined to happen. It will be wonderful, yet . . . both of you will have to learn to let go of your fears. And if you give it all you have, Ms. Bradley, you'll gain the world. If you don't"—she paused—"your life will be a mere shadow of what it is, even now." Dellia stood up. "I hope I have helped you." She offered Vanessa a handshake. "Good-bye."

Vanessa had had one eyebrow raised during Dellia's speech. She looked at the outstretched hand. "So how much do I owe you?"

"The fee for a half hour is thirty dollars, but I don't expect you to pay me if you are not satisfied."

"You're joking?" Vanessa looked into the woman's warm brown eyes.

"No. I don't take a gift such as mine lightly."

"Maybe you don't, but surely you can't make a living doing readings this way." Vanessa studied Dellia with renewed interest.

"I do make a living," Dellia assured her. "But not doing this. I came into this business because I had a gift to share, not to milk susceptible people out of their money. I only do readings on weekends. Most people from my day job would never expect to find me here. This is my way of serving."

"I see." Vanessa hesitated a moment, then reached inside her purse and gave Dellia the money. "Thank you." She smiled slightly. "Although this didn't turn out like I expected, I am satisfied."

"Good." Dellia looked deep into Vanessa's eyes. "Trusting yourself and those you love will be very important as the days go by. You'll be in a definite flow. Don't fight it. The people and the circumstances are your destiny."

one

"And the Volunteer of the Year is—" the emcee stalled. "Xavier Johnson."

"Xavier Johnson," Vanessa echoed through stiffened lips. *The Volunteer of the Year is a man?* Several claps late, Vanessa scanned the auditorium as she joined in the applause. Then she spotted him.

"Have mercy," Miss Bea leaned over and whispered. "The thoughts that kind of man brings to mind."

Vanessa kept her eyes straight ahead. "I'm not taking you anywhere else with me. I tell you, without Mama around, I can't keep up with you."

"If I was fifty years *your* junior I wouldn't admit that." Miss Bea shook her gray head. "And your mama doesn't have anything to do with my having good taste and fairly good eyesight. What this proves is you have no idea what your mama and I talk about." She smiled slyly. "I can't help it if he reminds me of a man I knew long, long ago."

Vanessa watched Xavier Johnson approach the stage. He walked with confidence, but there was an air of humility about him. Vanessa had to admit Miss Bea was right. This Xavier rang all the bells and that puzzled Vanessa. He didn't look like the type who'd be involved with the list of things the speaker had rattled off. Teaching adults how to read. Mentoring young boys. Volunteering his time at a battered women's and children's shelter. During Vanessa's six years of doing volunteer work, a man had never won an award. She had surmised most volunteers were women. As a matter of fact, Vanessa couldn't recall ever seeing a man's signature on any correspondence she had received from the charities and organizations, and no men attended the meetings. Which was what she expected. She had concluded that most men with any kind of drive were basically like her father had been . . . a workaholic who didn't know how to balance his personal life and his work.

She was interested to hear Xavier's speech as he took the plaque from the presenter's hands and stood in front of the podium. He eased a hand into his pants pocket, and one side of his dark, well-fitted suit jacket slid back, revealing a pristine white shirt.

"If you've ever seen the Academy Awards I know you've heard something like this said over and over again," Xavier began. "And at this moment I'm about as proud as someone who has received an Oscar, because this award means so much to me. Helping people realize and reach their potential is worth all the time I can give and more." Xavier paused. "Thank you." He smiled slightly. "Thank you very much." He stepped back and walked off the stage to thundering applause.

"See, I like that." Miss Bea leaned over again. "Short and sweet. Not like that other woman. I thought she was going to preach a sermon." She clapped a little louder. "We want everybody to have their moment but"—Miss Bea made a face—"that doesn't mean we want to hear them talk all night." Her voice rose above the applause. "I hate that your mama didn't get to come. She would have been right in her element in all of this. You know there's nothing Jackie Bradley loves better than dressing up and showing off. Maybe writing poetry ranks up there. But first and foremost your mother is a number one show-off."

"I know," Vanessa replied. "But the doctor threatened he'd put her in the hospital if she didn't follow his instructions to the tee, and that meant staying at home tonight."

"Oo-o, I don't think I've ever seen a woman with the flu so mad. Jackie was livid," Miss Bea continued loudly despite the dying applause. "And I guess you've noticed since your father died, she doesn't want anybody telling her what to do."

Several heads turned toward Vanessa and Miss Bea.

"Yeah, I've noticed," Vanessa replied in a softer manner. "And don't worry, they're going to sell videotapes of the program. I'll make sure I buy one so Mama can see the whole thing."

"We'll end this program with one more performance by the City Wide choir," the emcee announced as the singers filed onto the stage behind her. "But we want all of you to go next door to the reception and enjoy the fine spread we have for you. It's a small token for a job well done. Enjoy and . . . good evening."

The music began, and a very talented young man broke out in song. Before the number was over, the entire crowd was on their feet clapping and moving.

"There is nothing that can touch you like a good choir," Miss Bea declared as the music died away.

"I totally agree with you," Vanessa replied as the curtain closed and the attendees began to move out of their rows. Minutes later Vanessa and Miss Bea were in the reception area, where several tables placed in the center of the room bowed with an assortment of hot and cold dishes, breads, and desserts.

"Now this is the way to do it," Miss Bea said, her eyes gleaming. "You have the program late in the afternoon, and you feed everybody afterwards just like this." She looked at her watch. "And it's not too late to eat. Six-thirty is a good

time to fill up," Miss Bea advised no one in particular.

They ambled along, synchronizing with the
slow motion of the crowd. When Vanessa and
Miss Bea reached the buffet tables, they chatted as
they made their selections. Their plates were
quite full by the time they reached the desserts.

"Is that all you gone get?" Miss Bea stared at
the small piece of chocolate cake on Vanessa's
plate.

"This is all I need," Vanessa replied. "I've been
gaining a little weight lately."

"Pleez." Miss Bea pursed her lips, then her expression changed. "I've got a good idea." She
looked at Vanessa's plate. "You've got room for a
couple more pieces." Miss Bea started stacking
cake on Vanessa's plate. "I want to take some of
this dessert to the house for the card party."

Vanessa started to protest, but she decided that
at eighty-two all women should be able to have
whatever they desired, and if Miss Bea wanted to
take cake to her lifelong friends, Vanessa didn't
mind helping her.

"Put me one of those small fruit pies on there
while I look for us a place to sit."

"Okay," Vanessa replied, joining Miss Bea moments later. "There's two seats together," Vanessa
indicated.

"Let's sit over there." Miss Bea headed in the
opposite direction.

Vanessa watched her elderly companion make
a beeline for the empty table where Xavier John-

son was taking a seat. By the time Vanessa crossed the room, women were claiming seats around him fast and furiously.

"This seat is mine," Miss Bea said with authority as a woman tried to beat her to a chair.

The younger woman stopped, then focused on the seat beside her.

"And that is my play-daughter's seat. She was one of the honorees. Were you?"

The woman shook her head and looked from Miss Bea to Vanessa. "No, I wasn't." Irritation punctuated her words.

"Then I know you're going to let her have it for no reason other than that."

The woman looked flustered.

"C'mon, Vanessa," Miss Bea beckoned.

Vanessa looked at the thin, shapely woman who was still standing by the chair. "Look, it's okay. If you really want to—"

"I wouldn't think of it." The woman glanced at Xavier, then walked away.

Vanessa could feel several sets of eyes on her as she sat down. When she was settled, she looked around the table. How quickly the women had forgotten her. All eyes were focused on Xavier, including Miss Bea's.

"You have been a really busy man," a voluptuous woman with a very tall hairdo remarked.

"I try to keep busy," Xavier replied.

"Well, it seems like you're doing more than your fair share," she continued. "We need more men like you. Men who care."

There were several nods of agreement.

"Thank you," Xavier replied graciously. "But I think there are plenty of men who care. They may not know how to show it, but I believe they truly do care."

"You express yourself so well," another woman remarked.

Xavier looked down at his plate as one eyebrow rose. "Thank you." He paused. "With all the accolades I'm getting at this table, I'm going to run out of ways to say thank you very quickly."

"I want to do some volunteering," the voluptuous female proclaimed. "What groups do you work with?"

Before Xavier could answer, Miss Bea interjected, "So none of you women are volunteers?"

Low "nos" and hesitant shakes of heads followed.

"Vanessa started volunteering when she was in high school," Miss Bea said proudly.

Vanessa formed a weak smile and looked down at her plate. *Miss Bea is such a character. And I don't know what else she could do or say that could embarrass me more. But I'm sure she'll think of something.*

"So how many years have you been volunteering?" an almond-eyed beauty asked.

Vanessa looked at the woman, who was several years her junior. Other than Miss Bea and Xavier, she figured she was the oldest woman at the table. Her thirty-third birthday had just passed, and psychologically she was feeling every year of it. "I've been volunteering for a long time."

"Is eating lots of chocolate cake the secret to your long career as a volunteer?" Xavier asked with his lips slightly curved.

Vanessa looked at the four pieces of cake and felt even more embarrassed. "No, it's not. But chocolate does have other virtues," she added to mask her discomfort.

"Such as?" Xavier rejoined.

Now the women really looked at Vanessa—this time with a competitive interest. Vanessa patted her classy chignon sculpted from her micro-braids. "Eating chocolate helps the body release chemicals that make you feel good."

"I've heard as much," Xavier replied.

They searched each other's eyes across the table before Vanessa began to eat again.

"I guess if you want to be the kind of woman who depends on chocolate for satisfaction it's okay," the voluptuous woman quipped. "But I can think of some other things that are even more pleasurable." She gave Xavier a sly glance.

Most of the women pretended they didn't hear her. Everybody except Miss Bea.

"So are you trying to tell us you don't like chocolate?" Miss Bea leaned to the side and looked at the woman's ample backside.

"I beg your pardon?"

"Chocolate," Miss Bea enunciated. "You don't like it?"

Now the woman was seething. She looked at the rail-thin Miss Bea, who, by now, was calmly eating her food, and she held back. "Yes. I like chocolate."

"Just keeping things straight," Miss Bea said without blinking.

Vanessa thought she saw Xavier put his hand up to his mouth to hide an impending smile.

The remainder of the meal went smoothly. A few perfunctory conversations about volunteering were exchanged, but it was obvious the young women steered away from anything that might spark Miss Bea. Soon people began to leave, and everyone said their good-byes. Vanessa wasn't certain, but she thought Xavier exhibited more than a passing interest in her during the meal. Yet when they parted, he never said a word, and neither did she.

"I've got to go to the little girl's room before we head for the car," Miss Bea said as she wiped her mouth with a paper napkin.

"I'll wait for you outside the door where we came in." Vanessa pointed. "Beneath the flood-light."

Miss Bea nodded, and Vanessa joined the crowd exiting the building. Once she emerged outside, the cool night air was refreshing but nippy, and Vanessa gathered the thin jacket of her outfit close around her neck.

"Excuse me." A woman squeezed past her.

Vanessa stepped aside and out of the way of

the flowing crowd. To pass the time she gazed at the sky, which was empty except for a sliver of moonlight.

"The temperature has dropped quite a bit, hasn't it?" a male voice said from beside her.

Xavier.

"Yes, it has," Vanessa replied, surprised. She hadn't expected to see Xavier Johnson again. At least not so soon. It had occurred to her that she might see him at the next state awards event. But what difference would that make? A man as good-looking as Xavier normally spelled trouble, and she had decided back in her twenties that she was done with that sort of thing. Vanessa glanced up into his face. His skin was as smooth as caramel. She looked away. It had taken a bit of restraint at the table not to ogle him like the other women. But now she realized the truth was that she might have, if Xavier hadn't been studying her every time she attempted to study him.

"But it's not too bad for this time of year," Xavier remarked. "I spent a year in Chicago so I can appreciate temperatures like this in September."

"So you live here in Atlanta?" Vanessa examined his face, which towered above her.

"No. I live in Columbus."

"I live in Columbus too," she replied, surprised. "What a coincidence."

"It is, isn't it?" They searched each other's eyes before Xavier continued. "I was born in Atlanta.

We lived in College Park. My mother moved us to Columbus when I was around fourteen. She wanted to get me away from the group of guys I was hanging out with. She wanted to get me back on the right path."

"And obviously it worked," Vanessa said.

"To a certain degree." Xavier looked at her. "But what really happened was that I decided to change. I wanted to take advantage of the new start. If I hadn't made up my mind to change, moving me to Columbus or any other place wouldn't have made a difference."

Vanessa looked away as she caught a tantalizing whiff of Xavier's cologne. "I've seen examples of that over and over again. My mother has a saying, 'You can lead a horse to water but you can't make him drink.' "

Xavier nodded. "I can't tell you how many times my mother said that to me. That's why volunteering for a group like Each One Teach One is so rewarding. The people are eager to learn and so appreciative. Seeing grown men like myself swallowing their pride and trying to broaden their world is worth witnessing."

"Now that's a fact," Vanessa agreed. "Between men and women, I think men can be the proudest and the most stubborn."

Xavier looked at her. "We can, can we?"

"At least that's been my experience." Vanessa's gaze didn't waver.

"I guess there's some truth there," Xavier acquiesced, then added softly, "but I don't know if it's pride or a sense of predestination that makes a man take the downward spiral."

"The downward spiral?" Vanessa asked, perplexed.

"To do things that seem to be against his own good."

Vanessa could feel how this issue truly concerned him. "That's something men *and* women can claim."

"And no doubt we both have." Xavier paused and gazed off into the night. "For years I've wondered why."

"Did you come up with any answers?" Vanessa felt moved by the depth of his thoughts.

"Not yet. I'm still searching. High and low. Far and near." Xavier looked at Vanessa again. "Which brings me to, where are you from?"

"From near." She looked into his eyes and smiled. "I was born in Columbus, spent my growing up years right there."

"And are you married?"

"No," Vanessa replied with a slight laugh. "Are you?"

"No."

They looked at each other meaningfully.

"Boy, we've covered a lot of ground real quick." Vanessa felt compelled to say something.

"I'd say so," Xavier agreed.

"Where you're from." Vanessa counted off on her fingers. "Volunteering. Human frailty. Where I'm from. And last but not least . . . marriage."

"I think it's a good idea to get the preliminaries out of the way," Xavier replied. "Wouldn't want to stagger into any big obstacles later on."

"Later on?" Vanessa's eyes filled with question.

"Yes. Later on. That's another thing about men. At least I can speak for this man." Xavier placed his palm over his heart. "I know what I like right off the bat. I think most men do. When we're beating around the bush and talking about how uncertain we are . . . it's just that. Talk."

"Really," Vanessa replied.

"Mm-hmm." Xavier looked into her eyes. "I have the feeling you're the kind of woman I've been looking for all my life."

The air around them suddenly felt warmer.

"Now that is quite a line," Vanessa said.

"I'm too old and busy for lines, Vanessa." She noted he remembered her name. "If you'll let me, I'd like to call you tomorrow."

"So you're telling me you're serious."

"Very."

She probed his steady gaze and checked for the whir of red flags . . . but there was none. "Then I'd like for you to call me. I'd like it very much."

"Good. Because I don't recall a time when I've been so certain." Xavier searched inside his jacket pocket.

"What's so different about me?" Vanessa asked pointedly.

"You mean, besides being a beautiful woman?"

Vanessa looked up toward the sky and shook her head.

"No. Seriously," Xavier continued. "There's something special. A sincerity." He scanned her hair and face with his gaze. "Never once did I see a calculating look in your eyes."

"A what?"

"It's this look," Xavier explained. "I've seen it over and over again. It's when a woman wants you to fill out her questionnaire. To find out who you really are hiding behind that mask."

Vanessa laughed.

"She determines that by asking what you do for a living," Xavier continued. "Then she decides if you are worthy of her. It's all a part of the hunt. The game."

Oh, the game. Vanessa's lips turned up slightly. *Something Mama wishes I had more of.* "I guess I didn't have to go through all that. Your worthiness is pretty obvious. The Volunteer of the Year award is heavy-duty stuff."

"Another reason for me to be glad I gave of myself and my time," Xavier said, pulling an ink pen from his pocket. "Write your number on the back of my program."

"Don't you want to save it? You were the star of tonight's show."

"I intend to save it, and with your number written on it, it'll be that much more precious."

Vanessa threw up her hands. "Don't say anything else or I might think you're full of . . . you know what."

"So . . . because I tell the truth, you think I might be full of crap. That's a pity. We'll have to change that starting with my phone call tomorrow. I will call you tomorrow, Vanessa."

She believed he would. She took the pen and paper and wrote down her phone number, then gave the program back to Xavier. Electricity passed through her when their fingers touched. It was a relief to see Miss Bea emerging from the exit. Xavier made Vanessa feel like a schoolgirl experiencing her first real crush. It was powerful. Unnerving.

Xavier walked over to give Miss Bea a hand down the stairs and escort her to Vanessa.

"Why thank you, young man. It goes to show there are perks to being an elderly woman." Miss Bea eyed Vanessa. "Hope I didn't keep you waiting too long."

"I'd say your timing was perfect." Vanessa's gaze strayed to Xavier. In her mind she captured the texture of his hair, the color of his skin, and the clarity of his eyes.

"Goodnight, Miss Bea," Xavier said. "It was nice to meet you. And Vanessa" His eyes softened as he looked at her. "I look forward to talking to you tomorrow."

"The same here," Vanessa replied.

He turned and walked across the street.

"My goodness, seems like you two made a real connection." Miss Bea searched Vanessa's face.

Vanessa smiled. "As usual, Miss Bea, you're right on the money. And maybe Dellia was too."

"Who? Who's Dellia?"

"Never mind," Vanessa said as she took Miss Bea's arm. "The car is over here."

Miss Bea chatted away while Vanessa drove home. By the time they arrived in their neighborhood Miss Bea had worked herself into a state of excitement. She couldn't wait to share "their evening extravaganza" with her friends.

"Look who's back," Mrs. Bertha exclaimed no sooner than the door opened.

Lillie and Mrs. Bertha had already settled into their familiar places at the card table. Jackie, Vanessa's mother, was in the kitchen, pouring popcorn into a bowl.

"Yes. Yes. Yes." Miss Bea strutted in. "We are back. And we had ourselves a time."

Vanessa couldn't help but smile. Miss Bea had rightfully earned a reputation as a mighty storyteller, and from the way she removed her hat with aplomb, Vanessa knew they were in for a treat.

"Ladies, you should have been there," Miss Bea continued.

"Aw right, Bea. Don't make me mad now," Jackie warned. "You know how bad I wanted to go, and you come in here bragging. Talking about how we should have been there. Don't do this to me, Bea. Just don't do it."

"Aw Jackie, don't be mad. You're the reason I'm talking like this. I wouldn't dare keep the evening to myself. I want to share it with you. Make you feel like you were there."

"Well you need to find another way to do it," Jackie insisted.

"Don't pay her any mind, Bea," Lillie jumped in. "We've been here all of ten minutes and she's been fussing the whole time."

"No, I haven't," Jackie retorted.

"Yes, you have," Mrs. Bertha claimed. "If we had known it was going to be like this we would have had the card game at my house tonight and made sure you took some more of that medicine that makes you sleep. That way we wouldn't have to be bothered with your cranky butt," she finished with a chuckle.

"I'm not thinking about y'all," Jackie replied. "I want to talk to my daughter." She stuck her nose in the air and turned toward Vanessa. "How you doing, Sugar? How was your evening?"

"Doing great, Mama. I was given a plaque." Vanessa waved it in the air.

"That's not all she got out of the evening," Miss Bea insinuated.

"It's not?" Jackie looked from Miss Bea to Vanessa.

"No it's not." Miss Bea warmed to her subject. "I'll have you know your daughter pulled the handsomest man there. And not only was he good looking, he received the Volunteer of the Year award."

"You hush up," Lillie cried. "Vanessa, girl, how did you manage to do more in one evening than you've done in the past two years?"

"Oh, Lillie." Mrs. Bertha slapped her friend's forearm. "You leave her alone."

"I want to know," Lillie insisted. "It's been

years since I've seen her with a man, I was beginning to wonder."

"Wonder what, Lillie?" Vanessa tried to keep a
straight face as she put her hand on her hip.

Jackie smacked her thigh. "I knew something
special was going to happen. I had a feeling.
That's why I told that stubborn doctor he should
let me go tonight."

"Here you go with those nudgings of yours."
Vanessa chuckled.

"But I did know," Jackie insisted. "And don't
change the subject, Nessa." She placed the popcorn bowl on the card table. An eager gleam entered her eyes as she asked, "What is Bea talking
about?"

"I met a nice man tonight. That's all," Vanessa
said as nonchalantly as she could.

"This sounds serious." Lillie leaned over the
card table and pretended to whisper. "And did
you hear how she said it, Bertha? 'I met a nice
man tonight.' Her voice was so sweet, bees might
start swarming in this room any minute." She
patted the table three times in rapid succession. "I
tell you that man struck a chord with Nessa."

"Vanessa's right." Miss Bea came to Vanessa's
defense. "He is a really nice young man. I told
Vanessa if I was younger I'd give her some competition. Not that every woman's eye in the place
wasn't on him already."

Jackie raised her eyebrows. "Seems like this
man's got Bea's vote as well. Do you think you
might see him again?" She applied her most non-

chalant tone, but Vanessa knew her mother was anything but nonchalant about her finding a possible mate.

"I think so," Vanessa replied with confidence.

Mrs. Bertha smiled. "Vanessa says don't play her short. She knows he's interested."

"I certainly do, and I'm definitely interested in him." She looked at each one of the ladies. "Now I'm going to leave you to your weekly card game and let Miss Bea fill you in on the rest of the evening. Suddenly, I want to make sure I put all that stuff I've been paying too much for on my face. Maybe after all these years it's going to pay off." Vanessa winked and headed for the hall.

two

"Congratulations, Xavier." The secretary's morning cup of coffee sloshed onto the desk as she set it down. "I heard the good news. Seems like you're going to be able to bring that Aboriginal art exhibit to the museum after all. Your hard work is finally going to pay off. I'm glad for you."

"Thank you, Sand." Xavier stopped in front of her desk. "It feels absolutely great." He leaned toward her. "I've been working here for three years and this is the first project that I can claim as mine."

"It's about time we brought some color to this place." Sand's dark eyes shone conspiratorially. "I've been here much longer than you and I can tell you this will be an absolute first." Her voice went even lower. "When they hired you I was so glad I was no longer the one and only minority.

And now this," she said in a tongue-in-cheek manner. "I don't know if my heart can take it."

"Yes, this exhibit will broaden some horizons, and that means a lot to me." Xavier's tone turned serious.

"You are something else, you know that?"

"Am I?"

"Yes, you are," Sand said. "And when you first started to work here I tried to get your attention, but you wouldn't give me the time of day."

"I had other things on my mind back then." Xavier gave her a slight smile.

"Yeah, like that woman who used to call here two and three times a day."

"Who? Karen?"

"Yep. Karen."

"I'm not going to take the blame for her obsession. I made it clear where I stood on our relationship from the beginning. She just—"

"All you men are alike." Sand fanned her hand at him.

"No, don't do that. Don't lump me in with 'all' men," Xavier cautioned her. "I don't know what they do, but I try to be honest. Now it may not be what the women who have been in my life wanted to hear, but I tell the truth."

"Well, you're a rare one." Sand began to back down.

"I think so."

"And none of those women were powerful enough to make you want to do anything permanent, huh?"

"It wasn't that. The chemistry just wasn't there." Xavier thought of Vanessa. "You know it when it's right. It kind of snaps your head back and makes you pay attention." He gave a demonstration.

"I guess if I haven't snapped your head back by now, I won't."

"Aw Sand." He patted her cheek. "You know you're my girl. How would I get along around here without you? Wish you could help me prepare for this trip."

"Do you really need me to?" Sand brightened at the prospect. "You've got to leave tonight."

"I know," Xavier said. "Curtis said—with all the authority he could muster—that if I want to go to Australia I need to get myself on a plane tonight."

"That sounds just like Curtis. He's always giving directives even if they're not his to give. And he's even worse when it comes to you."

"Ye-es, there's something about me that gets to Curtis. But I can't let him or any other man be an excuse for my not living up to my own expectations."

Sand nodded with approval. "I need to tell myself that from time to time."

"So how did I get a plane ticket on such short notice?"

She took a sip of coffee. "At the last minute Mr. Marshall told me to get online and find one. So I did. I guess someone cancelled their flight and we were able to get you a ticket at a really good price.

If it hadn't been for that, you might have had more time to prepare. You know pinching pennies is very important around here."

"You can say that again." Xavier looked at his watch. "Well, I guess I better give my thanks to the Internet gods." He gave a thumbs-up sign.

"You never did answer my question." Sand put her hand on her hip.

"What?"

"Do you want me to help you get ready for your trip? I'd love to see the inside of your house." She smiled enticingly. "I've driven around in your area a couple of times. It's nice over there."

"I like it. I've been there about five years. I bought the house after my mom died." He looked down, then up again.

"Oh-h," Sand sympathized. "Do you still have your dad?"

Xavier shook his head.

Sand paused. "Well it's a pretty house." She turned the conversation to a more upbeat note.

"And it's a good investment," Xavier replied. "Plus I like having a yard to hang out in."

Sand smiled.

"But back to your question, no, I'll be all right," Xavier said. "I've got only a couple of things to do—ask my neighbor to watch my house and pick up my mail. And then I'll throw some things in a couple of suitcases and after that I'll be ready to go."

"Sounds unbelievably simple," Sand replied.

"That's all you have to do? A couple of suitcases . . . are you going to have enough clothes for a six-week stay?"

"I'll manage," Xavier replied. "I'll probably take one pair of dress pants and a dress shirt, but basically I'll take some jeans, shorts, and a few T-shirts. I don't expect to do any socializing that will call for a suit and tie."

"Oh, no?" Sand questioned.

"No-o," Xavier replied definitively. "I'm going to have lunch with a man by the name of Phillip Ramsey, and he's going to take me around for a bit, but mainly I'll be on my own. Ramsey's company, World Import and Exports, are the middlemen, and I'm sure they want to protect their position, so they probably won't introduce me to their contacts. But I plan to seek out Aboriginal art exhibitions in Australia, become a little more intimate with the medium and hopefully the people. Being in the country will give me a feel for the land, and that will help me better understand the art. After that I should be able to put together a first-class exhibit." He squinted with determination. "The Aborigines are perceived to be so different from everybody else. Some people believe they are telepathic, and others say they have a different number of chromosomes than any other family of human beings."

"Really?" Sand's mouth dropped open.

Xavier nodded. "True or not, that's how different a lot of people feel the Aborigines are. I want the people who come to the Marshall Art Museum for the Aboriginal exhibit to leave with a feeling that they should embrace diversity. Not shun it or ridicule it." He paused to gather his thoughts. "And to show them that people who have a history and a culture like the Aborigine can be so similar to them, me, Curtis, or anybody else. That diversity—being different—simply is who we are. And maybe one less person will turn away from, or mistreat, someone because he's different."

"Sounds like you're on a mission, Xavier."

His dark eyes came back and embraced hers. "I guess I am. We've all got ghosts from our past that shadow our lives. I haven't forgotten some of the teasing I received while growing up."

"What did they tease you about?" Sand asked. "You had to be a darling little boy."

"It's a long story, Sand. Skeletons in my family closet."

"Is that why you tend to keep yourself so busy, so you won't have to think about these things?"

A wry expression took over his face. "No, that's not it." But Xavier wasn't sure.

"Whatever the reason may be, you end up not having much of a social life."

"You're looking at a much more settled Xavier. It wasn't like this when I was in my early twenties."

"I'm sure you gave us women a rough time." Sand shook her head slowly.

A devilish gleam entered Xavier's eyes. "And a good time as well, I hope."

"You need to get some of that fire back. You lead too dull of a life."

"That's a matter of opinion," Xavier replied as he headed for the door. "Maybe I'm just saving it up for the right woman."

"If it could only be me," Sand threw out with abandon.

"You couldn't handle it, Sand," he tossed over his shoulder.

"That's not the problem," she called after him. "You won't give me the opportunity to find out."

"Going to do a little overtime, huh?" Vanessa's coworker stood over her cubicle.

"Yeah. I need to straighten a few things out." Vanessa looked at the computer code on her screen. She'd completed her work for the day a half hour ago.

"Well, good luck." The man tapped the plastic molding. "I'll see you tomorrow."

"Bye," Vanessa replied mechanically.

I've got a few things to straighten out, all right. And one of them is my mind. I can't believe how I've been counting the minutes until I get home. I am so excited! I can't recall the last time I felt like this. Just because Xavier Johnson said he's going to call. Vanessa looked down and covered her eyes with one hand. *I refuse to leave here like this. I am going to get a hold of myself before I walk out of this office.*

She opened her desk drawer and started organizing the contents. There was the ordinary clutter of ink pens, markers, stamps, and rubber bands. But there were also Tootsie Rolls, Starbursts, and Lifesavers. Some of the perks of five years of office life at Apex.

Vanessa unwrapped a cherry Starburst and popped it in her mouth. Apex was a small but friendly company, and she got along fairly well with everyone. Being a computer programmer was a solid way to make a living, a good living. It wasn't the kind of job she'd dreamed of having when she was a child, but back then computers weren't the end all and be all that they were today. Vanessa had envisioned herself growing up to be a writer until her mother had insisted she study computer science as a backup. She didn't believe Vanessa had what it took to be a writer. Jackie didn't believe Vanessa had what it took at all. At least that's how Vanessa saw it. That day she stopped keeping a journal—something she had kept since she was twelve years old. Vanessa paused in thought, closed that drawer, and opened another.

Vanessa was determined to control her raging anticipation, but mentally hashing over the complicated relationship she shared with her mother was too taxing a replacement. True, her life had not been a romance novel, and for the past couple of years it hadn't been a novel of any kind. Vanessa could feel her stomach begin to quake again, and she held her hand against it. But her life *had* been calm and orderly.

Vanessa sighed. She thought she wanted excitement, but she wasn't sure she could handle it if it was going to make her feel like this. "I refuse to let the promise of a phone call affect me this way," she firmly declared. "Think about something else."

She straightened her second desk drawer and reflected on some recent office politics. A new position had opened up . . . and a rare can of worms along with it. Vanessa hadn't bothered to apply, and it wasn't because she didn't feel she was qualified. It was because she couldn't see herself working for Apex for the rest of her life. Outside of writing a book, Vanessa didn't know what she could see herself doing, but living in a gray cubicle world for another thirty years was not it. And she had sworn not to let herself do just that.

Vanessa cleaned off her desk, shut down her computer, and finally left. In completing those tasks she regained a sense of control—a sense that all but disappeared when she walked through the door and saw her mother engaged in one of her favorite pastimes: talking on the telephone. Over and over Vanessa had suggested they acquire call waiting in order not to miss incoming calls, but her mother kept insisting that she hated the disruptive beeping. Jackie believed it was common courtesy for a person to give all their attention to the person they were talking to. *Friends should never be put on hold as if they were calling a business. We don't need any of those bells and whistles,* she'd said. This was only one of her mother's idiosyncrasies that had plagued Vanessa since she'd moved back home after her father's death.

"Hi, Mama."

Jackie gave a preoccupied wave as she continued with her conversation.

Vanessa let go of a nervous breath, looked at the clock, then headed for her room. She tried to ignore the nagging thought that she may have missed Xavier's call. What if she had? If he were truly interested he'd call again, her logical side said, while her emotional side worked up feelings of dismay. By the time Vanessa changed her clothes and left her bedroom, her mother was off the phone and in the kitchen.

"Let me set your mind at ease, Nessa. I wasn't on the phone a long time," Jackie proclaimed. "I could tell by the look on your face you were thinking I had been."

Vanessa continued to look down. "Not really."

"Not really . . ." Jackie gave her daughter a side look. "Okay. But you know I know ya. And there's no need to pretend with me."

Vanessa was feeling that hyper-anticipatory feeling again. It was uncomfortable enough without her mother adding to it. "Mama, I simply walked through the door and went to my room. You barely looked at me, so how much can you read into that?"

"Plenty." Jackie pointed to the teakettle wall clock. "For one thing, you're late. You're never late. And knowing the way you think, you probably made it your business not to come straight home just to prove you're not hyped up about that young man calling."

"I don't believe you." Vanessa tried to look offended.

"No. I don't believe *you*." Jackie took a bite of chicken before she walked out of the room.

Vanessa watched her mother disappear before she raised her splayed fingers to the ceiling. "Okay. Okay." She made a funny face. "I am not going to discuss this any further with Mama no matter what she does or says. She's probably almost as excited as I am."

Vanessa busied herself with putting baked chicken, rice, and greens on a plate. That was one positive thing about living at home again: the home-cooked meals. She looked at her plate and put a piece of chicken back. Her appetite had grown with her sedentary lifestyle. *Thank God for fairly good genes,* she thought as she glanced at her mother's slim shoulders in the next room. *But who would have thought in two years my life would end up like this? Before I moved back I had started walking and going to aerobics, but now all I do is watch television and read. Maybe I'm depressed,* she thought as she put the lids back on the pots.

By the time Vanessa entered the dining room, Jackie had turned on the VCR and settled in on the living room couch. Absentmindedly, Vanessa watched the tape on the television screen. A man with a Russian accent was speaking excitedly. He was talking about being in several locations in a matter of moments. Vanessa tried to make sense of it, but the more she listened the more confused she became. "What is this, Mama?"

"It's called *Life After Life*," Jackie replied. "He's telling what happened to him right after he died."

"After he died?" Vanessa's brows furrowed. "But how can he be sitting there talking about it if he actually died?"

"He had a near death experience. An NDE."

"Now I get it." Vanessa let go of a long sigh.

"I heard that."

"Mama . . . I didn't say a word. I am eating my dinner, which is very good, by the way." Vanessa did not want to discuss the subject any further. No more than three months after her father died, her mother had begun to show an increased interest in the paranormal. At first Vanessa had decided it was a natural part of her mother's grieving process, a manifestation of her desire to see her husband, William, again. They had been married for fifty-three years. His passing had almost killed Jackie. It was during that time—at her mother's request—that Vanessa had moved back home.

She looked at the back of her mother's gray head, then sprinkled more hot sauce on the baked chicken. But that was two years ago, and Jackie's interest in the mystical had not waned. If anything, it had grown, and to tell the truth, Vanessa felt a bit uncomfortable with it.

"So you don't believe there's life after life?" Jackie asked without turning around.

"I'm sure there is some kind of existence, Mama, but that doesn't mean I'm going to believe everything I hear on the subject."

"I don't believe everything I hear. This video is based on years of research by a doctor. Dr. Raymond Moody." Jackie extended her hand toward the screen. "This stuff is documented."

"I'm not saying it isn't. But there are other doctors who say what these people are experiencing is a natural biological occurrence. All those things they think they are seeing are happening in their minds."

"Well, if it's nothing but their imagination, how did one guy who had a near death experience know there was a shoe on the hospital ledge several floors above him? It couldn't be seen from the ground. And it couldn't be seen from his hospital room. He said he saw it when he was floating outside of his body." Jackie turned around. "Or the woman? Her body was flat-lining on the emergency room table, but she knew the horrible things her in-laws were saying about her while they waited in the hall. She got to tell them about it too . . . after she came back and got well."

"I don't know how they knew." Vanessa shook her head. "But how do you know all that? The tape just came on. Have you watched this before?"

Jackie faced the television again. "Yes. Is there anything wrong with that?"

"No, there isn't. But I wish you wouldn't allow yourself to get so worked up over this stuff."

"I am seventy-six years old. I'm old enough to get worked up over anything I choose. And I'll have you know I think getting worked up over the possibility of life being eternal is a good thing. Just as you have the right to get worked up over the possibility of that young man calling."

"I knew we were going to get back to this."

"No. I'm just saying—"

"Mama, I know what you're saying. I didn't mean to interrupt your video program. Please . . . continue."

Jackie pressed the pause button. "Oh, Nessa. I didn't mean to rib you."

Vanessa nodded. "Apology accepted."

"Good." Jackie focused on the television set again.

Dinner progressed uneventfully from there. By virtue of proximity, Vanessa had no choice but to listen to the parade of people claiming to have had near death experiences. How, while out of their bodies, they only had to think of a place or a person and they would be there. That there was no time or space.

Some of their accounts were fascinating, but Vanessa had difficulty believing what they were saying. Yet she had to admit it made her consider the possibility of time being a human creation.

When Vanessa finished eating she put the dishes in the dishwasher and cleaned the kitchen. Afterwards she took several magazines and went outside. In the backyard, she plopped down in a chair beneath a large maple tree that had grown through the years as she had grown.

The minutes passed excruciatingly slowly, but in another way, time as a whole went far too fast. On two occasions the telephone rang, and Vanessa held her breath and waited for her mother to call her name. She never did. Finally, when it was too dark to read, Vanessa stood up to go back inside the house. A flash of bright blue in the window caught her eye. It was Jackie moving away so Vanessa wouldn't see her. When Vanessa entered the house, Jackie was back in the living room, pretending to read a book.

"Oh, you're back." Her mother continued the farce.

"Yeah."

Jackie looked at her watch, then cheerfully said, "I was thinking about going to bed, but it's only eight-thirty." She looked at Vanessa. "I don't know why I'm so tired."

Vanessa's eyes softened as she looked at her mother. "Mama, you don't have to pretend. I saw you standing at the window."

"Oh." Jackie looked down. "I guess I want that young man to call you almost as much as you do." She laced her fingers together. "I've already had a full life with you and your father. I want the same for you, Nessa, if that's what you want."

"There is more to life than getting married and having children." Vanessa felt her old truth didn't ring with the familiar conviction. "I have my career," she added out of habit.

"I know that. And I know it has given you a lot of satisfaction, but . . ." Jackie's voice trailed off.

"It's not like this man is my last chance, Mama."

"I know he's not, honey, but he's the only one who's brought a sparkle to your eyes in years."

Vanessa's eyes softened. "Well, I guess he'll call if he wants to. If he doesn't there's nothing I can do about it."

"If he doesn't call he's a fool," Jackie steamed.

Vanessa didn't trust herself to respond. A familiar, vulnerable feeling pressed against her insides. As a child she hadn't had a name for it, but as an adult Vanessa knew the feeling was abandonment. Xavier had looked her straight in the eyes and said she was special. He had promised that he would call—today. It was the same kind of promises her father had made.

Vanessa glanced at a photograph of herself as a little girl. She was waiting on the front steps of the house in her favorite yellow dress. Waiting for her father to come home. Miss Bea had snapped the picture because she'd said Vanessa looked so pretty. Later Vanessa found out she had also taken the photo because Vanessa had had on two different-colored socks. She was three years old and had dressed herself.

Vanessa tore her gaze away from the photograph. That day had been like so many other days when William Bradley had promised to return on a specific date. He never made it home that day either. Not only could Vanessa remember, but she could also feel it.

If Xavier doesn't call, he's a liar and he cannot be

trusted! Vanessa attempted to harden her heart, but the pain of it all quickly made itself known. *But most of all he is cruel.*

"I'm going to work on my poetry, Nessa," Jackie said softly from the other side of the room. "And then I'm going to bed." Although she attempted to hide it, Vanessa could hear the disappointment in her voice.

"Okay. See you in the morning."

Vanessa turned on the television, but by ten-thirty she couldn't recall the theme of the programs she had watched. As she turned out the lights, Vanessa poured cold water on the spark Xavier had lit, vowing that if she ever saw him again, she would turn her back and walk away.

"This is the last boarding call for Delta Airlines flight number One, four, four, eight."

Xavier looked at his watch and cussed beneath his breath. It was 10 P.M. Time had run out, and all he could do was stare at the endless lists of phone numbers in the telephone book. *Why didn't I enter her number in my PalmPilot instead of writing it on that stupid program?* he thought, watching the last passenger disappear through the double doors.

The attendant kicked away the doorstop before Xavier closed the phone book and ran across the terminal.

"I thought you had already boarded the plane," the attendant stated, surprised. "I printed out your boarding pass over an hour ago."

"I know," Xavier said. "I was trying to make an important phone call."

"It must have been really important." She took the boarding pass from him. "You almost missed your plane."

"It was," Xavier replied.

"Enjoy your trip," the attendant said in a practiced personal tone as she waited for Xavier to walk into the jetway.

"Thanks." Xavier took a few steps, when the door closed behind him. "Damn. I'm going to be gone for six weeks, and I promised Vanessa I would call her today." He shook his head as he continued toward the aircraft.

"Smile. You made it." A very cheerful woman greeted him with an outstretched hand.

Xavier showed her his ticket.

"Continue to your right, and you'll find A-16."

"Thanks," Xavier said before he turned toward the narrow aisle. When he reached it, a man and little boy who shared the row with him slid out of their seats so he could sit by the window.

"Almost missed it, did ya?" the slim child remarked.

Xavier greeted the boy's statement with a half smile. He wasn't in the mood for small talk. "Sure did."

"My dad and I are meeting my mom in Perth. Do you have a son?"

Xavier looked at the little boy, who was obviously excited. He couldn't recall a time in his childhood when he'd felt so carefree or his eyes had been as bright. Xavier studied the boy. He could easily have a child that age. Before his mother died she had been looking forward to having grandchildren. Xavier was uncertain about fathering a child. Uncertain as to how it might turn out. If it would be . . . healthy. The thought saddened him for himself and for his father. "No," Xavier replied. "I don't have any children."

"Did your dad ever take you on trips?"

"Don't ask so many questions, David." The boy's father put his hand on the boy's blue-jeaned thigh.

With eyes that appeared wider because of his glasses, the boy looked from his father to Xavier.

"It's okay," Xavier said, although his Adam's apple seemed to harden. "No, my father never took me on trips." The weakened state of his own voice surprised him. He hadn't realized the pain of his childhood was so close to the surface. "You're very lucky," Xavier managed to say.

The child leaned over as if he wanted to whisper something. Xavier bent his head down. "I'm going to be just like my dad when I grow up. That's what everybody tells me, and boy am I glad."

Xavier gave the exuberant child a forlorn smile, then looked out the window into the darkness. As a boy he would have given anything to say that about his father. But Xavier had never had the luxury of really knowing him. Then when he was a little older, he began to hear the gossip. Things that weren't very complimentary. *Drugs took Zeke's mind. Drugs are more important to Zeke than anything and anybody.*

Xavier buckled his seat belt and put away the images from his past. He was keyed up and tired from preparing for the trip. But most of all Xavier was disappointed that he had not contacted Vanessa before he left. He'd been so busy with last second plans that by the time he'd realized that he hadn't transferred her phone number to his PalmPilot, he'd been at the airport already. He thought about her face and the sincerity that had emanated from her dark eyes the night before. *This is a woman who will understand. She's not the kind of person to play games, and I'm sure she'll recognize that quality in me*, Xavier concluded. He balled up his sweater and placed it behind his head before he closed his eyes.

three

Seven weeks later

"This street festival gets bigger every year," Jackie grimaced. "It's almost too many people for me. I don't know if I will come to Atlanta for the next one." She placed her hand at the base of her throat. "Let's plop down on that bench and rest a while."

"You go ahead, Mama. I'm not really tired." Vanessa looked at the homeless man who sat on one end of the weathered bench. She also noticed a man with a German shepherd eyeing the vacant seat on the opposite end. "But I think you better hurry. You're not the only person with that idea."

"If you're not tired . . ." Tiny beads of perspiration appeared on Jackie's brow, although the weather was cool and pleasant.

"Oh, you know me. I'm like the Energizer Bunny," Vanessa assured her.

"I used to be," Jackie said softly.

"What?" Vanessa looked at her mother.

"I said I better get on over there." Jackie replaced the forlorn look with a determined one.

She was lucky—another dog appeared, and the owner of the German shepherd had to battle to keep his dog under control as Jackie claimed the prized seat.

"I'll be back in fifteen to twenty minutes," Vanessa called.

Jackie glanced at the homeless man, who appeared to be aimlessly going through a stack of papers. She eased back against the bench. "I'll be right here."

Vanessa sauntered through the crowd, which flowed in and out of rows and rows of booths. It was a shopper's paradise with a wide range of items for sale. Vanessa tried on several rings but finally decided on an ankle bracelet made of cowrie shells and leather. As she fastened the jewelry around her ankle, Elvis Presley's "Jail House Rock" filled the air. Vanessa's eyebrows furrowed. *Why in the world are they playing that?* She stood up and looked around. A large number of people were walking toward an area marked by high-flying banners. Curious, she fell in behind them. Vanessa and the crowd ended up in the plaza where several swing dancing couples were performing. Pleasantly surprised, she watched the frisky dancers do their thing as the audience grew. Ever since her disappointment over Xavier, Vanessa embraced anything that gave her even the slightest bit of pleasure. She was determined to prove she didn't need Xavier or any other man to fulfill her.

Jackie wanted to close her eyes, but she felt uncomfortable because of the homeless man beside her—not that he had threatened her in any way, but just the thought that someone could be living on the street. Jackie wondered how he'd come to this. She wondered if he had any family or friends. She wondered if anyone cared.

She attempted to get a good look at the man without his being aware, but that was very difficult to do. From what she could glean, he was about her age and at one time had been a very handsome man. Although his mustache and the little bit of hair she could see beneath his skullcap were a dusty gray, there was a strange kind of charm about him.

Jackie tried to steal another glance, thinking how it would feel at this point in her life to be homeless, but when she looked his way the man was looking directly at her.

"We should be proud of our young men," he said.

Quickly, she averted her gaze. But she could still feel his eyes on her. Jackie felt afraid. *I am not going to sit here and be intimidated.* She replaced her fear with resolve. *Even if he wanted to attack me, we're both much too old and out of shape to run.* She turned bold eyes in his direction and was surprised to see him holding a torn piece of paper out toward her in his tattered, gloved hand. Jackie started to pretend she didn't see it, but the thought *If not for the grace of God there go I* floated through her mind. Slowly, she reached out her hand and took it.

"Give it to him." The man pointed a worn finger before rising from the bench.

"What?" Jackie glanced in the indicated direction, but her eyes were drawn to the scripted words on the paper: *Love does not fade when darkness descends. Love is the light that defines it. He is not his father's son.* The name *Xenophon* was signed beneath that.

"What in the wo-orld," Jackie remarked after reading the strange words. She looked up just as the man passed by a small group of people standing in front of a Walk For Literacy booth. The homeless man gazed intently at a younger man handing out free T-shirts. Jackie stood up when she recognized the handsome young man from a recent television interview. Her eyes raised to the sky as she held the slip of paper in her hand. "This must be a sign, William," she said to her deceased husband. "What else could it be but a sign?" Excited, Jackie hurried across the grass to speak to the young man.

The swing dance couples were so good that Vanessa stayed for another performance before she decided to head back. She browsed as she went. The only thing that stopped her was a Kettle Korn stall. The lightly sweet aroma wouldn't allow anything else. After a sample of the salty-sweet popcorn, Vanessa was convinced the diversion was worth it. She arrived at the bench holding two steaming bags, but her mother wasn't there.

Vanessa searched the area. Finally, she spotted Jackie in a pack of people jockeying to get to a man standing at a booth. She crossed the grass and sidled up to her mother. "I've got something you're going to like." Vanessa held out a bag of popcorn. "I had never heard of Kettle Korn before, but it is absolutely delicious."

Jackie gave the bag of popcorn a side glance as the woman who had been standing in front of her walked away. Instead of reaching for the Kettle Korn, she stuck her hand out toward the man, but the slip of paper was in the way. Jackie stuck it in her pocket, then extended her hand again. "Hello, my name is Jackie Bradley. Weren't you on television a couple of days ago?"

"Yes, I was," the man replied.

Vanessa glanced up and nearly dropped both bags of Kettle Korn.

Xavier Johnson.

"I knew it was you." Jackie shook her finger in the air. "I read an article in the newspaper about your trip to Australia that same day. I found it very interesting because I've been reading about the Aborigines. I'm very—" Jackie stopped short. Xavier had barely looked at her. His gaze was focused on Vanessa. "Oh, I'm sorry." Jackie touched Vanessa's arm. "This is my daughter, Vanessa."

"Hello, Vanessa," Xavier said without moving.

It took everything Vanessa had to reply. "Hello."

Jackie continued. "As I was saying, I'm very interested in some of the cultural beliefs of the Australian Aborigines. I think they express all this spiritual stuff that is flooding the market, but in a really down-to-earth way. Is that the way you see it?"

"That is one way of looking at it," Xavier replied, forcing himself to look at Jackie. "For the Pintupi, the traditionally-minded group of Aborigines whose artwork I'll be exhibiting here in Columbus, there is no separation between spiritual life and daily life."

"And I love that." Jackie beamed. "I've been reading up on this. Everything is one and the same. Past, present, and future, overlapping. That is what the Aborigines' belief of the Dreamtime is all about." She revved up. "I believe when you're in the Dreamtime you can truly be in touch with all realms of existence. Even those that we cannot see," Jackie replied fervently.

"Yes," Xavier said in a distracted fashion as he looked at Vanessa again, then took a step toward her. "How have you been?"

"I've been just fine." Vanessa squeezed the popcorn bag.

Jackie gave her daughter a quizzical look. "Do you two know each other?"

"Ye—" Xavier nodded.

"Not really," was Vanessa's terse reply.

Xavier stared at Vanessa, who was looking in the opposite direction.

"Nessa, this isn't—" Jackie's arm crossed her chest as she pointed.

"I'm ready to leave if you are," Vanessa interrupted again.

"Do I have a choice?" Jackie looked from Xavier to Vanessa, who gave her a meaningful look before she walked off.

Xavier looked down. "I guess it is safe to say she wasn't too happy to see me."

"I guess . . . I'm sorry I got in the middle of this." Jackie backed away, then glanced over her shoulder at Vanessa's retreating back. "I just wanted to talk to someone who had actually been to Australia and shared an interest in the beliefs of the Aborigines. Believing in the oneness of time and space is very important to me at this time in my life." Jackie's eyes were desperate.

Xavier was obviously preoccupied with Vanessa's abrupt departure, but he tried to remain cordial. "I hope there will be many more people as interested in the Aboriginal culture as you are," he replied, then added, "Maybe I should go after Vanessa."

Jackie began to nod. "That's a good idea!"

"Why, it's Xavier," a deep voice with a strong Southern twang remarked.

"Mr. Marshall." Xavier acknowledged the head of the museum. "How are you doing today, sir?"

"Just fine. We had some relatives in town, so we decided to bring them to the street festival."

He motioned as if he was about to introduce them.

Xavier smiled slightly to the people Mr. Marshall had in tow. "Can you give me a moment, please?"

"Sure," Mr. Marshall said amiably before he crossed his arms, waiting.

Xavier turned to Jackie. "Look." He reached into his pocket. "Here's my card . . . in case either one of you wants to get in touch with me."

"All right," Jackie said. "Are you really interested in my daughter?" The question shot out like a bullet.

Xavier looked surprised. He gazed intently into Jackie's eyes. "Yes." He paused. "I am."

Jackie waved the card. "I've got a feeling about you. I've got a feeling about all of this," she said and walked away.

Vanessa was shaking her head when Jackie caught up with her. "I don't believe it. Talk about coincidences."

"Believe it," Jackie replied. "Because there's no such thing as a coincidence."

"Not now, Mama." Vanessa continued to trudge across the grass.

"Maybe you should have asked why he didn't call," Jackie suggested.

"Maybe he should have volunteered to tell me."

"How could he? By the time he started talking to you, you cut the conversation short and walked away."

"Well, I see he didn't come after me." Vanessa stopped walking to make her point.

"He was going to, but his boss came and—"

"Yeah, any excuse will do." Vanessa started walking again. "I believe I have shown plenty of patience. It's just that after two months my patience has worn re-eal thin."

"From what I know about him he doesn't seem like the kind of guy who would stand somebody up without a good reason."

"What do you know about him, Mama?" Vanessa stopped beside the car.

"Well—" Jackie's chin tilted upward as she looked down. "I know that he's an art expert. That he is the sole force behind bringing a very extensive Australian Aboriginal art collection to Columbus. And that he is truly—"

"That doesn't say anything about his character, Mama. That says what he does for a living. Not who he is. For years you and Dad seemed to get that mixed up." Vanessa got into the car. Jackie followed.

"How did your father get into this?" Jackie threw Vanessa an irritated glance.

"I'm just saying . . . what a person does for a living does not say who they are. For all of my life, while he was alive, Dad thought being the best he could be at his profession was a clear statement of who he was. But he had it mixed up. Being the best person you can be with your family and friends is the most positive reflection of who a person truly is."

"Don't start in on your father, Vanessa. He worked hard all of his life so that you and I could have the kind of home-life that we are still enjoying. Maybe he didn't have the total picture, but his intentions were good."

"That may be true. But I still have a right to say what's in my heart."

"Yes, you do." Jackie set her chin. "But you didn't have the right to criticize your father when he was alive, and you certainly don't have that right now that he's dead."

"I don't want to talk about this any further. You've always taken up for Dad and followed him everywhere, even when you didn't want to. Or when it was to my detriment. You always talk about truth and such, but for once I wish I could hear you say 'You're right, Vanessa. It's not your imagination. Your father did place more emphasis on his work than on his family.' "

Jackie paused before she spoke. "When are you going to let go of this, Nessa? Your father and I made decisions that we thought were best at the time. Just as you and I are making the best decisions we can make at this moment. None of us is perfect. But for you to still hold on to this is only hurting you. I've expressed my remorse to you, and I've forgiven myself for anything I may have done that hurt you. But that hasn't been good enough. Something inside of you just won't let go."

"I'm trying to." Vanessa placed her hand on top of her mother's. "But I am not going to over-

look anyone's indiscretions because of who they
are. Nor am I going to decide a person must be of
good character because of what they do. How
they conduct themselves, and how they treat me
will be the deciding factor."

"And that's good." Jackie looked lovingly at
her daughter. "But you've got to let them get to
know you so they *can* treat you. Otherwise it's
impossible. Because if every man you meet is going to be judged by your past hurts and wounds,
even the good ones won't have a chance. And I
think that Mr. Johnson is a good one." Jackie
paused again. "He gave me his card." She placed
the card in the ashtray. "It's obvious he's interested in talking to you."

Vanessa took a deep breath and turned on the
car. Although she had apologized to her mother,
the tension between them could still be felt.
Vanessa grimaced. Here Jackie was, taking
Xavier's side—a complete stranger's side against
her own daughter—just because he was an art expert. What did that prove? Vanessa fumed, but to
look at her you would never know it. Her face
was the perfect mask.

It had come to be her strongest weapon at moments like this. Vanessa's most poignant way of
striking back was to give nothing when she knew
her mother wanted more.

She pulled out into traffic. Vanessa believed
her mother saw her as a failure. Yes, she had a
good job, but Vanessa had never pursued her career with any obvious passion. Vanessa knew her

mother would have accepted her love life suffering because of an all-consuming career. But Vanessa did not have passion for her work, nor was that spark of life present anywhere else.

But her mother had always been a very passionate woman, in the way she spoke, in the way she dressed and acted, but most of all in the way she loved Vanessa's father. Loved him so much that her love for her child paled in comparison. Vanessa gave her mother a sideward glance.

As a young child Vanessa had needed her parents' love, needed them to be near, but with time she'd felt she couldn't have either. At the moment of that realization Vanessa had intentionally toned down her life light. She knew a child who was as passionate about life as they were would have pleased her parents most. In Vanessa's heart of hearts she was that child, but for the pain Jackie and William's abandonment had caused her, Vanessa had decided a passionless child would be their just reward. Yet during those years, Vanessa had had no idea that that way of thinking, that way of quelling the fire within would spill over into her adult life and weigh down the intensity of her existence. Living life at a distance had damaged Vanessa's ability to feel passion. She was a bird that sought refuge and revenge in a complicated cage then lost its way out.

Vanessa thought of Xavier. Something about him had shown her the door. Perhaps it was the way he had looked at her that evening by the steps, the way he had spoken to her with such sincerity, such clarity, that had awakened her. Vanessa had heard of two people experiencing absolute chemistry. Now, because of that short meeting with Xavier, she knew what that meant.

Vanessa willed away the sudden feeling of sheer frustration and disappointment that threatened to overwhelm her. Yet it had all been an illusion, wishful thinking on her part. In the end she was abandoned once again, and reminded of why she'd distanced herself from life in the very beginning.

Vanessa drove home with her mother in silence, and against her will her gaze was drawn to the business card in the ashtray. Persistent mental images of Xavier in a pair of worn but stylish blue jeans and a white T-shirt covered with an Aborigine playing a *didjeridoo* stayed with her for half the ride.

four

Jackie cleared her throat before she picked up the telephone. She dialed the number to the museum. Quickly. The phone rang once, twice, three times, and Jackie was on the verge of hanging up when an automated voice offered a confusing list of options. *God, I hate these things. You call a place to speak to a human being and all you get is a machine. The world is going to hell in a hand basket with all this technology. If the folks who are making money off of this stuff have their way, none of us will know how to interact with each other because we won't have to.* Jackie fumed so long without making a selection that the automated service switched to the receptionist.

"Marshall Art Museum," the well-seasoned voice greeted her.

She cleared her throat again. "I'd like to leave a message for Xavier Johnson, please."

"Hold on. I'll connect you to his extension."

"No-no," Jackie blurted out, then tried to mask her apparent panic. "I don't want to disturb Xavier." She attempted to make her voice lighter, younger. "I know he's very busy with the Aboriginal exhibit. So please, would you give him a message?"

"Sure," the woman replied.

Jackie was relieved by the quick response. "Tell Xavier I know this is short notice, but Ms. Bradley would like to meet him at Bill's tonight, at seven."

"Is there a phone number?"

"Uh-h. He has it," Jackie stated.

"All right, Ms. Bradley. I'll pass the message on to Mr. Johnson."

"Thank you." Jackie hung up the telephone and exhaled. Then she began to nibble on the side of her thumb. "There's no turning back now," she said softly. "But somebody had to do something. Neither one of them has made a move, and they've got to get together soon." Jackie looked at the calendar, then closed her eyes and said a short prayer.

"What are you up to?" Miss Bea called through the screen door.

Jackie jumped. "Woman, don't do that. You're going to give me a heart attack, sneaking up here like some kind of Peeping Tom."

"I've been coming up here like this more years

than I can remember." Miss Bea opened the door without invitation.

"My heart isn't as good as it used to be." Jackie held her chest. "So unless you want me to have a heart attack, you need to make some noise or something."

"I'm not stud'n you. The other day you were bragging about the results of your last physical, and how your heart would last forever. So don't give me that." Miss Bea squinted and gave her friend a side look. "That's not what scared you. You're up to something."

"Aw-w, shoot." Jackie waved her hand.

"I don't care what you say," Miss Bea retorted. "We've been best friends for fifty-something years, and you were doing something you had no business doing."

"At this age I give myself license to do whatever I please."

"Un-huh. I bet." Miss Bea shook her head before she changed the subject. "How you feeling today?"

"I feel great. You want some iced tea?" Jackie walked over to the refrigerator.

"I could do with some." Miss Bea went and stood by a kitchen counter. "And I'm glad you're feeling good. Can't have you pooping out on me. I don't want to break in another bid whist partner."

Jackie stood inside the refrigerator with her hand on the pitcher of iced tea. A sad smile crossed her face before she closed the door and said, "You could win with any partner. Our winning has had little to nothing to do with me."

"I'm going to remind you of that when we play tonight." Miss Bea stuck her finger in the soil of an African violet blooming on the windowsill. "These plants love this window. They bloom all the time. I still can't get mine to bloom." She sat down at the table where Jackie had placed the iced tea.

"Violets can be a little fussy, but once you find a good space for them they're really easy to take care of," Jackie replied.

"You've told me that over and over again and it hasn't made a bit of difference," Miss Bea said as the low hum of a car pulling into the driveway filtered into the kitchen.

"That must be Nessa." Miss Bea took a drink of tea.

"Yeah, it is about that time." Jackie poured her new glass of tea into the sink, then walked into the living room and back into the kitchen again.

"Woman, what is—" Miss Bea started.

Jackie motioned for her to be quiet.

"Hello, Mama. Miss Bea." Vanessa's pumps clicked as she walked across the hard wood floors.

"Hey, Baby. You always look so nice in your work clothes." Miss Bea smiled at Vanessa before her gaze strayed to Jackie.

"Hi, Nessa." Jackie smiled brightly. "You had a

phone call." She took a square of paper off the corkboard.

"I did?" Vanessa's voice turned whispery.

"Mm-m huh."

"Xavier?" She still didn't move.

"Yes." Jackie walked forward and gave Vanessa the note, which she'd written and tacked a few moments before she'd called the museum.

Vanessa stared at the message. "Would you meet me at Bill's tonight at seven o'clock?" She stopped reading and looked at the clock. "What time did he call?"

"Oh, a couple of hours ago." Jackie poured herself another glass of tea.

"And he expects me to meet him in an hour and a half? I haven't really spoken to the man since I met him two months ago."

"Well, Nessa—" Jackie looked a bit uncomfortable.

"Baby, don't even worry about that," Miss Bea jumped in. "The way he was chewing your mama's ear off when he called, I'm sure he's very aware of how much time has gone by. Seems to me like he's trying to make it up."

Jackie's eyes widened. "Yes, he was very apologetic."

"He should have saved his apologizing for me." Vanessa's brows furrowed.

"You know how men are," Miss Bea retorted. "This one is just trying to get in good with your mama. And that's a good sign."

"That's a matter of opinion," Vanessa replied. "And I haven't been to Bill's for years. I didn't know it was still open."

"But that is the club you used to go to, isn't it?" Jackie turned her back and made an expression for Miss Bea alone.

"Yeah."

"And I thought you said it was a very nice place," Jackie pushed.

"It was back then," Vanessa conceded. "But that was over two years ago."

"If Mr. Johnson chose it, I'm sure it still is a nice place," Miss Bea said.

Silence filled the room.

"Well, are you going?" Miss Bea inquired over the rim of her large iced tea tumbler.

"I don't know," Vanessa said.

"Do you want to?" Miss Bea asked.

"Sure I want to," Vanessa admitted softly.

Jackie placed her hands on her hips. "Then you put on something pretty and you go. You don't pass up opportunities like this. You take advantage of them." From the tone of her voice, Jackie could easily have been advising Vanessa as a teenager considering her first date.

She looked at her mother. "You know, you're right. I think I will go."

"That's the spirit," Miss Bea chirped. "You can't catch a fish unless you bait the hook."

Vanessa gave Miss Bea a thumbs-up sign as she left the kitchen. "And I'm going to bait it, but good."

The two women leaned in unison as they watched Vanessa disappear through the adjoining room.

"Now what lie did I just participate in?" Miss Bea whispered with her eyes wide.

"It wasn't a lie," Jackie replied. "And when you think about it, nobody asked for your help."

"If I hadn't come in when I did, you were about to bungle it."

"It never fails." Jackie smacked the air. "You take credit for everything."

"No, I'm not taking credit for this. You cooked up that stew. I'm simply asking what was in it, since I added a little spice."

Jackie crossed her arms and leaned back against the kitchen counter. "I gave Nessa and that Xavier Johnson a little nudge, that's all. Helped them do what both of them were either too proud to do, which would definitely be Nessa, or too busy, which is probably Xavier Johnson."

"So you wrote that note?"

"Yes, I wrote it."

"Well, how is he suppose to know to show up at Bill's at seven?" Miss Bea was confused. "What did you do? Write him a note too?"

"No. I left him a phone message," Jackie explained.

"Lor-rd, you have become a humdinger in your old age."

"I simply believe in taking care of business. That's all," Jackie defended herself.

"Yours and everybody else's, huh?"

"Mine and Nessa's," Jackie said stubbornly. "She's been lonely, Bea, and you know it. This man is the man for her. I know it. I feel it in my gut."

"Really?" Miss Bea softened at her friend's conviction.

"Ye-es. I've been praying for it, Bea. I want my daughter to be happy and fulfilled in her young age. Although life is sweet when you get to be our age, sometimes physical limitations put a damper on things. Our bodies can't keep up with our mental and emotional desires."

"You've spoken more than a word, there," Miss Bea testified.

"I want Nessa to have it all." Jackie felt validated. "And Xavier Johnson is the biggest possibility that's come her way in years. She likes that man, Bea."

"I know she does. And from what I saw, he likes her too."

"See there? I just hurried things along a bit." Jackie paused. "I want to make sure my one and only child has someone in her life when I'm gone."

"Judging by what your doctor said, it's going to be a while before you have to worry about that."

"Death isn't the only thing that can take a person away." Jackie gazed out of the window.

"It's the main thing I know," Miss Bea replied. "Moving can as well. And sickness too."

"But that's just it, Bea. There are things in this world beyond the things we basically know. Wondrous things. All we've got to do is believe in them."

"Can't be too wondrous if they take you away from your loved ones." Miss Bea wrapped her boney arms around herself.

"I'm talking about the kinds of thing that will reunite you." Jackie looked at her friend intensely.

"Jackie, you know how I feel about all that stuff."

"I know exactly what you're feeling. Fear. It's nothing but fear, Bea. And you don't even know what you're afraid of. You certainly don't know what I'm talking about."

"I know enough." Miss Bea put up her hand. "I don't want to know any more."

"And you're supposed to be my friend," Jackie mumbled. "How is that when I can't share all the things I'm thinking with you?"

"I'm sure you could share them. It's my inability to accept what you're thinking that worries me," Miss Bea replied. "So let's leave it at that. We don't have to see eye to eye on everything."

"I know we don't, but sometimes I feel so lonely, Bea. I want to share the things I'm discovering with somebody. Bill and I used to share so much. Travelling to all those different countries, seeing life under all kinds of circumstances." Jackie paused. "It was after William died that I realized just how much we shared."

"That's because you miss him," Miss Bea explained.

"It's true. I do miss him. We had a good life together. And we explored some interesting ideas about life and death and the beyond."

Miss Bea's shut-down expression said it all. "When it comes to that, just like there were other things William did for you that I can't do and wouldn't want to, I can't handle this, Jackie. But I *can* be right here with you pushing, even if it's underhanded, for Nessa's happiness."

Jackie patted Miss Bea's shoulder. "And nobody but a true friend would do that."

Miss Bea hesitated. "Jackie."

"Huh?"

"Why do you think it's been so hard for Nessa to really connect with a man?"

Jackie considered the question in silence before she said, "Things are different than they used to be, Bea. For a long time I don't think *getting* a man was important to Nessa. See, you got to think modern, Bea. Not what the kids call old school."

"Old school?" Miss Bea scrunched her face. "I didn't think wanting a man would ever get old."

"You know what I mean. Nessa's got her own career and a sense of self that, to tell you the truth, I don't have. She *knows* she can make it alone, without a man. I'll never know that," Jackie added, contemplatively. "I'm still living off of her father's accomplishments. I believe if I knew then what I know now, as a younger woman I could have made my own way. But even at Nessa's age

I had a very dependent way of looking at life," Jackie admitted to Miss Bea. "In that sense, Nessa's independence is a plus. But there's also a defiant part of her that says, if I stay single, I'll never be my mother, never be led around the country and the world on a leash called marriage." Jackie shook her head. "Getting to see the world not on her own terms, but on the terms of a man with insatiable goals. To Nessa, I didn't have the strength to live my life on my own terms. And Nessa's got to have that."

"Do you think she really sees you like that?" Miss Bea looked unconvinced.

"Yes. I do. She's told me so in different ways through the years, and more clearly since her father passed away."

"Well, you can believe that's not the way your friends see you. And if we told the truth—" Miss Bea's body moved as if she were letting Jackie in on a secret—"most of us wanted to *be* you. You were the neighborhood heroine, coming back with your fancy stories, being of the world, but never being above those of us who never traveled outside of Georgia."

Tears glistened in Jackie's eyes. "Oh, thank you, Bea."

Like the best of chameleons, Miss Bea crossed her arms abruptly. "So does Nessa really want a relationship or not?"

"Now . . . I think she does. But it's going to be tough to find a man who fits into that perfect little box of hers. When you think about it, most professional men, or men who are really into whatever they may do for a living, are dedicated. And Nessa might interpret that as their work being the most important thing in their lives. For her, that's a problem." Jackie paused. "But on the other hand, she surely wouldn't want a man who's not working, because Nessa's not going to take care of no man," Jackie announced with finality.

"That girl. That girl," Miss Bea repeated. "She's got the right idea, but she needs to be a little more proactive instead of reactive, if she's going to be so picky."

"We know that." Jackie pointed to her chest. "And that's exactly what we helped her with today."

"I'd like to be a fly on the wall in that club." Miss Bea smiled conspiratorially.

"I simply hope whatever happens at Bill's is good, because if it isn't, Nessa may never speak to either one of us again."

five

 anessa leaned toward the bathroom mirror in Bill's. She applied a coat of gloss to her cherry-colored lips. The salesgirl at the Origins counter had assured her that gloss was in. Vanessa flexed her shimmering mouth. She was so keyed up over meeting Xavier that she felt more uncertain than she could remember feeling in a long, long time.

The rest room door swung open, and two women entered in full conversation. "Why did you and Raymond bring me here to meet this guy?" one woman demanded of the other.

"This is my first time meeting him too," her companion continued to talk as she fastened the stall door. "Don't get mad at me. He's Raymond's homeboy."

"And that's where Raymond needs to send him. Back home."

Vanessa watched the unhappy woman smooth her French roll then look at her long, airbrushed nails. She was packing in all the right places, which made Vanessa scrutinize her own more modest form. *It ain't the best, but I have seen worse.* She took one last look at herself in the red form-fitting dress she'd chosen. Just enough cleavage and plenty of leg. At least that's what Miss Bea had said as she'd walked out the door. But Vanessa knew that could mean the dress was over the top, because Miss Bea never did anything in a mild manner. *If there's a time when I want to be a little over the top, it's now. I want to bowl Xavier Johnson over. I want him to regret that it took him so long to call me. But at the same time be glad that he finally did.*

"The man can hardly talk," the woman in the stall continued to vent. "And I'm supposed to spend my evening with him?"

"You don't have to. You can tell Raymond the truth." Her friend came out of the stall and began to wash her hands.

"Excuse me," Vanessa said, passing the two women. Embroiled in their own dilemma, they moved aside, giving her less than a second thought. Suddenly feeling unimpressive, Vanessa opened the rest room door and headed for the interior of the club.

The music was pumping an up tempo. It mirrored Vanessa's heartbeat. Happy hour was over, but some of the crowd remained, having placed double orders for drinks before the prices went back to normal. The lighting hadn't been turned down for the night crowd, and it was easy to see.

Vanessa entered the main area carefully. She didn't want to appear to be in a rush, nor did she want to pass Xavier by accident, but most of all she wanted to be prepared when she approached him. She did a slow sweep of the room and spotted Xavier at a corner table near the bar. Her preparation time was short, because as soon as Vanessa spotted him, Xavier laid eyes on her.

"Well, hello." He stood up as she approached.

"Hello to you," Vanessa replied.

"This was the only empty table they had. I hope it's okay."

"It's fine," she replied.

They both sat down.

"I haven't ordered anything to drink yet. I told the waitress to come back when you arrived." His dark eyes were steady, calm.

"How long have you been here?" Vanessa hoped her voice was casual. She felt anything but.

"About ten minutes."

Involuntarily, Vanessa looked at her watch. It was five after seven.

"Yes, you're late," Xavier said, lightly.

"Oh, I'm sorry. I've got a bad habit of checking my watch." She looked down at the table, feeling suddenly shy. "I was in the ladies' room."

He smiled. "Well then, you're forgiven."

Vanessa looked up at him from beneath curly lashes. *But should I forgive you for keeping me waiting for two months?*

The waitress appeared at the table. "Care for anything to drink?"

Xavier motioned toward Vanessa.

"I'll have a glass of white zinfandel."

"And you?" The woman settled into one hip.

"I'll take Jack Daniel's on the rocks."

"Got it. I'll be right back," the woman said, then headed for the bar.

"A man's drink," Vanessa remarked.

"That's one way of looking at it. Do you have a problem with that? Because I don't drink very often." He seemed to turn serious.

"No, just making an observation." Vanessa studied Xavier's face.

"An observation." He nodded his head, slowly. "Come to any conclusions?" he asked with what felt to Vanessa like an underlying purpose.

"Yeah. That this isn't your first time in a bar," Vanessa replied with her own smile, but she wondered what had triggered his change in mood.

Xavier seemed to relax again. "You've got good deductive reasoning skills."

Vanessa looked around. "Do you come here often?"

"Over the years I've been here a few times. But it's not a place that I frequent. How about you?"

"Pretty much the same. I've been here before. But it's been a while."

The waitress returned. She placed the drinks

on the table, and Xavier placed a ten dollar bill on her tray. "Keep the change."

"Thanks," she chimed before walking away.

Xavier shook the glass and watched the golden liquid tumble over the ice cubes. "I must say it's good to see you again, Vanessa."

"Did you come to the conclusion late today that it might be?" Vanessa couldn't help but refer to the time of Xavier's call and his hurried invitation.

"No." Xavier's brows furrowed. "I came to that conclusion while looking at you sitting here."

Vanessa studied his face. She wanted to be more blatant, but his eyes were so sincere that she remained quiet.

"From the look on your face I'd say you don't believe me."

"Your deductive reasoning skills are very good." She tossed his words back.

"They are?" One of Xavier's brows went up and came down, slowly. "So I guess that means you *don't* believe me."

"Considering the circumstances, I do find it difficult to believe."

"And why is that?" Xavier asked.

Because two months passed before you called me like you promised! Vanessa took a sip of wine. "I find that people tend to do the things they want to do. And . . . if it's so good seeing me again, I would think you would have attempted to see me before today."

Xavier leaned back in his chair. He studied Vanessa as he took a swallow of Jack. His gaze did not waver, and Vanessa began to feel uncomfortable. Finally, Xavier said, "To set the record straight, I had every intention of calling, but I had to leave for a last-minute business trip the day after we met. I was gone for a month and a half. I had been back a couple of days when I saw you at the street festival."

Part of Vanessa rejoiced at hearing why Xavier had not called when he'd promised, but her inner child heard a familiar excuse: that business was more important than she was. Vanessa looked down at the table. She wanted to accept what Xavier had said, to put the incident behind them, but the old emotional scar was a deep one.

She took a deep breath as Xavier looked at her intently. Waiting for a response. *Isn't he reaching out to me now? Didn't he call and make this date so that we could start all over again?*

A few seconds passed as Vanessa thought it over. Meanwhile, the lights lowered, and Natalie Cole began to croon about falling in love forever. Suddenly, the small corner table seemed even smaller.

More than a little aware of the cozy atmosphere, Vanessa shifted in her chair, and her knee bumped Xavier's leg. She flinched.

"Are you all right?" Xavier asked, in an all too knowing tone.

"Of course I am."

"You seem a little nervous." His silky voice pressed through the darkened atmosphere.

"Do I? Well, I'm not," she said, denying the truth. "I was on the verge of saying something, but I bumped into yo—"

"Into my leg. And that made you forget it?" He was toying with her. She didn't know what to make of that.

"Not really," Vanessa replied.

"So have you thought it over? Have I been forgiven?" Xavier's dark eyes bore into her.

Vanessa paused before she nodded. "I think so."

"Good," Xavier said. "Because you should have seen me in the airport as my plane was about to take off, trying to figure out how I was going to get your phone number. Remember, I wrote it on that program."

"I remember," Vanessa replied.

"And as much as I wished I had, I didn't take it with me."

Vanessa couldn't help but smile. "No, I guess you wouldn't have."

They both took sips of their drinks as the music flowed around them. Vanessa could feel herself relaxing, and Xavier appeared to settle back as well.

"Music is a wonderful thing," Xavier said. "It can relax you, excite you, bring back memories."

"Yes," Vanessa replied. "I can hear a song and remember approximately how old I was, what I was doing when it came out—"

"Who was in your life at that time." Xavier continued the train of thought.

Vanessa nodded.

"When this song came out I was about sixteen and I had two girlfriends." His eyes gleamed.

"Two girlfriends?" Vanessa stuck her fingers in the air.

"Yep."

"Did they know about each other?" she asked.

"Not at first, but when they found out . . ." He made a face. "There was a fight and it was all over the school. I tell you, it was too much action for me."

"So you're saying you didn't like them fighting over you?" Vanessa prodded.

Xavier smiled. "No. That wasn't it. I just didn't like all that attention. It seemed like the entire school knew my business. I'm a very private guy." He looked down. "I guess I was even back then."

"So which one did you end up with?" Vanessa was curious.

"Neither one. And I've been a one-woman man ever since."

Vanessa raised an eyebrow. "That's hard to believe."

"I didn't say how long I was with each woman," Xavier slyly rejoined. "I just said it was one at a time."

Vanessa shook her head, and the conversation lulled as Natalie repeated that she refused to stop falling in love.

Vanessa placed her wineglass against her lips, then asked in a matter-of-fact fashion before she took a sip, "Have you ever been in love?"

"Never," Xavier replied without skipping a beat.

"No hesitation there," she quipped, although Vanessa felt anything but laissez-faire.

"There was no need to hesitate. I know I haven't." He tilted his head so that he was looking down into Vanessa's face. "I believe love is a very powerful thing. And I'm certain I'll know it when I feel it. I also think love is very serious and it's not to be taken lightly."

All of a sudden Vanessa felt tingly inside. "Do you always give mini-lectures when it comes to subjects like this?"

"I wouldn't call that a lecture," he said smoothly. "I like to express myself clearly so I will be well understood."

"Yes, you don't want any mistakes made when it comes to that. You can save a lot of grief." They looked into each other's eyes. "And I agree with you, love is both powerful and serious."

"Am I speaking to an expert?" Xavier leaned forward, using the full extent of his tall frame. It brought him close to Vanessa. Very close.

"Of a sort. Not from being in love, but I have had a close-up view of two people who loved each other. My parents."

"Loved as in past tense?"

"Yes. My father died a couple of years ago."

"How sad for you," Xavier said. "But obviously you were very fortunate when he was alive."

"You could say that." Vanessa looked down at her hands, feeling conflict within her own heart.

"Many people grow up without two parents," Xavier continued. "But to have parents who truly loved each other, and who loved you . . . in today's society that is a gift." He nodded his head slowly. "Take me for instance. For as long as I can remember it was only my mother and me. My father," he hesitated, "died when I was young. I never knew my mother to have any other serious relationships."

"Your mother never had a boyfriend?" Vanessa was shocked.

"Not that I recall. No one ever came to the house, and she never went out."

"She was either very lonely or you were her life." Vanessa could picture Xavier as a cute little boy that any mother would cling to.

"I think it was the latter."

"That was spoken like a true mama's boy," she contended.

"No-o. I was too headstrong to be a real mama's boy. Then I moved away from Columbus and clipped the few apron strings she had managed to tie. Not that she didn't try to hold on." Xavier looked down. "And then she was killed in a car accident. It was after the accident that some of her lessons came back to me stronger and clearer."

"That must have been horrible," Vanessa said softly.

"It was rough." Xavier's head took a stubborn tilt. "It made me realize how impermanent we are." He blew air into his cupped hand. "After that I became interested in cultures and beliefs that look at life differently than most of us see it. Cultures that believe in reincarnation, for instance. I needed to think that there was a possibility my mother would experience life as we know it now, at least once again."

Vanessa released a deep breath. "You and my mother would get along quite well."

"Really?"

"Maybe that's why she's drawn to you. With all of their travelling, my parents were pretty broad-minded about a lot of things. Then after my father died, my mother seemed to immerse herself in 'metaphysical'—Vanessa made quotation marks with her fingers—"and Eastern books and spiritual videotapes. She also went to several conferences."

"I can understand that." Xavier shrugged. "She is probably trying to prove to herself that your father is not really dead as a lot of people perceive death to be. Like the Aborigine's Dreamtime. It embraces the continuity of life and death. In the Dreamtime, time doesn't flow in one direction. Past, present, and future are happening simultaneously. There's a oneness of existence. Some of our great minds, Albert Einstein, Isaac Newton, had similar beliefs."

"Maybe so." Vanessa crossed her leg. "But I think exploring that kind of thinking has allowed you and my mother to turn your grief into something constructive."

"I never thought about it that way, but I guess that's true." Xavier paused. "Another way I dealt with it was through travelling. I just took off and did a lot of exploring right after my mother died. I saw a lot of the world and I learned so much."

"I think a person can open their life up without travelling." Vanessa reacted to one of her old childhood demons. "Travelling can become a kind of running away. I mean, there are other things to be learned through the mundane day-to-day human experiences. You can learn from human relationships," she added more softly.

"I'm sure you're right," Xavier replied. "I bet you learned a lot from your parents' relationship."

"Yes, I did," Vanessa conceded, caught off guard.

Xavier's eyes took on a faraway look. "I've never been around . . ." He paused and seemed to adjust his words, "at least not for an extended period of time, two people who were in love. And I don't have a true grasp of that. Short-term romance, yes. I understand that. Short term without the romance, yes," he added wryly.

"I bet you've had your share of that," Vanessa retorted.

Xavier took another swallow of Jack. He was about to put the glass down, but he held it in midair instead. "But you know, I don't think you really need a blueprint when you truly love someone." He looked into Vanessa's eyes. "I believe your heart will guide you, and you will never want to hurt that person because their happiness will be your highest concern. I think two people in love is probably one of the most naturally self-perpetuating things in the world."

Vanessa felt almost hypnotized by his voice, but she wondered if Xavier was speaking from his heart. Or were these just lines that he had spoken before? Lines Xavier knew worked well on the female psyche.

For a moment Vanessa considered leaning back in her chair and putting a little more space between them. Perhaps that might help her think more clearly. But Vanessa's body remained where it was, leaning forward, soaking up every word Xavier spoke, along with the smoothness of his skin, his mustache, the sincerity of his eyes. Such eyes. . . . *Lord, don't let me close my eyes now. Not even to blink. I'd probably swoon like those silly women in the old movies.* She looked at his lips, which were so close. Finally Vanessa replied, "From what you just said I don't think you'll have any problem at all. Not one bit."

There it is! Xavier recognized the moment Vanessa was emotionally present. *That openness I glimpsed the first night I met her. So pure. So powerful.* He continued to gaze into Vanessa's clear eyes. Alluring eyes that held so much. He knew that if he pressed his lips against hers, she would respond. But Xavier held back so he could admire the fullness of her lips, the curve of her cheek, and the way a soft swirl of fine hair framed her face. Just as he was about to lean forward and kiss her, lightly, he heard Vanessa say, "I'm glad you invited me here tonight."

"What?" he replied in a whispery tone.

"I said I'm glad you invited me here tonight." She smiled. "At first I didn't like how you left the message with my mother instead of calling and talking to me directly. But as you can see, I came anyway. I came because I wanted to see you again."

"I'm glad that you came, Vanessa," Xavier said. He paused, then continued, "but I never called you and left a phone message with your mother."

Vanessa's expression melted. Her dark eyes, which had been soft and inviting, turned confused. "I beg your pardon."

"You called and left a message at the museum, remember? Inviting me to meet you here at seven o'clock," Xavier explained.

"No. I didn't," Vanessa said. She sat back slowly. "What are you saying? You never called me?"

A dawning realization surfaced in Xavier's eyes. "I never called, but—"

"My mother said . . ." Vanessa's voice trailed away. When she looked at Xavier again all she could think was, *This man never called me.*

Xavier glanced down at the table, then up at Vanessa and said, "I've been in some awkward situations but I must admit this is one of the strangest." He looked as if he didn't know what to say.

Vanessa cringed. "My mother."

Xavier's eyes turned hooded. "Do you think your mother is behind this?"

Vanessa looked down. "It's possible."

"Goodness. She surely has gone to great lengths to get us together."

His pointed comment heightened Vanessa's embarrassment and also sparked her anger. "You've heard the old saying, a mother will do anything for her child. Well mine will do anything to get what she wants."

Xavier shifted in his chair. "Which is?"

The full impact of what had taken place descended on Vanessa. She felt like the hopeless daughter who needed help getting a date, who had been set up by her mother! She looked at Xavier's guarded features. He had been unknowingly drawn into the plot. It hadn't been his idea to see her at all!

Vanessa felt like a fool. "Your guess is as good as mine" was Vanessa's tart reply.

The tiny corner space squeezed in on them.

Xavier studied the myriad of emotions shifting across Vanessa's face. "Look," he finally said, "I—" He placed his hand on top of her clenched fist.

"You what?" She removed her hand as the shame continued to mount.

Xavier exhaled and sat back in his chair. "Let's just forget about how we got here. What does it matter? We're here now. And I think we should make the best of it."

But Vanessa couldn't look at Xavier. She couldn't recall a time when she had been as embarrassed. Her mother had overstepped her bounds in a major way, but it didn't change the fact that Xavier had *never* called. Hadn't called when he said he would. Hadn't called to apologize or explain. Hadn't called after seeing her at the street festival. And hadn't called tonight. When she glanced up into his face again Vanessa thought she saw a tinge of impatience. *How dare he judge me now? Doesn't he care how this makes me feel?*

Xavier could only guess what was going through Vanessa's mind. He had said what he could to put her at ease, that it didn't matter how they got there, that he had truly wanted to see her. *What else would she have me do or say?* He watched her eyes turn dark with anger. *She seems to insist on being angry with me, when it's her mother that she should take this up with.* His lips turned a smirk at the irony of it all. *We finally get together and this is what happens.*

Vanessa looked at Xavier as one side of his lip took an upward turn. *Now that's the last straw! He is laughing at me. I'm not going to sit here and be ridiculed. I cannot!* Vanessa stood up and looked down into Xavier's upturned face. "There's nothing to make the best of." She walked away from the table and out of the club.

six

Vanessa entered the house slowly, closing the front door without a sound. She felt dead inside, as if a vacuum had sucked all the life out of her. Vanessa knew it wasn't just about Xavier. It was much bigger than that. Much deeper because of her mother's involvement. Jackie would not have committed such a desperate act out of a concern that she and Xavier would never get together.

There had to be a deeper motivation. A deeper fear that her mother carried. *Does she feel there is something so inadequate about me that I will end up spending my life alone and it won't be my decision? And is that fear not so much for me but for herself? Will my inability to find a mate, in her mind, be proof of her inadequacy as a mother?*

Miss Bea, Lillie, Mrs. Bertha, and Jackie looked up from the card table. Embroiled in her thoughts, Vanessa had forgotten it was card night. She stared at the four sets of familiar eyes as if they were strangers'.

Jackie placed her cards face down on the table. "You're back so early." Her voice was apprehensive.

Vanessa didn't reply.

"Nessa, are you okay?"

Vanessa looked at her mother for a prolonged moment. "How can I be, Mama?"

"What happened?" Jackie got up from the table, crossed the room, and stood in front of her daughter.

"What did you expect would happen when you set me up on a blind date and don't tell me?" Vanessa replied.

Jackie opened her mouth a couple of times, but nothing came out. Finally, she said, "It wasn't exactly a blind date. I thought if I gave you and Mr. Johnson a little push, I'd get the ball rolling and you and he would take it from there."

"You call that a little push?" Vanessa's low voice trembled.

Jackie bit her lip and looked away.

"I'm thirty-three years old, Mama. A grown woman. You just don't do things like this to a grown woman."

Jackie's hand went up to her mouth before she got control of herself and brought it down slowly. When she replied her tone was rather matter-of-fact. "I know you're grown, Nessa, but . . . things have been moving so slowly."

"My life has always moved too slowly for you. It has never been what you wanted it to be." Vanessa took a deep breath, and her body trembled on the exhale. "But there are two key words in that, Mama—*my life*." She patted her chest. "Maybe if you had been around more when I was a child, things would have been different." The comment sliced through the air.

"There you go digging up the past," Jackie said nonchalantly, but she was squeezing her own hand so tightly that her veins protruded.

"Maybe we should call it quits for the night," Miss Bea announced, breaking the awful silence that had descended. "The score's about even, so it doesn't matter if we scratch tonight."

Lillie and Mrs. Bertha placed their cards on the table when Miss Bea gave them a silent command to do so.

"No." Jackie formed a stop sign with her hand. "We are not going to end the game. I want to finish it, and that's what we're going to do."

Uncomfortable, the women at the table looked at one another. Vanessa looked at her mother, and the words she had suppressed and feared since she was a little girl surfaced in her mind. *I hate her. I hate my mother.*

A horrible, sad feeling came with them, and Vanessa knew at that moment that all the apologies and the backing down she had done through the years stemmed from the fear that one day she would come to this conclusion. *Could it be true?* she asked herself. *Do I really hate her?* Vanessa prayed to God that it wasn't as the guilt poured in.

"Jackie, I think it would be better if we went home and let you and Nessa talk this thing through," Miss Bea said, looking guilty because of her part in the fiasco.

"Nessa and I can talk later, if she wants." Jackie turned tired eyes on her daughter. "But we're going to finish this game tonight because it'll be a while before we get to play again." With a sigh of resignation Jackie walked back to the card table and sat down.

"As usual you deal with me on your own terms." Vanessa remained motionless as she felt pity for herself. The debilitating feeling emanated throughout her being as a thought dawned on her. *If it is possible that I hate my mother, is it also possible that she hates me?* Vanessa watched her mother sit down with a new sense of loss. To have a mother who neglected you was one thing; to have one who hated you was totally another.

"If that were true I wouldn't have done the things I've done through the years," Jackie replied, "including what I did tonight."

Vanessa felt a huge knot in her throat as she started for her bedroom. *Why did she ask me to move back? Why did she ask if she hates me so?*

"Don't we have a game scheduled next Friday?" Lillie asked Miss Bea in a lowered voice.

"Of course we do," Miss Bea reassured her. "I don't know what Jackie's talking about."

"I'm saying I'm not going to be here next Friday." Jackie situated her cards.

"You're not?" Lillie remarked. "Where you gonna be?"

"In Australia."

"Say what?" Mrs. Bertha blurted out.

Vanessa stopped dead in her tracks.

"In Australia?" Miss Bea repeated.

"That's right." Jackie didn't look at anyone. She continued to study her cards.

"And when did you decide all of this?" Miss Bea questioned.

"Yes, Mama. When did you decide *all* of that?" Vanessa called out with slightly veiled criticism.

"I made up my mind a week ago."

"And when were you going to tell me?" Vanessa's voice broke.

"Tonight," Jackie replied. "After you and Mr. Johnson had gotten reacquainted. I was hoping to see you two off to a running start before I left."

"Oh, I see." Vanessa couldn't believe what she was hearing. "So the setup was for your benefit, not for mine. I'm too old for a nanny so you decided to pawn me off the best way you could. And then you could do what you have always done . . . leave."

Jackie stacked her hand and placed it on the table. "I can see we are not going to have a reasonable conversation right now, Nessa. You are too upset." Jackie used her best parental voice. "I think we should discuss this in private." She dismissed her daughter. "It's your turn, Mrs. Bertha."

Vanessa's eyes never left her mother's face. "You're right, Mama. This is not the time for me to say what I am thinking and feeling. But I don't think that you will ever be ready to hear what I have finally come to understand."

The way Vanessa spoke made Jackie look at her daughter once again. Their eyes locked before Vanessa crossed the room and disappeared down the hallway.

The four friends resumed their game under an awkward silence.

Finally Miss Bea leaned on the card table and said, "Are you really going to Australia?"

"Yes," Jackie replied, her heart palpitating. She looked at her cards, not at her friend. "I've got my ticket and everything's been arranged."

Miss Bea looked astounded, but Lillie and Mrs. Bertha were obviously impressed, although they tried to mask their excitement because of the look Miss Bea gave them.

"What part of Australia are you going to?" Lillie inquired after an appropriate pause.

"Alice Springs. It's in central Australia," Jackie replied.

Mrs. Bertha's eyes widened. "I've never heard of it. I've heard of Sydney and Melbourne, but not Alice Springs."

"Yes." Jackie brightened a bit under Mrs. Bertha's attention, but she was remembering the look in Vanessa's eyes before she'd walked out of the room. "It's near the Western desert, which takes up a large portion of the land. There are several Aboriginal tribes living in the area. I want to go see them. Some Aborigines still remember things that their ancestors taught them. Things that are thousands of years old."

"My goodness," Lillie exclaimed. "I guess it will be like stepping back in time."

"No, I don't think so," Jackie continued. "Modern times have affected them as well. But there are Aborigines who can tap into states that we might consider to be miraculous. There is a book called *Mutant Message Down Under*, that it is almost impossible to believe because of some of the things the author writes about." Jackie paused. She had never really been able to talk to her friends about these things. Things that she and William had begun to discuss a few years before he died. Whenever Jackie would bring up this kind of subject, her friends would become frightened. Eventually she gave up.

Jackie had hoped that having Vanessa back home would allow her to share with her daughter the things that intrigued and consumed her. That discussions about life, death, the forces of nature, and countless other profundities would create a new bond between them, and allow Vanessa a glimpse of the world that had become important to her mother and father. In short, it had been very lonely having these things buzzing around in her head without William to talk to.

But Vanessa had shut out her attempts to be

closer, as she had done time and time again since she was a child. Jackie could feel her heart become heavy again. "I hope to experience at least one of those miracles while I'm there," she added.

Lillie and Mrs. Bertha seemed uncomfortable, while Miss Bea gave her a kind of *what-are-you-up-to?* look.

Lillie tore her gaze away from Miss Bea's disgruntled expression. "When do you leave?"

"Tuesday," Jackie replied.

"You mean to tell me you're going to Australia in four days and you are just now telling us about it?" Miss Bea was incredulous.

"I had to make up my mind. And when I did, I went straight to the travel agent's office and made all the arrangements before I could change it back again."

"That should tell you maybe you've moved too quickly," Miss Bea said, continuing her strong position. "From the little I know of Australia, it seems like it could be pretty rough, Jackie. Are you going with a group?"

"No." Jackie placed her left hand on top of her right one, which had begun to shake.

"What in the world possessed you to think you should go to Australia alone?" Miss Bea insisted.

"If I had asked you, would you have come with me?" Jackie was tired of Miss Bea's interrogation.

Miss Bea hesitated, then began, "I don't th—"

"See there," Jackie retorted. "I wanted to go. I knew I couldn't count on you or Nessa or anybody else to go with me. I've travelled with William all over this planet and this is a trip that I've got to take. It's important to me and to W—" She stopped before she said her husband's name. "I'm going and I'm going on my own," Jackie said with finality.

"How exciting!" Lillie couldn't hold back any longer. "It sounds like quite the adventure to me. Just the kind of thing that I would expect of you, Jackie."

"Oh, hush, Lillie." Miss Bea waved her hand in the smiling woman's direction. "This is no time for fancifulness. Jackie isn't Indiana Jones and we are not some young Girl Scouts whose troup leader is going off to summer camp. Here she is talking about going somewhere that probably doesn't have bathrooms or running water, and you're cheering her on."

"Alice Springs is a city. Granted, a very small one. But it does have bathrooms and running water. And as far as the Western desert goes, I'm sure there are provisions for tourists like me." Jackie defended her decision. "Xavier Johnson has been there, and he came back here in one piece."

"Xavier Johnson is a good-looking, young buck. I'm sorry, but you and he can't be placed in the same physical category," Miss Bea pointed out.

"Bea, I don't care what you say. I'm going to Australia, so you might as well wish me well," Jackie said stubbornly.

Miss Bea pursed her lips, then looked down. "If you are set on going, you know I wish you well. But this is one decision, Jackie, that I pray you don't regret."

"I won't regret it, Bea. No matter what happens. I swear I won't regret it. And nor should you."

The old friends' gazes met.

They finished the game, and Jackie walked her friends to the door, then locked up for the night. She started down the hall, and stopped outside Vanessa's bedroom. Jackie could hear the television playing inside. She raised her hand to knock, then changed her mind. Jackie needed to prepare herself before she talked to her daughter.

She entered the bedroom that she and William had shared for fifty-three years. Then she sat on the side of the bed and opened the night stand drawer. She removed their one and only wedding picture, and stared at the young faces that looked back at her joyfully. And that's when Jackie started to cry. "What did we do, William?" she asked the portrait. "What did we do to our little Nessa?"

At that moment Jackie realized how much she and Vanessa were truly alike. There she sat, crying her eyes out like she had done so many times before, but Vanessa had never seen her cry. Had never seen the times when her eyes were full of love and dismay over how to regain her daughter's trust. Jackie had kept her true feelings hidden from her child, and as payback Vanessa had locked herself away from her parents and from life.

When Vanessa had been small, Jackie had thought a strong, invincible image was what she'd needed to present to Vanessa so that Vanessa would learn to cope. *A person needs to be strong and clear about what she wants and no one will perceive her as weak. People take advantage of the weak.*

That's what Jackie's life had taught her. She had been a sensitive child who had had to develop a thick skin to weather the bumps and bruises of life. It had been a painful way to grow up, and Jackie had wanted to spare Vanessa such an experience. But Jackie had eventually realized her staunch image had not created a good relationship between her and her daughter. By then they had both become so deeply entrenched in their ways that it had been hard to change. By the time Jackie realized the problem, she'd wanted to change, but it had been too late. Vanessa had gone into herself, locking her mother and father and life away because they had not shown her how much they'd cared.

"But we did love her, William," Jackie continued. "We had her late in life and she was quite the surprise, but we loved her because she was an extension of ourselves, a product of our love." Jackie choked on her own words. "Was it wrong for us to love each other so much that our child felt like an outsider because of it?" She wiped her eyes with the mound of her hand and shook her head. "Maybe I should have stayed at home more, or maybe I should have convinced you to stop contracting and take an engineering job that would have kept you at home." She touched her husband's face, and her tears fell on the photograph. Quickly Jackie dabbed at the picture with the bedspread. "But you would have died staying in one place, not physically, I know, but your free spirit, the one that made me love you so, would have withered away." Jackie swallowed hard. "Now I've got to go talk to her, William my love, before I leave for Australia." Her eyes beamed with determination. "But there was such a look on her face before she walked away." Jackie trembled as she replayed the scene in her mind. "I don't know what she will say to me." She shook her head once again. "I don't know what she's going to say." Jackie heaved a sigh. "But it was never our intention to hurt her." She began to dry her eyes. "Never. And no matter what happens, I'll hold on to that until I see you again."

Jackie waited until her face was totally dry and all the traces of her tears had vanished before she left her bedroom.

seven

$\mathcal{V}$anessa repositioned her pillow again. It seemed no matter where she placed it, she couldn't get comfortable. The late news was about to air on television, and Vanessa searched for the remote control to change the channel. She wanted to see something uplifting, not depressing.

Jackie tapped on her door. "Are you still awake, Nessa?"

Vanessa continued to change the channels. "Yes. I'm awake." There was a pronounced silence. Vanessa knew Jackie wanted her to invite her in, but she refused to do so.

"May I come in . . . please?" Jackie requested.

There was a tinge of hurt beneath the question, and Vanessa immediately regretted her defiance.

She's my mother. Doesn't that alone command a certain amount of respect and obedience? "Yes, Mama," Vanessa acquiesced. "You may."

She sat up in bed as Jackie came through the door. Instead of sitting in the empty chair near the bed, Jackie sat on the bed. Vanessa crossed her arms to combat the closeness.

"I want to apologize to you, Nessa," Jackie began. "I guess I did overstep my bounds by arranging that date with Xavier Johnson and I'm sorry."

"Oh-h Mama." Vanessa continued to look at the television. "Yes, you most definitely overstepped your bounds." She turned to Jackie. "But you've always felt it was your right to participate in my life in whatever fashion suited you. I've always been secondary, and you've never apologized before."

Jackie looked defeated. "But you have to admit I've never done anything like this." She bit her closely trimmed nails. "The truth is, I thought you'd never find out. I thought that you two would be so swept up by seeing each other, that how you got there wouldn't even come up. That's how your father and I were."

"Xavier and I are not you and Daddy," Vanessa said. "I hardly know Xavier." Vanessa shook her head. "What does it matter? All of this is partially my fault anyway."

Jackie looked confused, but hopeful.

"Don't get me wrong. You should never have done what you did." Vanessa wanted to make her

Finally, Jackie said with sincerity, "I love you, Vanessa. You're my only child. I've always loved you. Maybe not the way you wanted me to, but I loved you the only way I knew how."

Vanessa looked down at the bed. Her arms felt trapped at her sides. She wanted to reach out and hold her mother, but she had restrained herself for so long that it was impossible to do so.

Jackie looked at her daughter's bowed head. At that moment she wished that Vanessa was a little girl again, and that she had been given another chance to pull her onto her lap and rock and hug her hurt away. But Vanessa was no longer a child, and Jackie's arms weren't strong enough, nor was there enough history of physical demonstrations of love between them for her to pull her full-grown daughter into her arms and physically comfort her. The best Jackie could do was slowly reach out and pat Vanessa's hand.

Vanessa watched her mother's slightly puffy hand cover her own. She looked up and saw the sincerity in her mother's eyes, and in return she gave Jackie a weak smile.

"I want us to be closer, Nessa. I want us to really share our lives, our deepest thoughts." Jackie paused. "Since your father died I've had so many thoughts go through my mind. I can't believe he's really gone," she said softly. "Because I don't believe putting him in that box and covering him with dirt was the end of him. That's why I must go to Australia." Her eyes burned with intent.

"Unbelievable things are possible there. There, bridging the seen and unseen is a part of everyday life."

Desperation emanated from Jackie's eyes as she spoke, and suddenly Vanessa saw her mother in a different light. She was no longer an unbendable force to reckon with. Jackie was an elderly woman who desperately missed her lifelong partner. Missed him so badly that a part of her refused to let go. Missed him so badly that mental instability was a possibility.

For the first time in her life Vanessa truly feared for her mother's mental well-being. She was uncertain as she thought about how to phrase her next statement. "Mama . . . I don't know about your going to Australia alone."

"I'll be fine, Nessa. I'm an old hand at travelling. Your father and I went almost everywhere together."

"But that's just it, Mama." Vanessa touched her shoulder. "You won't be travelling with Daddy. You won't be travelling with anyone that you know, and I don't think that's a good idea at this stage of your life."

"My mind and my spirit are more vital now than they have ever been." Jackie looked at Vanessa defiantly.

"I don't deny that," Vanessa replied carefully, then took a deep breath. Her mother was seventy-six years old, and in good health as far as Vanessa knew, but that did not negate her age or her unsettling frame of mind. "I tell you what—" She paused again. "I'll go with you."

Jackie leaned back and stared into her daughter's face. "I don't believe this."

"Believe it." Vanessa thought of the videotaped program about near death experiences that her mother had recently watched, and the audiotapes she was constantly listening to, as well as the spiritual books stacked on their bookshelves. Vanessa had never thought they could be dangerous, but now, with her mother's conviction that she might be able to see her father again . . . she wasn't so sure. "I'll go and get a ticket tomorrow." Vanessa ran her hands over her braids. "It's been a mighty long time since I've been on an airplane, but I'm willing to go with you."

"Let me jog your memory a bit." Jackie crossed her arms sl   . "I believe you were fifteen when you dran   sp   vowed that you would never travel wit   best out one of us again. Even if we begged yo   out   ackie looked at Vanessa with a lowered ch   w   And if my memory serves me right, how t   ame about was, you wanted to go with us on   ip, and we turned you down. So that's how y   handled it. You said we would never get the   pportunity to do that again. Remember?"

"Of course   remember." Vanessa put on a poker face.

"And from w   know, you haven't travelled outside of Georg   You hate travelling. But that now, all of a sudden, you're willing to go to Australia?" Jackie looked unconvinced.

Vanessa nodded.

"What caused a one-hundred-and-eighty-degree turn like this?" Jackie studied her daughter's face. "Are you afraid that I'm too old to go on my own? Or are you thinking that because of the things I said about your father, I might be losing my mind?"

"I didn't say that, Mama," Vanessa replied.

"You didn't have to say it. The fear is right there in your eyes." Jackie smiled a sad, resigned smile.

At that moment she knew just how much she missed William. Was she going to spend the rest of her days an outsider, although she had family and friends? Once again she had tried to share her beliefs with Vanessa with less than satisfactory results. And Vanessa's fear that she may be losing her mind was far worse than Vanessa dismissing her beliefs with a shake of her head or an intolerant look.

Jackie looked in her daughter's eyes, which were too bright. No, she would go to Australia alone, although she didn't know what that would ultimately mean. Jackie had seen the Australian outback, and she'd read up on what to expect. It was not for the faint of heart. *But if my reuniting with William means I am to die there*, Jackie thought, imprinting her daughter's face on her mind, *I still go willingly*. She looked down. *I had hoped to see Vanessa on the road to a relationship as fulfilling as the one her father and I shared. My tactics were not the best this time, and I must admit I bungled it pretty badly, but if it's the last thing I do before I leave Columbus, I will make sure there is still hope for Vanessa and Xavier.*

Jackie suddenly thought about the untimely meeting at the street festival. The homeless man. The note. And the unlikely chance that Xavier Johnson, the man that she had focused on because of his involvement with Australia and the Aborigines, was the same man who had touched her daughter's heart. *There are no coincidences,* Jackie repeated in her mind with fervor. *There is purpose and meaning even behind the smallest thing, let alone circumstances like this.*

She gave Vanessa an unusual smile. Jackie didn't need anyone to go with her to Australia. And she certainly didn't want Vanessa there, who, as well intended as she might be, didn't understand what motivated her, and who might plant doubt in Jackie's heart about her expected reunion with William ever taking place.

Jackie stood up from the bed. "I am going to Australia, Nessa. And I am going alone. And no matter what happens afterwards, I want you to know I have always loved you, and I always will."

eight

"How are you holding up?" Curtis Martin stood in the doorway of Xavier's office.

Xavier looked up from his desk. Curtis rarely stopped by his office to "chat." As a matter of fact, as of late, he'd been keeping his contact with Xavier down to a minimum. Xavier knew it was because Curtis believed that Xavier was after his job as assistant curator of the museum. Although that wasn't Xavier's intent, if the opportunity presented itself he certainly wouldn't ignore it. "Just fine, Curtis."

"If you can say that, I guess you haven't heard the recent buzz."

Xavier put his ink pen down and sat back in his chair. "What buzz?"

"Seems like your Aboriginal art exhibit may

have run into a snag." Curtis could barely conceal his glee.

"Is that right?"

"Yes, it is." Curtis nodded with authority.

Xavier's gaze never left Curtis's face. "Mr. Marshall hasn't said anything to me about it. And I haven't had any calls from Australia indicating that."

"I'm coming directly from my uncle's office." Curtis made his customary reference to the boss, Mr. Marshall. "I told him I'd pass the information to you. My uncle's got more important things to be concerned about, so I thought I'd just put you on the alert."

Xavier rubbed his chin. "What's going on ... exactly?"

Curtis looked down, then quickly up again. "It appears you misled us about the solidity of the deal."

"I haven't misled anyone." Xavier's jaw clenched. "I did the research and selected a group of Aboriginal artists who were willing to send their paintings here to Columbus. That's what I promised to do. My involvement will commence again, once the paintings arrive." Xavier thought for a moment. "Maybe there's some problems with the contracts that I don't know about, but that's not my area. So you either tell me the details of this 'snag' as you put it, or let someone who's knowledgeable do it."

"I am knowledgeable, Mr. Johnson. I have far

more knowledge than you do about being a curator of a museum of this stature." Curtis's short fuse went off. "It would serve you well to remember that."

"I wasn't talking about being a curator, Curtis." Xavier's voice was low but powerful, making Curtis's name sound obscene. "I'm referring to the problem with bringing the Pintupi paintings to the Marshall Art Museum."

Curtis's nostrils flared ever so slightly. "I can tell you this. It seems the Aborigines that you met with in Australia didn't have the authority to make the deal."

"Well, if that's true, you need to talk to the group that you put me in contact with, World Import and Exports. They set up the meeting. I visited some Pintupi areas on my own, but in the end, the Pintupi artists I selected I met through the import/export company."

"Well-uh. Well-uh," Curtis stumbled. "You couldn't have explained what was going to happen to them very clearly, because now it appears the Aborigines are trying to pull out. Phillip Ramsey with World Import and Exports says they're working on keeping the deal together, but things aren't looking too good. He says they're going to turn to some other Pintupi contacts. But if they're not able to straighten it out," Curtis added, shaking his head, "and I mean shortly, we will have no choice but to allocate the money from the Aborigine exhibit budget elsewhere. We can't risk investing in a shaky project, Xavier." He gave

Xavier a condescending look, then continued on his way.

If Marshall Art Museum has so much stature, why don't we have more money? Xavier mentally fumed, more at the thought that the museum might pull its backing from the Aboriginal art exhibit than at anything else. *I've worked long and hard to interest the museum in a project like this, and I don't intend to let it fall to the wayside.*

Xavier stood up. *The Pintupi artists I spoke with at the Strehlow Research Centre in Alice Springs were reputable, and they were obviously known and respected by the people working there. I saw some of their paintings and I loved them. And they spoke sincerely about other paintings by Pintupi artists, who they were certain would be willing to participate in the exhibit. So what made them change their minds? Wouldn't they be able to speak for their own artwork even if they couldn't speak for the artists who weren't there?* Xavier was puzzled. *And now World Import and Exports has become the projects' lifeline. When I consider the double-talk surrounding that company, which Curtis had recommended, I don't feel very good about that.*

Xavier walked around his office. *I was going to select the paintings and artists on my own, but Curtis called me at home and suggested I contact World Import and Exports when I got to Alice Springs.* His eyes narrowed. *He said they could facilitate getting the paintings over here. How did he put it?* "We wouldn't have to get caught up in the maze of Australian import/export laws because World Import and

Exports are set up to do that kind of business." More wary than ever, Xavier sat back down again.

This exhibit is important to me. It's important to the museum. It will make the Marshall Art Museum a world player. Not just a museum with local, regional, and a few national pieces from time to time. But it's also important to the community. We need something to expand the views of people like Curtis, and this Aboriginal art exhibit will show Columbus that people of color are so much more than what history delegated us to. That there are people of color all over the globe who are making their mark on the world in a profound way. I want to be a part of educating people about that. Getting people to realize that although someone may not look like you, it doesn't mean they don't have worth.

And the Aborigines of Australia are a prime example of that. Of all the cultures on earth they seem to draw the most curiosity. People tend to see them as different. Think that their hopes and dreams and expectations are different. But I want to say even if they are, there is beauty in that diversity, just like the beauty that is so apparent in their art.

Xavier sighed as he thought of his father. *Now I know being different doesn't mean being without worth. If I can't say it to him directly, I will say it to the world through honoring one of the most unique cultures known.*

Xavier picked up the telephone, ready to straighten out this so-called snag. If Xavier had anything to say about it, Curtis wouldn't be celebrating Xavier's defeat anytime soon.

*   *   *

"Is this everything, Mama?" Vanessa called from the living room. "You're just taking two suitcases?"

"That's it," Jackie confirmed from the kitchen.

"Okay then. It's time to go if you don't want to be rushed boarding your plane."

"We'll be out in a second," Jackie replied. She turned to Miss Bea. "Now I want you to take my African violets over to your house and place them in that window that I keep telling you to use for your plants."

"Take your violets?" Miss Bea's mouth dropped open. "Why do you want me to do that? Nessa's here. All she's got to do is give them a little bit of attention. It's only two weeks. They'll be fine."

"You know how Nessa is with plants. They are not her thing."

"Then I'll take care of them over here."

"No, Bea." Jackie was adamant. "I want you to have them."

"What?" Miss Bea looked apprehensive.

"For the meantime. Until I return."

"I don't like the feel of this, Jackie." Miss Bea took hold of her friend's shoulders, then looked her straight in the eye. "There's something you're not telling me."

Jackie's voice held an unusual lilt when she spoke. "Don't worry. I plan to see you again." She reached for the two violets, then stopped. "And would you do me another favor?"

"Sure."

"Mail this letter a couple of days before I am to return."

"You are acting mighty strange, Jackie Bradley." Miss Bea shook her finger.

"There is nothing strange about asking you to mail a letter for me. I need it to arrive at a certain time, and this is private. I don't want Nessa knowing about it. So I'm trusting you, my best friend, to take care of it for me." She put the letter in the pocket of Miss Bea's duster.

"Well, when you put it that way, it doesn't sound so bad."

Jackie handed the flowers to Miss Bea. "It isn't. Now let's hurry. I've got a plane to catch."

They entered the living room as Vanessa returned from taking one of the suitcases to the car.

"Now Miss Bea, I want you to be my witness," Vanessa said.

"Witness to what?" Miss Bea looked uncertain.

"You heard Mama promise that she's going to check in with me every three days, didn't you?"

"I heard her, for all that means."

"That's all I needed to hear you say." Vanessa picked up the other suitcase. "If you do other than that"—she looked at her mother—"you won't be able to worm your way out of it, saying stuff like you don't remember, or you never promised or—"

"I promise. I promise." Jackie closed the door behind them and began to lock up. "You two act like I'm on probation or something."

"You're going to be on parole if you don't call

me," Vanessa warned, giving her mother a serious look.

"Ugh-h." Jackie turned to her friend. She couldn't deal with the concern in her daughter's eyes. "Bea, you did the right thing by never having children. That way you'll always be an adult. Sometimes they try to reverse the roles on you."

Miss Bea smiled.

"Well let me hug you." Jackie wrapped her arms around her friend, who did the best she could to return the favor with her hands full. Then Vanessa and Jackie climbed in the car. Eyes sparkling with tears held back, Jackie said, "I'll be seeing you, Bea," and waved as the car drove away.

Vanessa rushed to unlock the door as the telephone rang for the third time. She ran across the living room and grabbed it on the end of the fourth ring. "Hello. Hello," she said as the party hung up. "Damn." *Could that have been Xavier?*

It could have been, and once again her mother's insistence on not acquiring any of the more modern phone services was extremely perturbing. "There's going to have to be some changes around here when Mama gets back. If she doesn't want these services, that's fine. But I'm going to insist on getting my own phone line with call waiting and an answering machine," Vanessa said out loud.

Yet deep down inside, Vanessa felt good about the possibility for positive change in her relationship with her mother. Yes, they had been worlds apart for years, but they had spoken from their hearts the night that Jackie had dropped the bombshell of her trip, and Vanessa knew it marked a new beginning for the two of them. She closed the front door, her mind a jumble.

Time passed effortlessly, and Vanessa couldn't believe, after only a few days, how empty the house felt with her mother gone.

When she'd first arrived home from the airport, Vanessa had breathed a sigh of relief. Driving Jackie to the airport, which had included leaving work early, herding her mother out of the house, and waiting with her until she boarded the plane, had been a minor ordeal. So during the first few days, Vanessa was content with the quietness. But that came to an end rather quickly. Her mother's trademark constant chatter, which she had become accustomed to, was blatantly absent. There was no smell of food cooking in the kitchen, no discussions about possible programs to watch on television, and no telephone calls. The house was silent except for the occasional over-thirty-year-old house creaks, and Vanessa didn't like it.

Somehow it was different from when she had lived alone in her apartment. There had been a new feel about the place, and the possibility of things to come. But the ambiance here, in the house where she had grown up, was one of shadows. Things that had once been. Possibilities that had come and gone. It made Vanessa think about how it might feel to grow old alone. Without friends. Without children. Without a husband.

Deep in thought, she sat down at the kneehole desk where her mother did all her paperwork. First her gaze searched the desktop. Next she opened the long middle drawer. Vanessa had Xavier's card in hand before she truly realized what she was searching for.

The simple lines on linen paper were a class act, just like Xavier. Her mother certainly liked him, and so did Miss Bea, Vanessa thought, turning the card over in her hand and wondering once again if that phone call had been Xavier trying to reach her.

She thought back on their meeting at the club. Once the cat was out of the bag about her mother's meddlesome ways, Xavier had wanted to start their relationship anew, wipe their slate clean, so to speak. But Vanessa had been too embarrassed to see it. *I shouldn't have left him like that. I should have given him another chance*, Vanessa chastised herself. *Maybe it's not too late.* She picked up the telephone and dialed the numbers from the card.

"May I speak to Xavier Johnson."

"I'm sorry," a voice replied. "The museum officially closes at five."

"Oh. I didn't realize how late it was." Vanessa looked at her watch. It was six-thirty. "I'm sure Xavier has left by now."

"Is this a personal call?" The professional voice incorporated a more personal tone.

"Why . . . yes it is," Vanessa replied.

"Then hold on a moment. Let me see if he's still here."

A pleasing melody emerged on the telephone line while Vanessa waited. Then there was a click and Xavier's voice saying, "Yes."

"It's Vanessa." Her gaze rose to the ceiling as if calling for help.

"Hello, Vanessa." He sounded genuinely pleased. "This is a pleasant surprise."

Vanessa's smile was deep and satisfying. "I just thought I should give you a call to apologize for the way I left the club the other night."

There was a pause as if Xavier was distracted. "I appreciate that, but no apology was necessary."

The line went silent.

"How have you been?" Vanessa searched for a way to bring a normal tone into the situation.

"Not too good," Xavier replied.

"No?"

"No." She heard him sigh. "As a matter of fact, I'm in the middle of an important meeting."

"Oh, I'm sorry."

"No problem," he said quickly, then spoke as if he didn't want to be overheard. "It's good to hear your voice. Let's make sure we talk soon."

"Sure," Vanessa replied, but she couldn't deny that her feelings were still hurt when she hung up the telephone.

She'd wanted to apologize, and she had. She had no right to any expectations. So why did she still feel so stung?

* * *

"Sorry about that, Mr. Marshall," Xavier said to his boss as he hung up the telephone. "I had to take that call." And he wished he'd been able to continue the conversation. But right now the situation with the Aborigine exhibit was dire.

"That's okay." Mr. Marshall waved his hand in a gentle fashion. "Well . . . I thought I'd let you know about the sentiment that's brewing around this situation, because I like the idea of bringing that Aboriginal art here." His heavy jowls shook with the statement. "It would be a good thing for the museum, and a good thing for the community," Mr. Marshall stressed. "So I'm rooting for things to work out."

"I'm really glad to hear that, Mr. Marshall," Xavier replied with appreciation. "I've been placing phone calls to World Import and Exports, trying to speak with Phillip Ramsey, but I haven't heard back from him." Xavier shrugged. "I don't understand what's going on. He was friendly enough while I was there."

"We-ell . . ." Mr. Marshall stuck his blue-veined hands in his pockets.

"If I had envisioned that we'd have this kind of problem, I would have kept the middleman out of it and dealt directly with the Pintupi. That was my intention in the first place, but Curtis recommended this company and I trusted his judgement." Xavier voiced his concerns in a mild fashion because Curtis was Mr. Marshall's nephew.

"I understand, but I don't think Curtis foresaw any of this either." He looked at Xavier with clear blue eyes. "Anyway, I'm going to hold off the dogs from this project as long as I can. But I don't think I can do it for more than a couple of weeks." Mr. Marshall peered at Xavier from beneath shaggy brows.

Xavier simply nodded his head.

"If it doesn't come together by then, Xavier," Mr. Marshall continued, "we're going to have to seriously discuss the project's fate."

"All right, sir," Xavier replied as Mr. Marshall walked to the door. "I'm going to make some more phone calls. With the time difference between the States and Alice Springs, you can't make any business calls earlier than this. I'm going to stick around and try to dig up some other phone numbers from the Internet as well. Maybe I can shake up some new interest." He threw up his hands in frustration. "We'll see what happens."

"Good luck, son," Mr. Marshall replied before he walked out into the hall.

Xavier knew he'd need it.

nine

"I'm going to shoot that friend of yours." Vanessa dropped a piece of homemade lemon pound cake into her mouth. "Mama did great the entire time, calling me every three days, then two days before she's scheduled to come back home, nothing. Not a word. So I called the hotel. The hotel clerk said he had seen her that morning, but she wasn't in her room when he put the call through."

"Jackie's probably thinking, what the heck," Miss Bea said, securing the aluminum foil edges around the plate of freshly baked cake. "That she'll be home in a couple of days, so she might as well save that money."

"But that's not what we agreed on. And I'm going to tell her so when I pick her up from the airport this afternoon."

"Well, you know your mother. She can be as hardheaded as a rock."

"She sure can." Vanessa's brows furrowed. "Strange . . . when I was a child, I don't remember her being that way. Seemed like she couldn't do things fast enough whenever my father asked her to."

"Jackie was pretty pliable when she was young, but after she went through the change, she was different. If your father was still alive I'm sure he could attest to that." Miss Bea made a telltale expression.

Vanessa nodded, then released a sigh in the middle of the word "Yeah."

Miss Bea squeezed Vanessa's forearm with a boney hand. "What have you been doing to keep yourself busy while your mother's been gone?"

"Not much."

"Did you ever hear from that young man again?" Miss Bea looked out the window toward the mailbox, where she'd mailed Jackie's letter two days ago. It had been addressed to Xavier Johnson.

"Yes, I did." Disappointment blanketed Vanessa's face. "Spoke to him briefly a couple of days ago. But he was busy at the time, and obviously he's been busy ever since, because I haven't heard from him."

"Maybe he *is* busy." Miss Bea looked her straight in the eye.

"It's possible." Vanessa thought it over. "Then

on the other hand . . ." She threw up her hands in resignation.

"Why don't you call him, Nessa? Honey, you've got to learn to take your life by the horns, not watch it drift by as if it were some cloud out of your reach. Pretty soon you'll be my age looking back on the things you wanted to do. Should have done. And I can tell you from experience, there is nothing worse than that."

"I was the one who called. But the truth is," Vanessa confessed, "I just haven't had much experience being the aggressor when it comes to men."

"Then it's time to get assertiveness skills." Miss Bea smacked her hands in time with each word.

"That's easier said than done." Vanessa thought back on how hurt she'd felt after she'd called Xavier at the museum, only for him to hang up so quickly. "I don't have what it takes," she concluded. "Now with work, that's a different thing. Give me a computer program with a bug and I'm going to hang in there until the cows come home, until I find the problem. It's not that I love it. It's just that I'm stubborn, as you can attest to." Vanessa made a funny face. "But something is lacking inside of me when it comes to intimate relationships. You know . . . trusting that I can make them work. It doesn't feel good to me to look at you and say that, but it's the truth." Vanessa's eyes opened wider. "And by now I'm tired of trying to—"

"You don't know what tired is." Miss Bea cut her off. "Do you really want to know what the problem is?"

Vanessa looked at the expression on Miss Bea's face and prepared to be walloped. "I guess so."

"Life hasn't kicked your butt enough for you to really reach out to someone."

Vanessa began to shake her head.

"You can shake your head all you want to, but the truth is you grew up in a world like a little bubble. It was you and your parents, or you and those part-time nannies that Jackie and Bill hired. Whoever heard of a Black child living in this neighborhood with a nanny?" Miss Bea made a motor sound with her lips. "Yeah, you went to school, but when you came home you didn't want to leave the house. I guess you thought you were punishing your mother and father. If you couldn't go with them on their trips, you weren't going to go anywhere. And I think the only reason you went to school was because you truly loved learning. That's all. All those years of mental somersaults you were doing have come back to haunt you." Miss Bea rubbed her nose with the back of her hand.

Vanessa touched her forehead and began to squeeze her temples.

"And for years you really didn't want a relationship, that's what I think. You know how I could tell?" Miss Bea waited for Vanessa to reply.

"No, how?" Vanessa continued to squeeze her temples.

"You never got with anyone who was important enough to you for you to bring home. Never. And by the time your mama told me how glad she was that you were seriously thinking about a relationship, your father died, and you ended up moving back in with Jackie, where you allowed yourself to be lulled back into a second childhood." Miss Bea stood up and looked down on her. "But I want you to know something, Nessa, this arrangement you've got here has an expiration date on it. It's life's way that it's going to have to come to an end. And the way you and your mother bumped heads right before she left, thank God, it will. I simply hope you two can find peace on some kind of ground before it ends." She started for the door, then called over her shoulder. "And don't eat none of your mama's cake. I made you that small one so you wouldn't. I want Jackie's cake to be nice and perfect when she sees it."

Miss Bea opened the door. "Tell her she doesn't have to call me when she first gets home. I know she might want to rest a bit. But after that, I want to hear everything." She closed the door and disappeared outside, leaving Vanessa with plenty on her mind.

Vanessa watched two flight attendants emerge from the jetway behind a young man whose face was still swollen from sleep. The majority of the passengers had deplaned at least five minutes earlier. Vanessa watched them be greeted by friends and relatives as she waited for her mother, but Jackie never appeared.

Vanessa caught up with the flight attendants. "Excuse me. Are there any more passengers on the plane?"

A blonde replied, "No, there aren't."

"There's not?" Vanessa's dismay vibrated through her voice. "But my mother was scheduled to be on this flight."

"There's always the chance that she missed the plane," the brunette replied.

"I don't think so." Vanessa hedged. "My mother's done a lot of travelling. It would be so unlike her to miss a flight."

"How old is she?" one of the women inquired.

"Seventy-six."

"And she travelled to Australia alone?"

Vanessa's guilt was born anew. "Yes, she did. But she's in good health and . . . look, I don't want to be rude, but at the moment that isn't the issue. I need to find out where she is."

"I suggest you check with customer service to see if they can help you." The blonde donned a professional demeanor, but it was obvious she was ready to be off the clock.

"But I'm sure that was her flight." Vanessa searched the faces in the crowd.

"You should double-check," the brunette said. "You could save yourself some grief. I wish you luck."

Vanessa arrived at the Delta Airlines customer service counter. She spotted an employee who was not servicing customers. She walked straight up to her. "I've got a problem. I came to the airport to pick up my mother. She was supposed to return from Australia today on a Delta Airlines flight, but she wasn't on the plane. One of the flight attendants suggested that I check here to make sure I had the right flight." Vanessa spoke extremely fast. "I'm positive I did, but—"

"Let me see if I can help you. Would you step down here, please?" The woman walked over to an unoccupied computer. "For security reasons the best I can do is check to see if she had a reservation. What flight was it?"

Vanessa looked at the display board on the wall in front of her. "It's the one that just arrived from Los Angeles." Vanessa pointed.

The employee keyed in the information, then asked, "And your mother's name?"

"Jackie Bradley." Vanessa could feel a knot in her stomach as she waited.

"She was never given a seat assignment. So I assume she never checked in."

"Oh no." Vanessa placed her hands in a praying position against her lips.

The employee looked concerned. "I'm sorry, ma'am. All I can suggest is that you call the place where she was staying."

"I'll do that right away. I've got that information at the house." Vanessa looked off into space, as if the answer to where her mother might be were there.

"It's possible she missed the flight," the airline

employee continued, "although most passengers take extra precautions when they are out of the country to be at the airport on time. But there is always that possibility."

"Thank you," Vanessa replied.

Her mind raced from the time she left the ticket counter until she returned home. Jackie had not been on the plane! All of a sudden the connotations of that were enormous. What if something had actually happened to her? What if she were . . . Vanessa couldn't bring herself to even think the word. Now the arguments and the differences that she and her mother had shared during her lifetime vanished like snowflakes on pavement. They were nothing, nothing compared to the thought of never seeing Jackie again.

Vanessa unlocked the door to the house and rushed over to the kneehole desk where her mother had left her contact information. "The Plaza Hotel Alice Springs." Vanessa looked at her watch. "It's nine-thirty in the morning here. So it's about one-thirty in the morning in Alice Springs." Vanessa dialed as quickly as she could.

"The Plaza Hotel Alice Springs. May I help you."

"Hello. This is a call for Jackie Bradley. She was in room seven-oh-six but—"

"One moment please."

"Wait!" Vanessa cried, but there was a series of clicks, then the sound of a telephone ringing. It rang several times before a voice mail service kicked in. "I'm sorry. The person you are trying to reach is not available at this time. If you like, you may leave a message after the tone. Be-eep."

"I don't want to leave a message," Vanessa said, exasperated. She held the phone for a few moments longer, hung up, then called again.

"The Plaza Hotel Alice Springs. May I help you please?"

"I called a few minutes ago. I am trying to reach my mother, Jackie Bradley."

"Were you disconnected?"

"No, I wasn't. You put me through, but I'm not sure my mother is still registered at the hotel."

"I couldn't have put you through if she is no longer a guest."

Vanessa tried to hold on to her patience. "I understand that. But I'm not certain where my mother is, and I want you to find out if she checked out of the hotel. Please!"

There was silence on the line before the clerk said, "One moment." A couple of seconds later the hotel man said, "We still have a Jackie Bradley listed as a guest."

"You do?" Apprehension took a strong grip of Vanessa. "But she was supposed to return home to the United States today."

"All I know, ma'am, is that she has not checked out of the hotel."

"Could someone go up to the room and see if she is in there?"

"You said no one answered the phone when I put the call through."

"I know I said that, but—"

"Then there is no one there, ma'am."

"I don't think you're hearing me." Vanessa began to lose her cool. "My mother was to have returned home today. She was not on the airplane. You said she has not checked out of her hotel. She could be lying in the room sick or something. Can't you send somebody up there to see?"

"Oh, I understand." The clerk suddenly became sympathetic. "Yes. I'll get security to go up to the room. Can I get your name and the telephone number where we can call you back?"

"Please, if it isn't a problem, I prefer to hold the line until I know something." Vanessa's heart felt as if it were skipping beats.

"No problem. I'll get back with you as soon as I can."

"Thank you." Vanessa heard her line go on hold. "Oh my God. Oh my God," Vanessa repeated over and over as she paced the floor and waited. Several minutes later the hotel clerk returned.

"Ma'am, are you still there?"

"Yes, I'm here."

"Let me put security on the phone."

"Oh, no." Vanessa could barely breathe as she stood still in the middle of her living room.

"Hello." A male voice came over the line.

"Yes?"

"You say Ms. Bradley was scheduled to arrive back in America today?"

"Yes."

"I checked her room but she was not there.

However, I did see some of her belongings. And the bed was made up as if it had not been slept in since the maid cleaned the room early yesterday morning."

"Say what?"

"Excuse me?" asked the security guard. Vanessa's colloquialism clearly confused the man.

"Something must have happened to her!" Vanessa's fear spilled over.

"Is there a possibility that she might have decided on another excursion before leaving the country?"

"Not without telling me, there isn't," Vanessa insisted.

The line went silent. "Well, ma'am, I suggest you wait until the morning so we can talk with the daytime staff. They may be able to shed some light on her whereabouts."

"I don't know if I can wait that long," Vanessa replied.

"If I file a report with the police now, they will expect a report from my department, and I can't write one until I talk to the daytime staff."

"Oh no." Vanessa's mind went into overdrive.

"Ma'am?" The security guard waited for Vanessa to respond. "If you could hold out just a little longer, I'll have some more information to share with you."

"Can't you call the hospitals and check to see if she has been admitted to any of them?"

"I assure you, ma'am, if one of our guests had been admitted to the local hospital, our hotel would have contacted a relative or a friend shortly thereafter."

"I see," Vanessa replied.

"So if you could give us until the morning, say six o'clock Sydney time, we should have some more information for you."

"I guess I don't have any choice," Vanessa said for the man's benefit, as well as for her own. She gave the guard her name and telephone number.

"We will call you then."

"Okay." Vanessa hung up the phone and stared at it with sightless eyes. "Oh my God. Where is she?" She looked at the clock for the hundredth time. "It's ten o'clock. I'm supposed to go back to work." Vanessa had informed her boss that she had to pick her mother up from the airport and that she would be late. For a moment she considered going in, but Vanessa knew she wouldn't be any good to anyone until she had heard from Australia.

She picked up the telephone again. "Hello Janice, this is Vanessa. I told Jerry that I'd be late coming in this morning, but an emergency has come up and . . ." She swallowed hard just thinking about it. "I won't be in at all today."

"Okay. I'll give him the message. He's in a meeting right now."

"Thanks." Vanessa hung up without further adieu.

Where was her mother?

ten

Vanessa walked the house for hours until she couldn't walk anymore. Finally, she lay down on her bed to try to sleep, but her mind kept conjuring up images she didn't want to see. The day crawled by slower than any day she could remember. "If there was only somebody I could call." She sat on the side of the bed. Vanessa thought about Miss Bea and how upset she would be once she found out about her best friend. As if by ESP, there was a knock on the door.

"Hey, Nessa. Is that woman still resting from her trip?" Miss Bea chattered as she came in. "I just couldn't wait any longer. Don't tell me I'm going to have to wake her up." She put her hands on pure hip bones. "How is she going to get back

in rhythm with American time sleeping like
this?"

"Mama's not here, Miss Bea," Vanessa said
softly.

"She's not." Miss Bea's brows came together.
"Where is she?"

"I don't know."

"What did you say?" Miss Bea grabbed the
back of a nearby chair.

"I went to pick her up from the airport and she
wasn't on the plane. So I called her hotel. She
hadn't checked out, and some of her things were
still in the room. A security man at the hotel is going to call me in a couple of hours"—Vanessa
looked down at her hands—"and tell me what
he's found out."

"You mean Jackie's somewhere in Australia
and nobody knows where she is?" Miss Bea
struggled with the situation.

"That's a possibility," Vanessa replied.

"Oh Jesus." Miss Bea sat down. "I can't believe
it." She clutched at her chest.

"Now don't you get too excited. I can't take
anything else happening right now." Vanessa
placed her hand on Miss Bea's shoulder. "We've
done all we can do at the moment. Now we'll just
have to wait."

"Oh Jesus," Miss Bea repeated. "I knew she
was acting awful strange before she left here."

"What do you mean?"

"She was acting like part of her knew something was going to happen." Miss Bea looked at

Vanessa with tortured eyes. "She gave me her African violets and told me to take them to my place even though I told her you or I could take care of them right here." She clasped her hands together. "Then there was that letter."

"What letter?"

"The letter to Xavier Johnson," Miss Bea explained.

"A letter to Xavier!" Vanessa was shocked. "What was it about?"

"I don't have a clue. Jackie asked me to mail it for her a couple of days before she was due back here."

"Why would she have written Xavier a letter and asked that it be mailed at a specific time?" Vanessa mulled the question over out loud.

Miss Bea shrugged her shoulders and shook her head.

"The only thing I can think of is the letter was about me. What else connects her with Xavier?" Vanessa began to pace again. "Wait a minute. Mother went to central Australia. And Xavier is planning a central Australian Aboriginal art exhibit at the museum where he works. As a matter of fact, he is the reason the exhibit is coming to Columbus." She looked at Miss Bea as if she were putting together a puzzle. "That isn't a coincidence, and I wonder if Xavier, if the letter, has something to do with Mama not coming back."

"I don't know how it could," Miss Bea replied.

"But there's too many things clicking here." Vanessa's face darkened.

"Well there's one way to find out," Miss Bea replied. "Call Xavier and ask him."

"It's too late to try him at work, and his business card doesn't have his home number on it." Vanessa was at the desk again. "But I'm sure there can't be that many Xavier Johnsons or X. Johnsons in the phone book." She flipped through the pages, stopped, then began to scan. "Wayne . . . Willie Johnson . . . Xavier. Xavier Johnson. Thirteen fifty-three Cardinal. This has got to be him," Vanessa declared as she dialed. She waited for the telephone to ring but heard a busy signal instead. She tried dialing the number again and encountered the same thing. "It's busy." Vanessa hung up the telephone but held on to the receiver. "I can't believe he doesn't have call waiting." Her mother's face came to mind.

Miss Bea continued to sit on the couch looking helpless.

Vanessa dialed Xavier again with the same result. "Maybe he's got both lines tied up." She ran her hand down her face. "Or maybe he's on the Internet." She was completely exasperated. "But I can't wait for him to get off the phone. I've been waiting all day long. I'm sick of waiting." Vanessa grabbed her purse and her car keys. "I've got to talk to him now."

"Where are you going?" Miss Bea's eyes followed Vanessa around the room.

"To thirteen fifty-three Cardinal Street."

"What if it's not him?" Miss Bea asked.

"I'll find that out when I get there."

"Maybe I should go with you." Miss Bea started to rise from the couch.

"No. You stay here in case the call from Australia comes early." Vanessa walked back over to the desk and scribbled something down. "That's my cell phone number if you need to get in touch with me."

Miss Bea nodded, and Vanessa headed out the door.

She jumped in the car and drove toward the area of town where she believed Xavier lived. Part of her was aware of the significance of seeing Xavier again, but Vanessa's main focus was that Xavier was the last person, in the States, at least, who had been contacted by her mother.

She found the street. Carefully, Vanessa drove by each house watching the numbers ascend. When she reached thirteen fifty-three, Vanessa pulled over to the curb. There were well-tended plants in front of the modest home, and lights were on throughout its interior. Vanessa got out of the car, went straight to the front door, and rang the bell. When no one answered in what she considered to be a reasonable amount of time, Vanessa rang the bell again. Finally, an attractive young woman answered.

"Hello."

Vanessa was caught off guard. "Hello. I don't know if I have the right house." She took a step back. "But, does Xavier Johnson live here?"

"Why, yes he does."

"Who is it?" Xavier's voice called from the interior.

The woman glanced behind her as he approached. "There's someone here to see you." Her volume lowered as she stepped to the side. "Did you finish scanning in the material?"

"Yes," Vanessa heard him say. "I did. You can take the pictures with you," Xavier added as he came to the door. "Vanessa." He was obviously surprised.

"Hello, Xavier." The woman's presence had Vanessa feeling more awkward than ever. She paused, thinking he probably would not invite her in. "There's something I need to talk to you about."

"Come in." Xavier held the door open for her.

Vanessa eased through the small space. "Thanks."

"Have a seat," Xavier offered. "I'll be back."

Before Vanessa could sit on the edge of an overstuffed chair in the well-furnished living room, Xavier had disappeared down a hall. The enormity of the moment hit her. Her mother was missing, and Xavier might have the only clue to explain it. Xavier, whose door had been opened by another woman. Vanessa could hear them talking in the back of the house.

"You're such a sweetheart. I don't know how I would have done this without you." The woman's voice was crisp, familiar.

"Don't mention it, Sand," Xavier replied.

"I guess it would take something like this for me to see the inside of your house." Her voice got louder as they approached the living room.

"Don't start" was Xavier's silky reply.

The woman's eyes were bright when she spotted Vanessa. She wiggled her fingers. "Goodnight."

"Goodnight," Vanessa replied. Unconsciously, she checked the woman over.

"Let's keep our fingers crossed that this thing turns out the way you want it," she said, opening the door.

"Yeah. I think I'm going to need my toes too for this one," Xavier replied.

Vanessa wondered what they were talking about—for about five seconds. Then her mother's face flitted into her mind, and Vanessa felt her heart constrict. Xavier's love life and private business were none of her concern, and right now, of absolutely no interest.

Still, she couldn't help feeling a pinprick of jealousy over whoever this Sand person was.

eleven

Xavier closed the door behind Sand. "Now, to what do I owe this honor and surprise?"

Vanessa went straight to the point. "My mother sent you a letter."

"Your mother?" Xavier replied, taken aback. "I haven't received a letter from your mother. Are you certain?"

"Yes," Vanessa replied, anxiously. "Miss Bea said she mailed it the day before yesterday."

Xavier looked confused. "Why would your mother send me a letter?"

"I don't know why." Vanessa tried to calm her nerves by clasping her hands together. "That's why I'm here. I need to find out."

"Did you consider asking her?" Xavier didn't know what to make of the situation.

"If I could, I would." Vanessa's voice nearly broke.

Xavier stepped forward. "What's wrong, Vanessa? Tell me." His voice registered alarm. "Why can't you ask her? Is your mother sick?"

"I don't know the answer to that." Vanessa wrapped her arms around her body and began to walk around the room. "She's missing, Xavier." She turned tortured eyes in his direction.

"Missing?" Xavier repeated the word as if it were incomprehensible. "What hap— Wait a minute." He stopped abruptly. "I just realized something. Did Miss Bea mail the letter to my house or to the museum?"

"I believe she mailed it to the museum." Vanessa blinked back tears.

"I didn't go to the museum yesterday," Xavier replied. "That's one of the reasons Sand was here. She picked up some reports and letters, but she also brought me my mail. It's in my office." Xavier had already turned toward the hallway. Vanessa fell in behind him. In the room, Xavier picked up a short stack of letters from his desk. He flipped a small white envelope over. "This must be it."

Vanessa wanted to reach out and take it, but instead she said, "Please open it."

Xavier ripped open the envelope and removed a piece of paper. His eyes began to follow the writing on the page. When he was done, a puzzled look descended on his face. "This is difficult for me to understand." He passed the paper to Vanessa.

She took it and began to read the words aloud.

> *This poem will find me far away.*
> *In the land where the kangaroo*
>   *and the koala bear play.*
> *A land where the people called the Pintupi,*
> *Will hopefully set me on the road to be*
> *One with my husband of days past.*
> *The Dreamtime will take me there very fast.*
> *I thank you, Xavier, for opening the door,*
> *I thank you for that and so much more.*
> *Because it is you, Xavier, that I know will be,*
> *The one to set my Vanessa's heart free.*
> *Take Care of Her, Jackie Bradley*

More than a little shocked, and very dismayed, Vanessa read her mother's poetry again. " 'Take care of her.' It sounds as if she doesn't expect to come back." The words trailed from her lips.

"Your mother is in Australia?" Xavier's tone held a note almost as strange as Jackie's poem.

"Yes. Somewhere in central Australia." Vanessa took a deep breath, then added lamely, "I think."

Xavier was cautious. "What do you mean, you think?"

"She was supposed to return from Sydney today. I went to the airport to pick her up, but she wasn't on the plane." Vanessa's eyes locked with his as she spoke, her voice shaky. "I called the hotel where she was staying. They told me she had never checked out. Some of her belongings were still in the room."

"How long has she been gone?" Xavier's voice was purposefully calm.

"Two weeks," Vanessa replied, then turned away because she couldn't stand the look of heightened concern in Xavier's eyes. "Miss Bea told me about the letter no more than an hour ago." Vanessa continued to talk because she was afraid to hear what Xavier was thinking. "She was drawn to you, Xavier, because of this obsession she developed with Australia." Vanessa rattled the poem. "That's what she's referring to here."

"Yes. She did have an intense interest in Australia. That's what she spoke about at the festival, remember?"

"Barely." Vanessa's hand went up to her temple. "My mind was on other things that day."

"Mine was too." Their eyes met. "But I do recall that she spoke passionately about the Aborigines and their belief in the Dreamtime." He paused. "I think that's what the poem is saying. It seems like your mother believes that she can use the Dreamtime to contact your father."

Vanessa recalled the look of desperation in her mother's eyes the night she announced she would be going to Australia and that she would be going alone. "I should have gone with her, Xavier. I knew she was having these bizarre thoughts and I should have insisted on going with her, even when she told me no." Vanessa closed her eyes. It all seemed like a bad dream. Had her mother met an untimely death while trying to recapture the past?

Xavier watched Vanessa succumb to her own mental torture, and all he wanted to do was relieve it.

Slowly, a subtle warmth enveloped Vanessa, and her eyes opened. Xavier had placed his arm around her shoulders. Until that moment Vanessa hadn't realized how much she needed comforting. It was a luxury that she had not afforded herself since she was a little child. Even when her father died she had continued to be strong. Now it was as if the possibility of her mother's being gone as well opened the doors to the pain she had kept at bay. Vanessa allowed herself to lean heavily against him.

"Why don't you go and sit down in the living room," Xavier whispered, holding her. "I'll be there in a moment."

Vanessa heard him, but she leaned a second longer before she nodded. Her eyes filled with unshed tears as she walked away. She didn't dare look at Xavier. If she did, Vanessa feared she might throw herself in his arms again. *I mustn't fall apart now. Not here in front of Xavier.* She fortified herself as she made her way to the living room and sat on the couch.

Xavier followed minutes later. "Here. Drink this." He offered her a small crystal glass filled with Grand Marnier before he sat down not far away. "I don't know if this is your kind of drink, but it should do the trick."

"Thank you." Vanessa took a swallow of the heady liqueur. Afterwards she continued to gaze down into the glass. "So what is the Dreamtime, Xavier? Some kind of New Age jargon?"

Xavier placed his arm on the back of the couch. "Not at all. The Dreamtime is one of the oldest beliefs of the Aboriginal culture. Many indigenous cultures embrace the Dreamtime in one form or another. No, there's nothing new about the Dreamtime. It is one of the oldest belief systems on the planet."

"Okay," Vanessa sighed. "So let's say my mother has an interest in this Dreamtime. Let's say she went there to find out more about it"— she searched for the right words—"to find out how to become a part of it. Because that's what I'm beginning to believe was my mother's intention." She looked at Xavier. "Ever since my father died she has been on this endless search for something." Vanessa threw her hands up. "Perhaps a way to prove that death is not the end of life. Or that there is a way to reach into that realm, not just communicate with it. . . ." She stopped, and her coffee-colored eyes were desperate once again. "I know this is a crazy question but . . . is it possible that my mother could have disappeared as a result of experimenting with the Dreamtime?"

"I don't know the answer to that, Vanessa."

"But you know if you believe in it or not," Vanessa said. "Strangely enough, I prefer to believe that over her being sick or dead somewhere, alone in the desert."

"I've heard of some very strange, unusual things happening in the Australian outback, but I have never personally experienced any spiritual practices there," Xavier replied in an academic way that disturbed Vanessa.

"My mother saw *you* on television, and read about *you* in some newspaper, then suddenly decided to take a trip to Australia. You're supposed to be the damn expert," she added, frustrated.

Xavier sighed before he spoke. "I can tell you this. From what I know, the Dreamtime is basically the Aborigines' belief in the simultaneity of past, present, and future. And yes, I mentioned it during my interviews. But, Vanessa," Xavier said, his tone low, "you're upset. Maybe it's convenient for you to blame me for what's going on here?"

A protest was on Vanessa's lips, but when she looked into Xavier's dark eyes, she knew he had spoken the truth. "You're probably right, I guess I just needed someone to blame. Someone other than myself." She looked down at her hands. "You see, since my father died, my mother has tried to reach out to me, tell me about what was truly going on inside of her, but I refused to listen. I refused because I wanted to punish her." The tears rolled down her face. "Punish her for not being the mother I wanted her to be."

Xavier watched Vanessa struggle for control.

He understood wanting a parent to be different from the way they had been. He understood that because of his father, who had not been there for them due to his drug habit, and later because the narcotics had altered his mind.

"Sh-sh." Xavier made the soft sound as he placed a finger against her trembling lips. "Don't, Vanessa. Don't do this to yourself. We all have regrets, things that we wish we had done differently, wish that we could change."

Still Vanessa couldn't stop. "But the truth is there were times when I wanted to let go of it. I wanted to embrace her and release myself. To just let go. But I couldn't, and boy did that frighten me." The truth bubbled out. "And then I even blamed my parents, especially my mother, for that. That they were the reason I became what I am." Her voice shook with tears.

"And what you are is a beautiful woman," Xavier said, enfolding her in his arms, "who is trying to live her life the best she knows how."

Vanessa felt the little strength she had left exit her body when he touched her. She had held up as well as she could, but now Xavier's arms gave her license to be frail. License to feel the fear that there was a possibility she may never see her mother alive again.

"Oh, Xavier. I'm going out of my mind with this." She looked up at him with damp lashes and cheeks.

"No, you're not. You'll make it." He comforted her with tiny kisses on her forehead and near her eyes. When his lips touched her cheek it was a natural progression to place the next kiss on Vanessa's mouth, and her lips clung to his, drawing sustenance from their firmness.

Their tongues touched, and the introduction was a soft explosion of sensations. Even in her distress Vanessa was amazed at how she could feel Xavier's kiss throughout her body, throughout her being. It was so unbelievably wonderful, and she lost herself in the sensation until a guilty pang inserted itself. Vanessa opened her eyes as she thought about her mother, and she had to pull away.

"What are we doing, Xavier?" Vanessa looked back into Xavier's desire-filled eyes. "This is the wrong time for this. This is wrong."

"Wrong?" Slowly, Xavier removed his arms. *That was the most moving kiss I've ever had the pleasure of being a part of, and Vanessa is saying that it's wrong?* "I don't think that anything two consenting adults do together is wrong."

Vanessa looked uncomfortable. "It's just . . . the timing of it all. I should be thinking about my mother, not doing this." She looked in his eyes, then looked away. "But of course, I can't expect you to feel the same way, or to understand."

"I understand more than you think." Xavier's voice was silky. "But I think you need to remember in the future that the same thing applies to us when it comes to your just letting go. You need to allow the moment, Vanessa. I know how con-

twelve

"The hotel in Australia didn't call," Miss Bea said even before Vanessa had closed the door behind her.

Vanessa looked at her watch. "But I guess they could call at any time now."

Miss Bea bent further than her naturally bowed stature to look into Vanessa's downcast face. "You've been crying."

"I've been doing that on and off all day long. It's nothing new." Vanessa sat down heavily on the couch.

"So the letter Mr. Johnson received from your mother didn't help at all."

"Not really."

"Well, what did it say?"

"Oh, you know Mama, Miss Bea. All drama and fanfare." She looked exasperated. "It wasn't a note at all. It was a poem about Australia . . . and some of the people there . . . and—"

"Can I see it?"

"I don't have it," Vanessa replied.

"In light of everything that's going on I would think Mr. Johnson would have given it to you."

"I guess I left rather abruptly," Vanessa explained. "I don't think either one of us was thinking of that at that moment."

Miss Bea's small features crunched together. "What happened?"

"Things got rather—" The telephone rang, and Vanessa knew she had two reasons to be grateful.

"Hello."

"Miss Bradley?" the accented voice asked.

"Yes."

"This is Allen Dalton, the security chief at the Plaza Hotel Alice Springs."

"Yes, Mr. Dalton."

"We talked to the maid who has been servicing your mother's room. I'm sorry to tell you this, but she says there has been no activity in that room for the past three days."

"What do you mean *no activity*?" Vanessa's heart began to pound again.

"I mean she has not made up the bed or cleaned in the room for three days because no one has used it."

"For three days?" Vanessa was panicked.

"What is it?" Miss Bea touched her arm. "Three days what?"

Vanessa looked at her mother's longtime

friend with frightened eyes. "Mama hasn't been in her room for three days."

"Three days." Miss Bea covered her trembling mouth.

The security guard continued on the phone. "We have turned over all the information that we have to the police, and we filed a missing persons report."

"Is that all that can be done?" Vanessa implored.

"It is the main thing," Mr. Dalton replied. "The police department will put any other relative parties on alert. And they will probably be giving you a call."

"But what good is that going to do?" Vanessa snapped in frustration. "I'm sorry. It just all sounds so routine, and I can't do anything about it from here."

"As much as I hate to admit it, that's very true, ma'am."

The line went silent.

"I'm going to take the next plane to Australia," Vanessa announced.

"Nessa, are you sure?" Miss Bea looked at her with eyes full of concern.

Mr. Dalton replied, "Ma'am, I think I understand how you feel, but I don't know what good it would do you."

"A lot more good than my being here in the States waiting for a phone call."

"I understand." The security guard paused. "Let us know when you arrive and we'll fill you in on any new information that we may have. By then the entire case will be in the hands of the police department, and I'm sure they will assist you with any personal efforts you make to find your mother."

"Thank you," Vanessa replied. "Good-bye." She hung up the telephone.

"So you're going to Australia?" Miss Bea's eyes were wide.

"I don't see that I have any other choice. I know the Australian authorities are going to look for Mama, but maybe I can turn up something they can't."

"But that's their job, Nessa. You don't know anything about finding a missing person here in Columbus, let alone in Australia."

"I know that, Miss Bea, but I just can't sit here and do nothing. Mama isn't"—Vanessa paused and locked eyes with Miss Bea—"as young as she used to be, and every day counts. I have already lost three days, and I'm not going to lose any more."

"All right. Just tell me what I need to do to help," Miss Bea said. "And don't you go over there and not come back. You and Jackie are the only family I have, and I'ma tell you now, I wouldn't be able to take it."

Xavier got up from the computer and went into the kitchen. He opened the refrigerator door and took out a jug of water. It had been difficult getting back to work after Vanessa's visit. He felt responsible for her mother's decision to go to Australia. Deep down inside, Xavier felt he had definitely contributed to the situation, if only by making very recent information available to Mrs. Bradley. He drank straight out of the jug.

Xavier recalled how reluctant Mrs. Bradley had been to leave the festival that day, even though Vanessa had walked away. But he'd thought her mother had simply found a kindred spirit in him when it came to being interested in the Aboriginal culture. Xavier had had no idea what she'd been contemplating. He paused. But had she been contemplating? The poem indicated that she expected to have some kind of reunion with Vanessa's dead father. Xavier shook his head. Although he was a man with an open mind, that seemed impossible even by his standards. Yet he had to admit, Mrs. Bradley had seemed to be of sound mind when he'd met her. Xavier gazed off into space, thinking back.

But there was something else about the poem that puzzled him just as much. In sending it to him, Mrs. Bradley was actually asking him to take care of Vanessa as if she might not return. She had basically said that he was the man for Vanessa. Considering the state of mind Mrs. Bradley must have been in when she wrote the poem, this was something he had to think she seriously believed. But how seriously did you take someone who would travel to Australia with such unusual intentions?

He took another swig of water. Xavier could

contemplate this stuff all night, but the bottom line was that Mrs. Bradley appeared to be missing, and Vanessa was more than a little worried about her. How could she not be? She was her mother. And no matter how complicated their relationship might have been, she cared deeply for her, just as most children did for their parents, even the ones who were far from stellar.

A dribble of water escaped from the corner of Xavier's mouth when the phone rang. He looked at the kitchen clock. It was eleven-thirty. Could it be Vanessa again? There was a definite surge within him at such a prospect.

"Hello."

"Xavier," the male voice replied. "This is Curtis."

"I recognize your voice, Curtis." Xavier wandered into his office.

"I guess this could have waited until the morning, but I thought you'd like to know the decision that was made about the project right away."

"Well, I can glean from your being the one to make the call tonight that it wasn't in my favor."

There was a pause on the line.

"I get the distinct impression that you don't think I like you, Xavier."

"It doesn't matter to me if you like me or not. I simply want the respect that is due me for the caliber of work that I bring to the museum. That's all."

"And that's exactly what we're talking about

tonight," Curtis rejoined. "The money for the Aboriginal art project is going to be targeted for something, shall we say, a little more viable. World Import and Exports told me they don't think they will be able to salvage the deal, and we've already lost money because basically we still have to pay them a finders fee. There's no way of getting around that. It was in the contract." Curtis cleared his throat. "They pointed you in the right direction, and when you said it was a go, they drew up all the appropriate paperwork. If you hadn't done such a poor job explaining the deal to the original artists, maybe things would have panned out. Now it appears the Pintupi simply don't trust us."

Xavier lost his cool. "First of all, I don't appreciate you talking to me like this. And secondly, there's some kind of fly in the ointment. I haven't been able to talk to anybody at that office for over a week. And I find that strange."

Curtis gave a sarcastic laugh. "There's a fly, all right, and it's big enough for us not to lose any more money on this thing. If we were getting any positive feedback from World Import maybe, and I repeat *maybe*, that would make a difference. But as it stands now they say they're still beating the bushes. We can't chance investing in advertising and countless other venues to promote the impending exhibit on the possibility that World Import will be able to come through in time."

The muscles in Xavier's face were working

overtime. "How is it, Curtis, that you are able to get so much information out of them, when I can't get them to return my phone calls?"

"Beats me." Curtis's voice was smug. "Maybe I know how to use more finesse than you do."

I doubt that, Xavier thought and decided to take a different approach. He picked up the envelope that had held Jackie's poem. "You know how important this project is to the community at large, Curtis. It'll bring all kinds of people to Columbus. We've never had anything like this before. It could broaden the horizons of many folks, and our museum could be the glue to build a bridge between the Black and White communities. Then the Marshall Art Museum would be remembered throughout local history for that. And we would be the people who made it happen." Xavier appealed to Curtis's ego. "African Americans would come out because the Aborigines are people of color. Caucasians would come because it's Australia, not to mention fascinating. I think we should give World Import a little more time. The Pintupi I spoke to while I was there were very obliging. I don't know what happened, but I believe they can be convinced to go through with the exhibit."

"The committee feels they have already given your project enough time and money." Curtis emphasized the *your*.

Xavier put down the envelope and absentmindedly traced it with his fingers. "C'mon, Curtis. It hasn't been given nearly the time and

money some of the other projects have been al-
loted. You and I both know that. The only difference is, the other projects weren't managed by
someone whispering in his uncle's ear, talking
against them." He picked up the envelope and
noticed something inside it beside the letter. He
was surprised to see a strip of torn newspaper
with writing on it.

"You give me more power than I have, Xavier."

"But not as much as you want." Xavier took the
newly discovered piece of paper out. The writing
was picture perfect, almost calligraphic. *Love does
not fade when darkness descends. Love is the light that
defines it. He is not his father's son.* It was signed
with one name: Xenophon.

". . . falls to me because I can handle it. I'm
qualified." Xavier focused on the last portion of
Curtis's sentence.

"We're all qualified for something." Xavier examined the writing very closely. "Sometimes it
has to be made clear to us in ways we never expected." *Why did Vanessa's mother include this?*
Xavier stared at the scripted print. *Could she have
known my father's real name was Xenophon although
everyone referred to him as Zeke?*

Xavier thought about the day Jackie approached him at the festival, and her persistence
in reaching out to him. Was it all because of
Vanessa? *This is either some strange kind of coincidence or. . . .* He reflected on what Mrs. Bradley
had said to him before she'd walked away that
day. "I've got a feeling about you." Xavier won-

dered if she was only referring to a possible relationship between him and Vanessa, or could there have been something more? Something that pertained to his father? Xavier had to know.

"Clear or not, it would take a miracle to revive this project," Curtis replied.

"Well, a miracle is what you'll get."

"What?"

"I'm not going to let this just fall by the wayside," Xavier said, slipping the paper into his wallet. "If it takes my going to Australia again to revive it, I'll do just that."

"You're talking crazy now," Curtis retorted. "There is no money for you to do anything of the sort, and, on top of that, time has just about run out. There are advertising deadlines and others that must be met to execute any project."

"I know. But I'll present it to the committee this way: if I'm able to salvage the project by spending my own money on a trip to Australia, I expect to be reimbursed when it's flying high here in Columbus."

There was silence on the line before Curtis said, "You'll be wasting everybody's time on that pipe dream, and your own money."

"How can you be so sure?" Xavier thought Curtis sounded too certain of the outcome.

"Just what are you trying to prove, Xavier?" It was nearly a bark.

"I'm not sure yet. Maybe a couple of things. Professional and personal." He thought about how grateful Vanessa would be if he did some digging around to help find her mother while he was in Alice Springs.

For a moment Xavier recalled the warmth of Vanessa's body and the way her lips had parted with ease as he'd kissed her. *Yes, I can't lie, I would love to experience more . . . but what rewards I might receive from Vanessa would not be my only incentive in helping her find her mother. I know the agony of having a parent who you are not certain is dead or alive. I would spare anyone that if I could.*

"This could also put the death nail in your coffin when it comes to your job at the Marshall Art Museum," Curtis said. "Some folks might call your actions neurotic and obsessive."

"But if I win, I win big. And if I lose . . . *that* position will be all yours."

Again there was silence on the line before Curtis replied, "Don't say I didn't warn you."

"Thanks for your concern, Curtis. But I'll be in bright and early tomorrow to lay my cards on the table."

"It might be the last deck you ever play at the Marshall Art Museum."

"That's a chance I'm willing to take," Xavier replied.

There was a click before the line went dead.

thirteen

Frustrated, Xavier stared at the airport telephone. It was like a recurring dream. Although this time he had brought Vanessa's telephone number with him, he still had not been able to reach her. Xavier had called on and off all day, but the line had either been busy or there'd been no answer.

He left the telephone booth. Although Vanessa had not turned out to be the perfect woman, Xavier knew he had no intention of being done with her. Her moment of turning away from his kiss the night before couldn't have been more stimulating. As it is with any male who had been rejected, Vanessa had surely whet Xavier's appetite, and his mind had flitted from one possibility to another while he'd slept and while he'd been awake.

Reluctantly, Xavier headed for the check-in counter. One suitcase was all he'd brought with him this time. If he wasn't able to pull things together within a week, it wouldn't matter. Curtis had been right about the deadlines, and Mr. Marshall, as chairman of the arts committee, had given him ten days to salvage the project. Ten days. After that he could procure the Mona Lisa and it wouldn't matter.

Xavier rounded the corner and saw the familiar Delta Airlines sign. The waiting line was short, and he heaved a sigh. He was much more tired than he realized. In between confronting Mr. Marshall, making flight reservations, thinking about Vanessa and her mother, and packing, Xavier had gotten on the Internet to try and trace a Xenophon Johnson in Columbus, Georgia. There was none.

As he crossed the floor, Xavier mulled over the possibility of Jackie's Xenophon being his father. It was a very long shot. He recalled the day his mother explained what she had meant all those years when she'd said his father was dead. *Dead to them*, that is. Dead because of a drug-induced psychosis that had cost him his identity, and theirs for him. Now the thought of his father walking the street in a drug-induced stupor, or living in a ward because he was a threat to himself and others, pained him. But at the time of his mother's confession, Xavier had found it much easier to tell people the same twisted truth. It was much less complicated.

Xavier got in line behind a large man wearing a

Crocodile Dundee hat. He was a massive human being who was speaking to his companion with a definite Aussie accent. He watched as the man bent down to rummage through a pocket of his suitcase. Suddenly, a familiar voice brought his entire body to attention, and Xavier focused on what was taking place at the ticket counter.

"I don't have a ticket because I got an e-ticket off of the Internet," Vanessa explained. "It should be in your computer system somewhere." She rose up on her toes trying to see around the computer monitor.

"Next," called out an employee a couple of work stations away. The Australian man and woman responded by gathering their belongings and moving forward.

Xavier walked up behind Vanessa. His gaze took in the pronounced curve of her hip as she stood with one knee bent in a pair of well-fitted jeans. "What are you doing here?" He started to put his arm around her waist.

Visibly shocked, Vanessa quickly recovered, then focused on the attendant again. "What does it look like?" She tried to put her driver's license back in her wallet, but her hands wouldn't cooperate. "I'm going to Australia."

"That's what I thought." Xavier let his arm fall back down by his side. "But somehow, knowing you as I do, I can't picture you in the dusty outback."

Vanessa glanced over her shoulder but kept her back turned. "That goes to show how much you know me. Did you find it?" she asked the attendant.

"Yes. Just a moment, please." The man focused on the computer screen.

"And where are *you* headed?" Vanessa inquired.

"It appears that we're heading in the same direction." Xavier watched her try to keep a straight face. *If she would only show that she is as glad to see me as I am to see her.* He took a deep breath. *God, when I pick a woman, I really pick 'em.*

"You're flying to Sydney?" She turned wide eyes on Xavier.

"Yes."

"Right now?"

"Flight number Eleven forty-five," he read from a piece of paper.

"You're all set, ma'am." The attendant handed Vanessa her boarding pass. "You fly with us from here to Los Angeles, and there you'll take Qantas into Sydney. Your seat is Thirty-one A. You leave out of Concourse A, Gate 20." The attendant held his hand out for Xavier's information.

"But last night you never mentioned that you were going to Australia," Vanessa confronted him.

"Nor did you," Xavier replied.

"Your passport and visa, please." The attendant continued to do his job. Xavier placed the documents on the counter.

"But that's because I had no clue that I was going," Vanessa retorted.

"Yet you assume that I knew I was heading back to Australia," Xavier replied.

"Well, didn't you?" She searched his face.

"Considering our history, I think you would have learned your lesson by now. You should never assume anything, Vanessa. When I was a kid we said assuming made an ass out of you and me."

The airport attendant tried to hide a smile before he went through the security script. "Are you checking any bags, sir?"

"Just one." Xavier turned to Vanessa. "Are you sure going is a good idea?"

"I'm going to help find my mother," Vanessa announced.

The courageous tilt of her chin struck Xavier. He couldn't help but admire Vanessa's newfound determination, although he didn't think she had a clue as to what she was getting into. "Vanessa, you don't know anything about central Australia. It's a completely different world over there."

"More reason for me to help look for her." Her eyes beamed a serious light.

The airport attendant rattled off the same information to Xavier that he'd given Vanessa, then added, "Your seat number is Thirty-one B. Have a pleasant trip."

"Thank you," Xavier said before he and Vanessa headed toward the T terminal. "I don't think this is the time for you to become courageous, Vanessa. The Australian outback is not some place that you can control. Hell, the Aborigines, who've been there for thousands of years, can't control it, but unlike you, they know not to try." Vanessa threw Xavier a dirty look before he continued. "The place is alive with its own synergy. I would suggest that you give the Australian authorities a few more days to find your mother. She may be staying at another hotel where there isn't a telephone. Perhaps her transportation fell through. It can happen out there. You can be stranded for days."

"In your attempt to have all the answers, you've missed something." Vanessa's pace picked up with her perturbation. "I just checked in, right before you, remember?"

"But this is only the first leg of the trip. You could still postpone the overseas flight." He paused, looking straight ahead. "Explain it to them. That you need to let the authorities do their job before you go running over there half cocked. Has it occurred to you that you could possibly just be in the way?"

Vanessa stopped in the middle of the flowing throng of people. Xavier was a few steps ahead of her before he realized what had happened. He turned and came back. "Or you can allow me to look into it while I'm there." Telling Vanessa his intention to help find her mother hadn't come out quite like Xavier had imagined.

Vanessa readied a smart remark to say, but she stopped when she realized Xavier had offered to look for her mother. Vanessa couldn't think of anything another human being could have said at that moment that would have meant more. *This man does care.* Vanessa was so moved that her heart felt as if it were expanding, and her hand went up to her chest. The realization was delicious, yet foreign, and just a bit frightening. *But why would Xavier care? Why would he care what happens to me or my mother?* Then it hit her. He simply did.

It was so very simple, yet for years Vanessa had not allowed herself such ease with her feelings. She struggled with accepting it from another. "Wait a minute." She threw up her hands in an attempt to hold Xavier back, although for months this is what she had wanted. Vanessa stammered as she said, "I-I haven't asked for your help."

"When it comes to this, Vanessa, perhaps you should," Xavier replied.

"No. No, I can't." She shook her head, unable to trust Xavier with so much of her life . . . so much of her, so quickly.

Xavier could feel Vanessa's emotional retreat. *Whenever I reach out to you that's when you draw back. Damn you, Vanessa Bradley.* His reply mirrored his frustration. "Am I getting too close for comfort, Vanessa?" His dark eyes darkened. "Have I stepped into your space without permission?" He made a circle around his body with his arms, which made passersby stare. "I'm simply offering you my help. But you don't have the courage to accept it."

Stung that Xavier would twist her shortcomings, Vanessa retaliated. "That's not what you're doing, and if you think it is, you really don't understand. You don't offer someone help and in the same breath put them down." She began to walk off. "And I can promise you I will not be in the way."

Immediately, Xavier regretted his reply. He caught up with her and grabbed her arm. "Wait a minute, Vanessa. That didn't come out right." Xavier just wanted Vanessa to let him in. His voice softened. "I truly do want to help."

But Vanessa was still smarting from Xavier's statement. "I just want you to think about this. Have you ever really cared about anyone?" The insensitivity of her question hung in the air between them.

Xavier just looked at her.

"Have you?"

"What do you think?" His face turned into a mask.

"I don't know." She paused. "Because if you have, you would know it is impossible for me to sit and wait here in the States, when I have the means to go and try to do something to help find my mother."

Xavier heard Vanessa's words, but his feelings conjured up the past. He had wondered about his father, but it hadn't been until his mother was gone that he'd thought about trying to find him. Xavier knew his mother had been against it, and, right or wrong, he'd accepted his parents' relationship as an aspect of his mother's life that she preferred to shun.

He looked down. Xavier knew Vanessa had no way of knowing it, but the effect was just the same. She had unearthed the one thing Xavier felt the most guilty about. He had never searched for his father. *Yes, I did care. I care now, and I always have.* His thoughts reflected his turmoil.

When Xavier looked up again, his eyes turned stormy as he said, "If you have any thoughts that we might be together in the future"—he paused to let his words sink in—"don't ever ask me that question again."

Vanessa's eyes opened wide, and before she could blink, Xavier turned and walked away.

....

fourteen

𝒱anessa gazed out the airplane window at the darkening sky. The plane was filling up fast, and she had not seen Xavier come aboard. *My God, did what I say make him change his mind about coming? I had no idea when I said what I said that it would affect him so.* She watched the people walk up the aisle. *I have never seen anyone's face look the way Xavier's did when he told me, "If you have any thoughts that we might be together in the future, don't ever ask me that question again."* Her heart seemed to beat faster. *I didn't mean to hurt you, Xavier. I know what it means to be hurt, and I didn't mean to hurt you, of all people.* She didn't know if she would get the opportunity to tell him that, but she wanted to say it.

The number of passengers still boarding trick-led down to a straggling few, and Vanessa began to worry. Where could he be? Her gaze strayed to the aisle time and time again.

Finally she saw him. Grateful to see his face, she said under her breath, "Thank you."

Inside the confines of the airplane, Vanessa realized how tall Xavier really was. Even in his jeans and button-down shirt he was an imposing, alluring figure. Vanessa turned away and watched the airport workers scampering below, preparing the plane for takeoff. Now that Xavier had come aboard, Vanessa knew that regardless of what she said and did he had his hooks in her, and perhaps . . . just perhaps, she had her hooks in him as well.

Vanessa kept her gaze averted until Xavier stopped at the end of her aisle. They looked at each other before he put his bag in the overhead compartment. Then Xavier slid into the seat beside Vanessa and fastened his seat belt.

"I guess the ticket agent thought we'd like to sit together." His voice vibrated a low tone.

"Yeah, I guess he did." Vanessa felt as if she were holding her breath.

He gazed deep into her eyes. "Was he wrong?"

"No," Vanessa replied softly, so relieved he was there and that she might be able to make amends.

"Good," Xavier said. He spread his legs, laid his head back, and closed his eyes.

Slowly, Vanessa turned back toward the window. This time she closed her eyes as she faced the glass. She could feel a small quaking inside her along with the touch of Xavier's wide shoulders. Not knowing what else to do, Vanessa took a paperlike airplane pillow and placed it against the window. She scooted down just a tad and laid her face against the pillow.

Out of the blue, the reading with the psychic Dellia came to mind. Dellia had mentioned a man who would be in Vanessa's life. A man who would aid her, and together they would find healing.

Vanessa tuned into the warmth of Xavier beside her. Was Xavier that man? Would he help her find her mother? And would she be alive and well? Vanessa closed her eyes and repeated a silent prayer. As she drifted off to sleep, Dellia's words continued to return to her: "It is because of these wounds you are together." *Xavier has been wounded. Of that I have no doubt. But will he care for me enough to allow me to help* him? *That will be the true test of his feelings,* Vanessa thought as she drifted further into sleep, exhausted and comforted by Xavier's presence next to her.

"Would you like orange juice, ma'am?" the smiling flight attendant inquired.

"Yes. I would," Vanessa replied, groggily.

"And you, sir?"

"Yes."

The attendant placed juices on both trays, then walked away.

"Preparing for a breakfast snack at what would be five in the afternoon, but is actually five in the

morning two days later, feels rather strange,"
Vanessa remarked.

"Shows how big of a time difference there is
between America and Australia," Xavier replied.

Conversation had flowed easily between them
after Xavier had broken the ice when he'd first sat
down, although a certain sense that they both
were being extra careful remained. Xavier and
Vanessa had slept a lot as well. Still, by now,
Vanessa knew every nuance of Xavier's face. The
way his hands moved and the sound of his
breathing while he slept. They were such endearing small things, things that managed to comfort
her whenever she thought of her mother.

Another attendant came by with bread and
fruit; Xavier and Vanessa ate breakfast in a com-
panionable silence. The flight would be over soon
and they would be in Sydney, Australia. Vanessa
watched as the sun projected a flaming gold
beam across the sky. It was topped by a shadow
of billowy clouds, and underneath was a hint of
blue. "How magnificent," she said softly as the
plane flew alongside the gorgeous sight.

"Nature can be magnificent," Xavier acknowledged. "It can be many things, but I've learned
through the years, and through my travels, that it
should always be respected. Misjudging the
power of nature can make the difference between
life and death."

Xavier sat back as the attendants announced
that everyone should right their tray tables and
seats in preparation for the landing. He could feel

Vanessa stiffen. Although she did not say it, he believed she had picked up his warning: that Australia was an unpredictable land, and he hoped that her mother had taken that to heart.

"Sydney is a very large city." Vanessa diverted the subject.

"Around eight million people, and it is as modern as they come."

"But Alice Springs is a different story?" she asked, turning her head to look at him. He was so close that her lips brushed his face. Their eyes met. "I'm sorry," she said, admiring the thickness of his lashes while the prickliness of his morning stubble still tickled her lips.

"Sir, could you bring your seat to the upright position, please." The flight attendant waited for Xavier to obey her request.

He sat back and pressed the button, and the moment between Xavier and Vanessa was broken as the flight attendant moved on.

Xavier rested his head against the seat. "I know we both have other things on our minds. Very important things, like finding your mother, and I have important business to take care of, but"— Xavier licked his lips—"how are we going to handle this, Vanessa?"

"Handle what?" She knew what he was asking, but she was unprepared to answer.

"This thing between us."

"Oh, that." Vanessa paused. "I guess it depends on what we want to make of it. You have any ideas?"

"At first I did." He looked down. "But we didn't get off to a good start, and because of that, I think we both have misgivings."

"Baggage before we begin. Doesn't sound too good to me," Vanessa said softly, hoping Xavier would refute her. But he remained silent. "I guess we'll just take one day at a time, huh?" Vanessa finally said.

"One day at a time. A wise plan," Xavier replied, then closed his eyes.

Vanessa studied his still features, and she prayed the misgivings and the baggage weren't too much as she turned her body toward the window and watched the plane descend.

Xavier opened his eyes ever so slightly as Vanessa repositioned herself. She was an unexpected factor on this trip, and his job at the museum hung on its outcome. Xavier had expected to spend some time looking into Jackie's disappearance, but he hadn't counted on the new emotional entanglements that Vanessa presented. Maybe she would find her mother right away and her stay in Alice Springs would be cut short. Somehow Xavier felt that could be the best thing for everyone.

Vanessa talks about baggage. When it comes to my father she has no clue about the kind of baggage I could bring. Although I've never dealt with drugs, some scientists believe I have a predisposition to addiction. He swallowed hard. *So what would that mean for a child that I might father? Would my child also have a predisposition? And what woman would want to take that kind of chance? Anyway, what do I know about being a father when I didn't have one myself?*

Xavier studied her profile as he reflected on the piece of paper that remained in his wallet.

If my father was the one who wrote the note, was it a message intended for me? "He is not his father's son." *The words echoed in his mind. Did he somehow realize my fears, and was he trying to find a way to pacify them?* The noise inside the descending plane increased along with Xavier's thoughts. *If that is true, he is no more insane than any other father who cares about his son. And if that is true, why didn't he tell me himself?*

fifteen

"This is the key to your room, Ms. Bradley." The hotel clerk passed it across the counter. "And it won't take but a second to register you, Mr. Johnson. You want a nonsmoking room, is that correct?"

"Yes," Xavier replied.

Impatient, Vanessa searched the lobby for the security guard again. "Do you think it would pose a problem if I went to his office?" she asked the clerk.

The clerk looked up from the keyboard. "No, that wouldn't be a problem. But I have already radioed him, because he wasn't in his office. I'm sure he will show up at any—there he is." He looked across the lobby.

Swiftly, Vanessa shortened the distance between them. "Mr. Dalton, I'm Vanessa Bradley from the United States. I talked to you on the phone a day or so ago concerning my mother, who has been missing."

"Oh. Yes. Yes," the portly man acknowledged.

"Have they found her? Or have you heard anything else?"

"As far as I know, no, they have not."

Vanessa's face fell.

The security guard hurried on to say, "But of course, as I told you, we turned the situation over to the police and they may have some information that we don't know about. I am certain, though, they would have informed us if she had been located."

Xavier joined them. "Any news?"

"No." Vanessa pinned him with tortured eyes.

Mr. Dalton looked uncomfortable. "Let me give you the phone number and address of the police station. I'm sure they will be very willing to talk to you about this." He walked over to a nearby desk and started writing.

Vanessa and Xavier followed. Their eyes met over and over again. Xavier reached out and put his arm around her. "We'll put our things in our rooms, then we'll go straight to the police station. I've got a couple of phone calls I need to make, but I'm sure they have a public telephone I can use."

Vanessa nodded.

"I know this sounds too pat at this point, but try not to worry." Xavier looked down at her. "It won't do you or your mother any good."

"At the moment I feel like I can barely think." Vanessa spoke softly, not wanting the security guard to hear her. "I realize I thought I'd get here and they'd tell me Mama had been found, or that she was in her room or something. Now reality is setting in, Xavier." His name held a desperate note. "I may never see my mother alive again."

Xavier enfolded her in his arms. "You don't know that to be true. Don't lose your footing, Vanessa. Hold on to the bright side." He looked at the security guard, who was holding the note and watching them with a guarded expression.

"Here's that information, ma'am."

Vanessa pulled back from Xavier, whose shirt was now wet from her tears. She wiped her eyes, then turned and took the paper.

"I do wish you luck, ma'am."

"Thank you," Vanessa replied.

"The elevators are over here," Xavier directed, touching Vanessa's back. "They put us in rooms right beside each other."

Xavier had barely touched the Up button when the elevator doors opened. They stepped inside.

Vanessa stared at the designer carpet. "I don't know what I was thinking when I jumped on that plane and decided to come here alone. From the way I feel right now, Xavier, if you weren't here . . . someone that I can lean on, if only a little. . . ." Her voice broke.

"I understand. You don't have to say it." He put his arm around her again as the elevator doors opened. They walked down the hotel hall in silence. When they reached their rooms, Xavier waited for Vanessa to open her door.

Vanessa held on to the doorknob. "I want to thank you."

"Look, there's no need. I—"

"Yes, there is a need. I don't know if I could deal with this alone, right now. But I feel so strange opening up to you this way. You don't really know me, and here you are in this situation with me. It's hard for me to let you see me at such a vulnerable time. I swear, Xavier, normally I'm not so pitiful. But it's my mother and—"

"I understand." He gave her a sympathetic smile. "Now, go inside. The bellman should be up in a second. When he's done we'll be on our way."

Vanessa nodded again, and wiped away more tears.

Xavier turned to go to his room, then looked back. "And it's my honor to be here for you, Vanessa."

The statement only created more tears as she closed the door.

Xavier entered his room, sat down on the bed, and opened his PalmPilot. He searched for the information he needed with his stylus. "Phillip Ramsey." He closed the device and dialed the number.

"World Import and Exports."

"Calling for Mr. Ramsey," Xavier told the receptionist.

"Just a moment."

Xavier held the line until the woman returned.

"He's not answering his line right now. Would you care to hold, or is there a message?"

"What time does your office close?"

"We close at five, sir."

Xavier looked at his watch. It was five minutes after three. "And you're located on Gap Road, correct?"

"Yes, we are." He could hear the bellman outside the cracked door.

"No message. I'll just drop by. Thank you." Xavier hung up the telephone.

Once the bellman delivered the bags and the tips were paid, Xavier and Vanessa were in a cab headed for the police station.

When they walked into the building it hit Vanessa that she was halfway around the world. At the Plaza Hotel Alice Springs, anticipation about her mother had blocked out the nuances that made Australia different from the United States. But in the police station, the contrasts were right in her face. The uniforms were decidedly different, but there was also a less intense atmosphere. Yes, Vanessa could tell the Australian police officers were about keeping the law, but the station didn't have the rough-and-tumble feel of American police stations.

"G'day. May I help you?" the officer behind the counter inquired.

"I hope so," Vanessa replied. "About two weeks ago my mother came here as a tourist. She was expected to return home to the United States three days ago, but she wasn't on her plane."

"Oh yes, I heard about that." The man's piercing blue eyes looked from Xavier to Vanessa before he turned around and addressed another officer sitting behind a desk. "Is Charlie handling the missing persons case from the Plaza Hotel Alice Springs?"

The other officer barely looked up. "I think so. You can check with him and see. He's in Frank's office."

The officer returned his attention to Vanessa and Xavier. "Excuse me. I'll be right back." Moments later he returned with a taller man at his side.

"I'm Officer Hughes. I'm handling Jackie Bradley's case. And you are?"

"Vanessa Bradley. Her daughter."

"Hello, Ms. Bradley." He presented his hand. "The security guard at the Plaza Hotel Alice Springs told us that you planned to make a trip over." He looked at Xavier.

"This is Xavier Johnson. A friend of mine," Vanessa explained.

Officer Hughes shook Xavier's hand. "Could you both come this way, please?" He unlocked the counter door and led them to his desk, which sat in the open along with several others. Officer Hughes dragged a third chair over to his desk. "Have a seat."

Xavier and Vanessa complied.

"I don't know what you've been told . . ." Officer Hughes began with his hands folded on top of a file folder.

"All I know is my mother didn't return home to the States three days ago when she was scheduled to return." Vanessa sat on the edge of her chair. "And at that time it appeared her room had not been occupied for a few days as well."

Officer Hughes nodded. "All of that was in the report provided by the Plaza." He paused. "Well, the good news is we do have some additional information."

"What's the bad news?" Vanessa's voice became a whisper.

Officer Hughes sat back in his chair. "The bad news is we still haven't located your mother."

"But she isn't dead?"

"We don't know that, Ms. Bradley," Officer Hughes stated carefully. "So at this time we are simply investigating this as a missing persons case."

Vanessa sat back. "You say you have more information."

"Yes. Your mother was last seen six days ago booking a tour to Ross River Homestead."

"Ross River Homestead?"

"It's a touring destination that allows people to see some of the Eastern MacDonnell Ranges."

"Okay." Vanessa wanted to hear more.

"We were able to verify that she did buy a ticket that day, and she went on the tour." Officer Hughes paused. "But she did not return."

"How do you know that?" Vanessa sat forward again.

"She never used her return ticket."

"My mother went to some mountain range setting and she didn't return? Why didn't the people from the touring company notify someone?" Vanessa's voice went up.

"Ms. Bradley, sometimes tourists don't intend to use the return ticket the same day. They may have plans to go on to other places. Then days later they return to Ross River Homestead and use the back end of the ticket."

"So you're saying it's possible my mother could have done what many other tourists have done."

"It's possible, but highly unlikely, seeing that she was scheduled to return to the United States, and as you stated . . . she never did."

Vanessa's hand went up to her forehead. "So what will you do now?"

"I want to go over the description we have of your mother." He started to twirl his ink pen. "We want to make sure our information is accurate, and that we're working with the best resources. We have already notified law enforcement officials in the surrounding areas of the situation. Beyond that we will keep this case open and wait."

"Wait . . ." Vanessa's eyes narrowed.

"Yes, ma'am." Officer Hughes gave her a sympathetic but law-enforcing look.

"My mother is seventy-six years old. What would you be waiting on? To see if she'll turn up dead somewhere?" Vanessa's voice shook.

"No ma'am. We'd be waiting on any and all information that could lead to finding her."

Vanessa clasped her hands together and leaned her face against them. "What's the name of the tourist company?"

"Range Tours," Officer Hughes replied.

"Is it near here?" Xavier spoke up for the first time.

"No, it isn't, but I can give you the address."

Vanessa squared her shoulders. "I want it."

sixteen

"Vanessa, I've got some business I must take care of," Xavier stated as they stood outside the police station.

"Please—" Vanessa placed her hand on his shoulder. "Go ahead. You've done more than enough already. I know you've got things to tend to. I'll be fine."

"What do you plan to do?"

"I'm going to that tourist company. I want to ask them a few questions. And who knows, maybe they've come across some new information and haven't turned it in to the police yet." Her words were hopeful, but her eyes were not. "All I know is I'll feel better if I go over there and talk to the people myself."

"I understand." Xavier looked down the street. "I don't know how long this is going to take, but I plan to be back at the hotel in a couple of hours. If I can't make it, I'll call and leave you a message."

"Okay. Two hours," Vanessa repeated. "And I'll do same thing if I'm not back by then." She reached up and placed her hand on his cheek. "Thanks."

Xavier looked into her eyes. "You're more than welcome." Then he stepped away and flagged down a taxi. When a cab stopped, Xavier opened the back door. "You take this one."

Obediently, Vanessa climbed inside. "I want to go to Range Tours on Todd Street."

"I know the place," the driver replied, and set his meter.

"Bye." Vanessa placed her hand at the base of the window.

"Good-bye." Xavier embraced her hand with his own before the cab drove off.

Minutes later, Xavier was also in a taxicab. World Import and Exports was only a short distance away. Xavier paid the driver and hopped out. He walked into the familiar building and went to the second floor. The company announced itself in bold engraving on a metal plate outside a nondescript door. Xavier went inside.

"Good afternoon. May I help you?"

Xavier didn't recognize the brunette behind the desk from his previous trip. "I called about an hour ago. I want to talk to Mr. Ramsey. Is he here?"

"Yes, he is. May I tell him who wants to see him?"

"Tell him Xavier Johnson with the Marshall Art Museum in the U.S."

The receptionist pressed a couple of numbers on the telephone. "Mr. Ramsey, a Mr. Xavier Johnson is here to see you from the Marshall Art Museum in America."

"Sir?" She gave Xavier an uncertain look. "Yes, sir." She hung up the telephone and stood. "I'll be right back."

Xavier watched her disappear down the hall. He had paced the floor several times before the woman returned with another man.

"Mr. Johnson," the man said with a wide smile and his hand extended.

"Yes." Xavier was a little slower to return the greeting.

"I'm David Paige. I've been taking over some of Phillip's workload while he's on vacation."

"But I thought Mr. Ramsey was here." Xavier looked at the receptionist, who kept her eyes averted.

"No. Julie came from the temporary service. She didn't know." He held the plastic smile. "Come back to my office, and I'll see what I can do for you." Mr. Paige turned back toward the hall.

Xavier followed the man past Phillip Ramsey's office door, which was closed.

"Please sit down." Mr. Paige motioned toward one of two leather chairs.

Xavier sat, but his distrust was growing. "Are you familiar with the Pintupi art exhibit that I hope to bring to our museum in Columbus, Georgia?"

Mr. Paige sat back. "Vaguely. You see, that is a project that Phillip was handling on the side. Not that we minded." He folded his hands. "But it was more or less directly under him."

"More or less under Mr. Ramsey." Xavier almost bristled at the double-talk. "It's obvious I need to talk to Mr. Ramsey." Xavier began to get up. "We're in the eleventh hour with this project."

"No. Have a seat." Mr. Paige put his palm up. "Please. I think I can still help you."

"But you just told me this was not a company project." Xavier remained with both hands on the arms of the chair. "Although this is the first time I've heard that."

Xavier couldn't believe what this man was telling him. What did he mean this wasn't a company project? There had never been an indication of that while he was in Australia, and had Curtis known this he would surely have thrown it in Xavier's face. That *his* project could only be a sideline for a major company like World Import and Exports.

"Yes, that's true. But because of what happened"—he made a motion like a bird with his neck—"I am familiar with the snafu, if you don't mind my using that term."

Xavier sat down and observed the man who was sweating profusely although the office was quite cool. "Why don't you tell me about it."

Mr. Paige touched up his forehead with a handkerchief. "From what I understand, it was the Pintupi artists that pulled out of the deal. At least that's what Mr. Ramsey told me."

"And why would they do that?" Xavier didn't waste a second with his question. "The negotiations were all in good faith. We had placed everything on the table—the time length of the exhibit, how the art would be cared for. The contracts had been drawn up, and we were waiting for the signed copies. From our view, it appeared everyone would come out a winner from this. The Pintupi. Your company, or Mr. Ramsey, rather. Our visitors and our museum."

"But you have to understand the Aboriginal mind." Mr. Paige gave a superior chuckle. "Some of the tribes function out of ways that are difficult for modern man to understand."

Xavier didn't crack a smile. "Try me."

Mr. Paige cleared his throat. "Phillip says the Pintupi believed that their art would not be honored in the spirit in which it was created." He crossed his arms. "Meaning in the spirit of the Dreamtime. Are you familiar with that term?"

"Quite familiar," Xavier replied. "What made them come to that conclusion?"

"Nothing logical, of course. Those people have defied acculturation every step of the way. At least most of them have." Mr. Paige spoke freely, then looked at Xavier's brown skin and recanted. "I mean, we mainstream Australians have tried to bring them into society. Make them productive citizens."

"Is that why the majority of the Aborigines who were forced to discard their tribal ways ended up very much like some Native Americans in my country? With drinking or drug problems while living on reservations? All because you were trying to make them worthy of society, Mr. Paige?"

Mr. Paige's amiable expression faded, and a more hard-nosed man appeared. "That's one way of looking at it. But the truth is, the art exhibition that we're discussing has nothing to do with that."

"You were telling me about how difficult the Aborigines are to acculturate when I asked why they felt we would not honor their artwork in the spirit of the Dreamtime."

Mr. Paige smiled coldly. "What I should have said was they don't feel your museum would do it in the proper manner. The spiritual beliefs of those—of the Aborigines is as complicated as the personal protocol within their extended families. It comes down to the fact that they didn't believe you or your museum had the knowledge or the expertise."

"By no means do we pretend to understand all the nuances of a culture as old as the Australian Aboriginal culture. But by dealing with the Pintupi as an individual tribe, we intended to do our best to adhere to their request. We planned to make sure the public understood that these paintings were recordings of important events, some of them spiritual, linking the past, present, and future."

Mr. Paige made a show of looking at his watch. "I'm sorry I don't have more time." He stood up.

"I've got a meeting scheduled for five o'clock, but I hope our discussion has helped you, Mr. Johnson."

Xavier knew he was being put out. "You are a very hardworking man, Mr. Paige. I understand your company closes at five." He could tell there was much more going on than Mr. Paige was owning up to.

Mr. Paige came around his desk. "It's the only way to get ahead."

"You wouldn't happen to have the name of the Pintupi contact that Mr. Ramsey was working with, would you?" Xavier remained in his seat. "Of course, if I was able to salvage this deal, I would give World Import and Exports full credit, since Mr. Ramsey had worked so hard and long."

"No. I don't have it." Mr. Paige stood by his office door.

"I didn't think you would," Xavier replied, getting up. "If you happen to come across it, I'm staying at the Plaza Hotel Alice Springs. You can contact me there."

"I certainly will. Good evening, Mr. Johnson," Mr. Paige quickly replied as he stuck out his hand.

"It could have been better," Xavier said, and headed down the hall. He heard Mr. Paige's door close, and he saw Mr. Ramsey's door ease shut.

These people aren't cooperating one bit. They're going to make money either way, so what happens to the exhibit no longer matters. And to think that Curtis was the one who put me in contact with them. Xavier walked past the receptionist, who bid him a hasty good-bye. *I can't help but wonder if Curtis is more than a little responsible for the shaky ground this project is experiencing. And I'm going to make it my business to find out.*

Vanessa entered the Range Tours building. The business appeared to be no more than a long counter with a few feet to spare.

"Could help you?" a Chinese man behind the counter asked.

"I hope so," Vanessa replied. "Six days ago my mother was in here. She bought a ticket to Ross River Homestead, but she never returned to her hotel. You've spoken to the police about her. Her name is Jackie Bradley." Vanessa looked at the man expectantly.

"One ticket." The man stuck his finger in the air. "Ross River Homestead?"

"No. I don't want to buy a ticket." Vanessa shook her head. "I want to ask you about my mother."

"Two ticket." He put up two fingers.

"No. I don't want to buy a ticket. I'm trying to find my mother."

"Ting bu dong." The man shook his hands and head. He opened a door behind him. "Zhou Yun Chung, lai le."

A pretty young Chinese woman appeared.

"Bong ta." The man gently flapped his hand toward Vanessa.

"Sorry," the woman began. "I normally work counter. May I help you?"

"I'm trying to find out about my mother,"

Vanessa began again. "She was in here six days ago and bought a tour ticket to Ross River Homestead, but she never returned to her hotel. The police were here—"

"No," Zhou Yun Chung corrected her. "The police did not come here, but they called. Asking if American Black woman come here. I tell them yes. Not many American Black women come here. So it is easy for me to tell them yes."

"So you were the one who saw her?"

"Yes. She come here, early. Very nice. Smiling. Buy one full ticket to Ross River Homestead. Many tour stops between here and there. She want to go to Aboriginal lands, but we no have tour to Western MacDonnell Range that day, and your mother no have permit," Zhou Yun Chung explained. "So go eastward to Ross River Homestead. While she wait for bus, she talk. Tell me she from United States."

"Did she say anything else?"

"She talk about her family. You." Zhou Yun Chung pointed at Vanessa. "Her husband. She seem very excited about meeting him here."

"My mother told you she was going to meet my father here?" Vanessa pointed down toward the counter.

"No. No." Zhou Yun Chung shook her head. "She meet him in Australia. Not say in Alice Springs."

"Oh-h. I understand." Vanessa looked down. It was difficult to hear the bizarre concept voiced so naturally from an unsuspecting stranger. "Have you seen my mother since then, or heard any-thing about her?"

Zhou Yun Chung shook her head. "No."

Vanessa could feel her body droop with disap-pointment. "If you do hear something, anything, please call me at the Plaza Hotel Alice Springs."

"The Plaza Hotel Alice Springs? Yes." The woman tore a piece of paper off a pad. "Write down your name and number. I call."

Vanessa took the ink pen. "I don't know the number, but my name is Vanessa Bradley." She wrote as she spoke. Vanessa gave the pen and pa-per to the woman. "Thank you," she added softly.

"You come all this way to try to find her?" Zhou Yun Chung asked.

"Yes. I got here today," Vanessa replied.

"So sad." Zhou Yun Chung's dark eyes were full of compassion.

"Good-bye." Vanessa turned away quickly. She couldn't take the emotion in the woman's eyes. It brought tears to her own.

"Wait," Zhou Yun Chung called. "I think of something. Family is very important in my culture. We have family in Ross River Homestead. Maybe they see your mother." Her eyes brightened.

A ray of hope dawned as Vanessa looked at the woman. "It's definitely worth a try."

"Yes. We try." Zhou Yun Chung smiled, which prompted her father to interject. He spoke to his daughter in Chinese.

Vanessa waited until the exchange between fa-ther and daughter died down.

"My father say the cleaners that his younger brother owns in Ross River Homestead is near the place where tour bus let people off."

"How close is Ross River Homestead to Alice Springs?"

"Almost two hour away," Zhou Yun Chung replied.

"Can I drive there myself?"

"I think so." The Chinese woman appeared concerned. "You come to Australia before?"

"No. I've never been here before," Vanessa replied.

"Ross River Homestead is not like this. Not so modern." She paused. "Maybe you should wait and go on tour bus. It leave tomorrow morning. It much better than go alone."

"I don't think I can wait until tomorrow, and I hope I can talk to your uncle tonight." Vanessa tried to calm down when she realized how pushy she sounded. "But if I can't, I'll be there whenever he's available."

"We call them now and see. You wait." Zhou Yun Chung entered the door behind her.

Vanessa looked at Zhou Yun Chung's father and smiled, but he turned away as if he did not see her. She wondered if the young woman's uncle would be as open to helping her as Zhou Yun Chung, or as distant as her father.

Moments later Zhou Yun Chung returned to the counter. Her father asked more questions. She answered them before she spoke to Vanessa. "I talked to my uncle's wife. She say he not there now. Will be home later. Perhaps you can talk to him early in morning."

"That's fine. I'll rent a car this evening and drive to Ross River Homestead and take a look around. I'll talk to your uncle bright and early."

"His name Yan Laoshi. He a teacher. This is where to go." She gave Vanessa a card. "You will see the cleaners. It has a big sign out front. Express Cleaners, it say."

"Thank you so much," Vanessa replied, feeling better than she had since leaving the police station.

"Mai wenti. No problem."

"Good-bye," Vanessa said to the woman and her father just as the man began to speak again.

"My father say, 'Xiao xin.' Be careful."

"I will. Tell him thank you," Vanessa said again.

Vanessa flagged down a taxi and asked to be taken to the nearest car rental business. As she waited for the paperwork to be drawn up, she placed a call to Xavier at the hotel. The phone rang and rang before a recorded message came on. "Xavier, I've got a lead on my mother, so I've rented a car. I will call you once I get to Ross River Homestead. Hope things went well for you." By the time Vanessa hung up, the attendant was handing her the keys.

Please be all right, Mama, she prayed silently as she clutched the keys. *Please be all right.*

seventeen

"If it wasn't for bad luck I wouldn't have any luck at all." Vanessa leaned closer to the front window in an attempt to see through the pouring rain. She had been driving for nearly two hours and feared she had missed her turnoff. Vanessa tried to block out the foreign feel of the land, the redness of the soil and the cliffs that she drove between and beneath. "Damn it! This is horrible. The weather was beautiful, then all of a sudden—this."

She gripped the steering wheel harder than ever. The rain was so forceful that it turned the soil into liquid. It was like driving over a melting clay-red painting.

Within headlight range, a road with an indiscernible sign appeared to the right of her. It was the first indication of human life Vanessa had seen for a while. Desperate, she turned onto the unpaved road. The car began to rock and roll like a boat in choppy water. Vanessa thought of Xavier safe and sound at the Plaza Hotel Alice Springs. She hoped he got her message just in case she, like her mother, ended up missing.

She had driven for no more than three minutes, but it seemed like an hour before she saw lights in the distance. Vanessa could tell by the number of lights that it wasn't a large establishment, and she wondered what kind of reception the people there would give her. There was no way to ignore the fear that surfaced as she pulled up in front of an old ranch house. Vanessa turned off the lights, then the car, and tried to make up her mind about what she would do if the residents turned out to be unfriendly.

Suddenly, a dog started barking; he was joined by another. Moments later they were at her car door barking in the rain, their coats drenched, their teeth bared.

The vicious dogs so unraveled Vanessa that she didn't see the front door open. When she finally looked toward the ranch house, a man was standing there with the door wide open, rain and all. He did not motion for her to come in, nor did he act as if he was coming over to see what she wanted.

"This does not feel good." Vanessa's tone was ripe with fear. "I should have waited for the tour bus." She regretted her impulsive actions. Then a shorter figure shooed the man away from the door. It was a woman wearing an apron. Vanessa could barely hear her thin voice through the rain. "Are you going to come inside or not?"

"I'm coming," Vanessa replied, not knowing if the woman could hear her. She started to open the car door, but the dogs renewed their most aggressive behavior.

In response the woman stomped her feet. "Stop all that noise and get back under the house." The words cut through the weather, and the dogs offered a few more yaps, then disappeared.

Vanessa climbed out of the car and ran to the ranch house. The woman stepped aside so Vanessa could enter. She closed the door behind her.

"What are you doing out here in this weather?" the thin, bright-eyed woman with more gray than blonde hair inquired.

"I was looking for the turnoff for Ross River Homestead, but I guess I didn't see it because of the rain."

"People miss that turnoff even when it's not raining," the woman replied. "Come in. Come in. Have a seat." She motioned toward a couch.

"Thank you." Vanessa shook the excess rain from her clothes. She saw the man who had been standing in the doorway. He was much taller than the woman, but not as tall and imposing as he appeared from the car.

"My name is Geneen. My friends call me The Fixer because I'm always trying to fix someone else's life. That's Evin, my son." She indicated the big fellow. "And that's Steve, a friend."

"My name's Vanessa." She looked at the group, who were obviously surprised by her visit. "I live in the United States."

"We gathered that," Steve replied.

"How did you know?" It was Vanessa's turn to be surprised.

"By your accent," Steve said.

"Yes, we didn't think you were from around here," Geneen concurred. "And as you can tell, you're not quite in Ross River Homestead. We live on the outskirts. Sometimes we put up tourists who want to explore the outback."

"You do?" Vanessa tried not to obviously assess the size and contents of the house, but from what little she could see, there didn't appear to be room enough for guests. Especially strangers.

"Yes. We consider ourselves one of the Station Stays in this area. We've got a couple of shearer's quarters that have been turned into guest cottages." Geneen donned a comical expression. "Not that my family ever successfully raised sheep on this challenging land," she went on. "One of the quarters is occupied. But we do have an empty one if you are interested."

"I certainly am." Vanessa couldn't say the words fast enough. "God certainly takes care of fools and babies."

"What did you say?" Geneen leaned forward.

"I was just being thankful for being led here to your place," Vanessa explained. "I was almost frightened out of my wits. I couldn't see a thing once it started raining."

"When it comes down, it comes down," Geneen replied. "But it will stop raining soon, and the sky will be so clear it will provide a perfect map of the stars," Geneen assured her. "Care for a little something to eat?" She walked over to the stove. "One meal a day is usually included with the stay, but since you have come under such dire conditions we will share dinner with you tonight for free."

"Oh, no thank you. I'm very willing to pay," Vanessa stated.

"Don't." Geneen put up her hand. "It is done. I was about to serve it up anyway. You'll be our guest tonight."

"And if you know what's good for you, you will not argue," Steve added. "Geneen may be the smaller one of the two, but she's got a tongue sharp enough to keep this one in line." He indicated Evin, who was sitting quietly watching.

"Evin's no problem. Are you, Evin?" his mother called.

He looked at Vanessa and shyly shook his head.

"He's like a big child. He comes in handy when you need brute force." Geneen picked up several plates. "You can all sit at the table. I'll have the food ready in a matter of minutes."

"It smells mighty good," Steve complimented.

"It really does," Vanessa added as she sat down at the table for four.

"It's emu, vegetables, and potatoes," Geneen informed them.

Vanessa's eyebrows went up, but she quickly brought them back down again.

"I bet you've never had emu before," Steve, who seemed to be the most cosmopolitan of the group, quipped.

"No, can't say I have," Vanessa replied.

"Well, when Geneen prepares it, it's a food fit for the gods."

"My mother's cooking is very good," Evin announced softly.

Vanessa looked at him and said, "Well I'm glad I've been invited to dinner."

Evin smiled slightly but never looked up.

Geneen placed the food on the table. "What brings you to central Australia?"

"I'm trying to find my mother. She didn't return home when she was scheduled to a few days ago. The police have her listed as a missing person, but I decided to come and see what I could do to help find her."

Geneen stopped in midair while serving a spoonful of potatoes. "That must be such a worry."

"I can't tell you when I've been more concerned," Vanessa confessed.

"Did you come alone?" Steve asked.

"Actually, a friend of mine came too. His name is Xavier Johnson. Although he came here on business, his being here has been a godsend for me."

Geneen sat down and picked up the plate of emu. "Are you staying in Alice Springs?"

"Yes, at the Plaza Hotel Alice Springs. I'm going to Ross River Homestead to ask a few questions."

"I hope you find your mother, Vanessa. Life has enough worries without an unfinished burden like that," Geneen stated sympathetically. "I hope she's simply stranded at one of the Station Stays that doesn't have a working telephone. That happens, you know."

"That's good to know." Vanessa sighed.

"Was your mother travelling alone?" Steve asked.

"Yes." Vanessa's guilt increased a notch every time she heard that question. Maybe she should have insisted on coming. Maybe she should have been a better listener. A better daughter.

"My-y." There was a deep sigh in Geneen's voice. "I've lived here all my life, and there are parts of the outback that I wouldn't travel in alone." Her hazel eyes met Vanessa's. She seemed to realize she had only added to Vanessa's worries, so Geneen piped up and announced, "Let's eat."

The meal began, and the discussion turned more banal, almost as if Geneen strove to keep Vanessa's mind off her mother. They talked about central Australia, the wide range of topography that could be found there, and the plethora of Aboriginal reservations that it housed.

"I don't know that much about the Aborigines," Steve stated. "The little I do know I can't say I find attractive."

"And why is that?" Vanessa questioned, very aware of her own brown skin.

"They are a hard people to understand," Steve replied. "And I'm not just saying that because their skin color is different from mine. There are Africans here in Australia who have come and started their own businesses and prospered, but the Aborigine. . . ."

"I've gotten to know some Aborigines pretty well," Geneen jumped in. "Their culture and the foundation of how they have lived life for thousands of years is just different. So when you try to give them a way of life that has only been around for a couple of hundred years, how can you expect to replace what is a part of their spirit, their soul? It's not that easy."

"They sound like a very interesting people," Vanessa said.

Steve made a mocking expression. "They can be interesting and much, much more."

Evin bristled. "Joseph is an Aborigine. I like Joseph. We're mates."

"Joseph is staying in the other shearer's quarters," Geneen explained. "He comes through here from time to time. He is Arrernte, but he has one foot in Western culture and the other in Aboriginal culture. That's a very difficult thing to do." Geneen got up and started taking the empty plates from the table.

Vanessa gathered the remaining dishes. "Where does he live?"

"Outside Alice Springs. And he has relatives on one of the reservations. Evin has more of a rapport with him than he has with anybody. Don't you, Evin?"

Evin nodded.

"I'm going to leave the dishes here until later," Geneen said. "It's stopped raining now, so I think I should show you where your quarters are."

"I'm ready whenever you are," Vanessa replied.

Geneen wiped her hands on her apron, took a key from a hook, and opened the front door. "I'll be right back," she said to Evin and Steve.

Vanessa followed her outside. "Wait. I need to call my friend at the hotel. I'm sure he expected to hear from me by now."

"I'm sorry. But whenever it rains like this my telephone isn't worth the wires it's made with. It'll be usable, but that won't be for quite awhile. Maybe by morning."

"I see." Vanessa tramped across the yard. She felt a twinge of disappointment. She knew she would not see Xavier that night, but she had hoped to speak to him. He had been such a comfort, and Vanessa realized she wanted the intimacy that they had shared throughout the day.

"That's it right there." Geneen pointed. "It's within seeing distance of the house, just like the other." She indicated a carbon copy of the building they were approaching.

Geneen opened the door with ease and lit an oil lamp that was sitting on a simple table. "It's not much, but it's clean and warm. You've got a bed, a light, and a place for your belongings. If you want to bathe in the morning, there's an outdoor shower around back, along with an outhouse."

"Thanks," Vanessa replied, suddenly realizing how good she had it back home.

"I've got a couple of magazines in the house. I'll bring them out for you to read." Geneen stepped outside again.

"I'd like that," Vanessa replied.

"You just wait right here, and I'll bring them to you," Geneen said.

Vanessa watched the woman retrace her steps across the yard. Steve was coming out of the house as Geneen was going in. They exchanged a few words, he waved, got into his car, and drove away. Minutes later Vanessa had locked herself inside her cottage.

If only she could speak to Xavier, hear his voice. Vanessa knew it would help her feel stronger. No matter how kind Geneen and her group were, they were strangers to Vanessa. Strangers in a strange land that had swallowed up her mother. Yes, Xavier's warm, familiar voice would feel so good right now.

But like so many things so far, it wasn't to be.

Alice Springs and she told me that the woman, Vanessa Bradley, wanted to get in touch with you."

"You've seen Vanessa?" All of Xavier's antennas went up. He looked at the stranger with renewed interest.

"Why yes, I have. A very nice woman," Steve answered with a large smile. "But that big downpour gave her quite a scare, she lost her way, and ended up at Geneen's place. Thank God for that. Geneen's such a lovely woman, wouldn't hurt a fly. Vanessa's staying in one of her shearer's quarters for the night. Geneen asked me if I would look you up when I got here, to let you know Vanessa's all right and that she wanted to contact you. Geneen's telephone is a little on the poor side right now."

"How close is your friend's place to Alice Springs?" Xavier asked.

"I'd say it's a couple of hours away."

"Can you tell me how to get there?"

"I can, but you're going to have to be a very determined man to find the turnoff after sundown. There's a darkness there that only a blind man knows."

"I'll take my chances," Xavier replied.

"Want to get to the little Sheila, eh, mate?" Steve picked up a tourist area map from the concierge desk. "I truly understand. Here are the directions." He traced one of the darker lines with his finger. "You get on Ross Highway and you just keep on going. If you reach the turnoff for

Ross River Homestead you've gone too far.
There'll be a sign on your right about twenty kilo-
meters past Corroboree Rock."

"Thank you for delivering the message,"
Xavier said. "And for the directions."

"You're more than welcome." Steve placed his
hat back on his head and walked out of the lobby.

Xavier wasted no time in renting a four-wheel
drive. Although he had limited personal experiences with the harshness of the Australian outback, he knew of stories that made its danger
clear; central Australia was amazingly beautiful,
but, like a taipan, it could be deadly as well.

By the time Xavier was on his way, the rain had
stopped and night was descending. Darkness
blanketed the land, and Xavier turned on his high
beams, but the lights only illuminated the road so
far. Outside of their path was pure, natural night.
A blackness that only a vast land, not altered by
technology, could produce.

As Xavier drove he wondered what possessed
him to take such a chance in a land so full of risks.
It was only a cursory thought because he knew
full well the answer. Vanessa. It was also sober-
ing, because Xavier wasn't sure Vanessa was
truly capable of letting him in.

His eyes narrowed as he thought about her,
about them. *A man's ego and his spirit are always
touched by rejection. And the truth be told, I had never
been rejected by a woman before. There is always the
chance that she moves me so because of that.* He
mulled the thought over. *I mean, how do I know*

*what I feel for her is any different than what I have felt
for other women? Lust can be quite the chameleon.*
Xavier tried to convince himself as he drove on,
but his heart told him his thoughts were the real
deceivers.

If it wasn't for the white cloth tied to the sign,
signaling the turnoff, Xavier would have missed
it. Still not certain that he had found the right
road, he drove cautiously. When he saw lights in
the distance he drove toward them until he an-
gled his high beams on a modest structure. Two
barking dogs came from underneath the house
and made his presence known. A woman in her
housecoat eventually opened the door. Xavier
rose up out of the car, placed one foot on the
ground, and left the other inside the vehicle. The
barking dogs went into warp drive.

"Sorry to disturb you so late, but I'm looking
for a Vanessa Bradley," Xavier announced.

"Get away from him," Geneen commanded the
dogs, waving her arms. "Are you Xavier?"

"Yes, I am."

"So Steve found you?" Geneen continued to
talk despite an occasional bark.

"With no problem at all," Xavier replied.

"Well I guess Alice Springs has grown a lot, but
it's still a little town." Geneen drew the robe
closer to her body as it started to rain again.
"Vanessa's here. She's in the building right over
there." She pointed and stepped back from the
rain. "My name is Geneen, if you need anything. I
serve breakfast in the morning between six-thirty

and eight-thirty. Cook it fresh for you right then and there."

"Sounds perfect," Xavier replied.

"And there's only one bed in there. I hope I don't hear any complaints from Vanessa."

"I don't think you have to worry on that account," Xavier replied, clearly aware of the rain and the night's possibilities.

"Fine. You have a good night," Geneen said.

"You do the same," Xavier replied before she closed the door.

nineteen

$\mathcal{V}$anessa pulled the sheet up over her bare legs as she read the sentence again. The vicious sound of dogs barking had broken her concentration. In the magazine that Geneen had given her, she was reading her third article about Alice Springs. Vanessa figured by the time morning came she would be an expert on the School of the Air, a school that broadcasted lessons over the radio to children living in remote outback areas. But no matter what she did to occupy her mind, not knowing her mother's plight was always there.

It was more than a little eerie inside the shearer's quarters, a rough-hewn building that oozed pioneer energy, mainly because of the night sounds that engulfed it in one low, but continuous, rolling vibration. Still, Vanessa felt safe enough with the heavy slide lock on the door that she had shed her pants and lay comfortably in only her T-shirt and underwear. She stopped reading to listen to the hearty downpour of rain that had just begun. The cozy sound made Vanessa pull the sheet closer around her.

A demanding knock at the door caught her off guard. At first Vanessa was speechless, then she finally asked, "Who is it?"

"Xavier."

"Xavier?" Overjoyed, Vanessa bounded out of bed. "How did you find me?" she asked as she fumbled with the lock.

"Never mind that. Just let me in. It's pouring out here."

Vanessa flung the door open, and a wet Xavier stepped inside.

"How did you find me?" Vanessa repeated, a huge smile dawning on her face.

"With difficulty," Xavier replied. He sat on the end of the bed, wet pants and all, and started removing his shoes and socks.

"No. Seriously," Vanessa said, her eyes bright.

Xavier turned his attention from his feet to her face, then casually dropped his gaze to take in the rest of her. Blatant disapproval shone in his eyes, but there was a definite fire beneath his gaze. "What possessed you to run off like that? You're not back in the States, Vanessa. This is dangerous, wild country."

"So you were worried about me?" she teased, smiling.

"I don't need another missing person on my hands." There was no smile on Xavier's face.

The light went out of Vanessa's eyes. "I didn't realize you had *one*," she retorted. "My mother is my problem."

"You'd serve her better by using better judgement than you've shown this evening." He began to unbutton his drenched shirt.

Vanessa put her hands on her hips. "Excuse me." The short T-shirt became shorter, and she was very aware of the scanty clothing she wore. Still, Vanessa refused to let Xavier know it. She wouldn't give him the satisfaction. "Let me tell you something. My father died two years ago, and I don't recall acquiring another."

"This evening you put yourself in a precarious, possibly dangerous, situation. And me along with you, considering my coming here tonight." He laid his wet shirt on top of the bed.

"I didn't tell you to come looking for me, Xavier Johnson," she fumed. "And get your wet shirt off of my bed." Vanessa reached over him and threw the damp top, but before she could stand up, Xavier had pulled her onto his lap.

"Don't do what you did today ever again." He spaced out each word.

"You can't tell me what to do." Vanessa struggled in his arms. "If you were really concerned about me you wouldn't say that. You talk as if I don't know how to conduct my own life." Her dark gaze flared as she looked into his even darker one. "All men are alike. You're all just like my father, judgmental. Expecting everything but giving so little."

"You call driving around cliffs in a night so dark I couldn't see my own hand in front of my face, giving so little?"

Vanessa stopped cold as the image of Xavier plunging over a cliff exploded in her mind. Wide eyes searched the face that had come to be so dear to her, and the thought created the feeling of the loss.

Amazed, Xavier watched Vanessa's eyes switch from anger to sorrow, and he wondered how much of this woman there was to experience. How much of this woman there was to know. He had to find out, and his face changed with the pressing urge. "There's something you need to know," he said softly.

At the change in his expression, Vanessa's concern increased tenfold, so immediate were her thoughts of possibly losing her mother, so present her fears. "What is it?"

Xavier looked deep into her eyes. "I don't want to be your father." And his lips crushed hers in a consuming kiss.

Surprised, Vanessa started to squirm again until a wave of heat rose up inside, so powerful that it nearly took her breath away. A dizziness followed, and her body became as pliable as soft butter. Vanessa's eyes were closed when their lips parted, and she heard Xavier say, "Don't ever run off like that again."

Through the pleasurable fog Vanessa gradually realized how Xavier had been able to manipulate her thoughts and her feelings with ease, and when she opened her eyes she could tell he knew it as well. She pushed against his chest. "Let me go, Xavier."

He resisted. "What's going on in that head of yours now? I can only imagine what is causing you to look at me that way."

"Just let go of me," she repeated. "How can I trust you when you openly manipulate me this way?"

Xavier could see a tinge of fear in her eyes. He had moved too quickly. Xavier had shown Vanessa the depth of her own desire and it had frightened her, and fear was not what he was after. Xavier relaxed his hold. Vanessa got up and backed away.

"You're acting as if you've touched a hot coal." He followed her with his eyes. "And now you don't know what to do about it?" Xavier spoke as if he were talking to a skittish colt. "This thing between us has been building up for a while, Vanessa. Don't act like you didn't know it. That you didn't see it coming." He lay back and rested his elbows on the bed beneath him.

Vanessa's mouth went dry as she looked at the picture he made. He was a magnetically handsome man, with a chest that was broad and muscular, sporting a hint of smooth hair. How many women had he shown himself to like this? she wondered. How many women had tumbled into bed without a second thought, and once done had to come back for more? But after the first time found "more" was only on his terms? Vanessa couldn't stand the thought of Xavier being in control of her in such a way. "I am not going to spend the night in here with you," she announced.

"You're not?" The words were almost taunting.

"No."

"Why? Because you know I plan to make love to you?" Xavier didn't move as he spoke, and his eyes remained riveted on Vanessa's face.

"I don't know any such thing," Vanessa replied.

"Yes, you do." His gaze seemed to cut through the cotton of the T-shirt. "Your body knows."

"But I'm more than my body, Xavier. Far more." Vanessa walked around the small room and finally found solace standing near the head of the bed.

"There's nowhere to go, Vanessa. Now it comes down to you and me." Once again he scanned her from head to toe, but this time it was a slow, deliberate process that made Vanessa tingle and shiver.

"Is this why you came here tonight?" Vanessa wanted to be indignant. Her mind supported her, but her heart and body did not.

"No. But I would be lying if I said it had not crossed my mind. And I'm not one to lie," Xavier said softly. "I may have my faults, but I'm not one to lie."

"But we haven't really talked about... about—"

"Us?"

"Yes. Us." Vanessa wrapped her arms protectively about her abdomen. "What would we be doing?"

"Maybe through this we'll find out if there is such a thing as *us*." Xavier stood up and started walking toward her.

"It may be your ideal way of finding out, but it's certainly not mine," Vanessa said as Xavier stopped in front of her. She looked up into his eyes as he began to stroke her face. Her heart pounded.

"Sh-sh-sh." The soft sound filtered from his lips as his large hand continued the stroking motion before it went down to her neck, smoothing and caressing.

Vanessa didn't move. Couldn't move. Eventually her breaths and heartbeats slowed down with the motion of Xavier's hands. His touch was so soft, just the opposite of the kiss he had planted on her lips minutes before.

"I want to know who you are, Vanessa." She trembled at the sound of his voice. "I want to know what you mean to me."

This time when he kissed her it was a pure, short invitation that caused Vanessa to reach for more. Masterfully, Xavier placed his mouth within her reach, and Vanessa's lips met his again, giving him license to slip his arms around her.

"Who were you trying to get away from? Me? Or yourself?" He spoke against her lips as he pulled her to him.

"I just don't . . ." Vanessa attempted to express her jumbled thoughts. "I don't know if I'm ready for this, Xavier."

"I will make you ready." He lifted her ever so gently and laid her on the bed. When he came down on her, Xavier kissed Vanessa again. This time their contact smoldered and Vanessa's lips were moist and trembling afterward, but her reservations had not been put to rest. "You can make my body ready, but what about my spirit, my mind?" she asked as he lifted the T-shirt over her head.

"I could never, would never, take on such responsibility." He looked deep into her eyes as he molded her breasts. But his gaze and his mouth were drawn downward, and he traced their tips with his tongue. "Your mind and your spirit are your jurisdiction, and always will be." Xavier stroked Vanessa's torso with one hand and removed his pants with the other. "But I can make love to your body, and some say that if we touch that special place within each other it will be a spiritual experience." The last stroke of his hand massaged the center of her femininity, before he opened it and stroked the wetness inside.

Vanessa's back arched at Xavier's caress, further offering him her breasts. Her unbridled response turned his dark eyes black, and he accepted them with reverence.

"Right now I couldn't care less if it is a spiritual experience," Vanessa said, breathless. "But I want it to be a loving one." She could barely speak as her mind melded with the sensations that Xavier's hands and tongue created all over her body. Sensations that were invigorating brands.

"Vanessa." Her name came as a husky tone from his lips. "How beautiful you are to me. How desirable." Xavier's lips cut a path around her navel and beneath. Moments later he explored the outer area of her womanhood, and Vanessa had no more words, only sounds that were the clearest communication of all. Then just when Vanessa thought Xavier would kiss the very center of her, he stopped. In one smooth motion Xavier brought his face parallel to hers again. "One day, I will taste you there, and on that day you will know you are truly mine." He entered her with that promise, and from that moment on his eyes never left her face. With each stroke Vanessa and Xavier experienced the other's pleasure and rode a wave of fulfillment that was greater than either had ever known.

twenty

$\mathcal{V}$anessa opened her eyes and felt the comforting heaviness of Xavier's arm. She continued to lay very still, but with a heightened awareness. She hoped Xavier was also secretly enjoying the intimate moment. Her eyelids became heavy with the memory of the night before. Vanessa had never known herself to be so passionate. She had never known she could. Her night with Xavier had gone far beyond anything she'd ever known.

Xavier stirred behind her, and moments later the warmth of his arm was gone. Still Vanessa remained quiet as she monitored his movements. He turned onto his back, sat up, and eventually threw his legs over the side of the bed. There was no hesitancy about his movements. No longing to remain beside her or to rekindle the fires of the night before. It was as if he had moved on without a backward glance or loving touch.

Disappointment flooded inside her when she realized Xavier had not reveled in the intimate spoon position that their bodies had shared. No sooner than he'd awakened, Xavier had felt inclined to remove himself from her and from their bed.

Vanessa stared at the wooden planked wall. Then with what she hoped was naturalness, she stretched as if she had just awakened. She turned over onto her back.

"Good morning," Xavier said.

Vanessa hid her eyes with her forearm. "Morning."

"I just looked at my watch. It's six-forty."

"It's early," she replied to the mundane statement.

"Not really." A nude Xavier picked up his pants. "We did good. Normally when you travel as far as we have, you run into a bit of trouble sleeping because your body clock is still on U.S. time. Waking up in the middle of the night is pretty much the norm. But we hit the ground running when we got here yesterday and didn't stop until last night. That was good." He zipped up his pants. "So we slept all night long."

Vanessa didn't know if she should turn away or watch him while he dressed. It was hard not to look, but there was something almost lewd about the way the morning had begun, as if nothing profound had happened between them. It was the absence of intimate looks and conversation that was turning their lovemaking into something unspeakable. Vanessa looked down at the bed. When she looked up again she caught Xavier watching her, but he lowered his gaze under her awareness.

"Geneen told me breakfast begins at six-thirty, so I thought we might as well get cleaned up, have breakfast, and be on our way."

"Be on our way to where?" Vanessa's hurt and disappointment were now turning to anger. "You never asked me what plans I had. As a matter of fact you haven't asked me anything."

Xavier stood with his shirt balled up in his hands and his legs like an inverted vee. "I plan to." His dark eyes settled on her face, just as his certainty about how much he cared for her enveloped him. Making love to Vanessa was unlike anything he had ever experienced, and he knew she was the woman of his dreams. But could he be the man of hers? "But I figured if I stayed in bed with you one moment longer, we would never make it out of this cabin." He tried to appease the confusion in her eyes, yet Xavier needed time to mull over the impact of their night together. "We've got important things to take care of. I know you are far more aware of that than I am."

The look in Xavier's eyes caused Vanessa's heart to hammer.

"So we'll discuss it during breakfast," he added after a meaningful pause.

Vanessa nodded. Xavier unlocked the door and went outside.

She felt exhilarated by what Xavier had said. She had touched him all right. Touched him as profoundly as he had moved her. Vanessa sat and allowed it all to sink in.

Finally, she got up and stood in front of a small square mirror that hung on the wall. Vanessa caressed her own face and thought of Xavier's hands. Immediately, sensations that reminded her of their lovemaking flooded over her. Vanessa looked deep into her own eyes, and the message there was clear. She was in love, and from the look in Xavier's eyes, he was too, but the profundity of it had unnerved him. That was empowering. It also made Vanessa feel bold and brazen.

She felt a sudden burst of desire to revel in her new sense of womanhood and to be as beautiful and alluring for Xavier as she could be. Immediately, Vanessa combed through her braids with her fingers. When they were smooth and orderly, she took a rubber band from her purse and styled them on top of her head, knowing the style would accentuate her almond eyes and high cheekbones. Afterward, Vanessa checked her purse for makeup. All she had was an eyebrow pencil and a tube of lipstick; Vanessa knew they would have to suffice. She would apply them after she showered.

Vanessa pulled her top over her head and looked in the mirror again. The image she saw

there made her stop, for the light she saw in her
own eyes reminded her of her mother. Many
times as a child she had seen the look of love in
Jackie's eyes when she'd looked at her husband.
Now, Vanessa understood those times, those moments, when her mother had been her most beautiful. "I hope I get to tell you, Mama, that I've had
a glimpse into the world that you and Daddy
shared, and it has helped me to understand."
Vanessa's eyes filled with tears.

"Vanessa." She turned away from the mirror
when Xavier knocked on the door. She opened it
and he was there, his hair still glistening with
water.

"I'm done. The shower is all yours."

"I'm right behind you." Vanessa stepped outside.

"The water's a little nippy at first. There's a gas
heater, but if you turn it on before you get in, it
could get too hot," Xavier explained from mere
inches away.

They stared into each other's eyes before
Vanessa said, "Thanks for the tip."

Xavier touched her face, then headed for the
main house.

Vanessa showered and applied her sparse
makeup with the aid of a small mirror that hung
on the outside of the wooden shower stall. When
she entered the house Geneen was at the stove,
and Xavier was seated at the table along with a
fascinating-looking man. His skin was far darker
than either one of theirs, but his hair was straight

with just a hint of curl. His pronounced brow provided an awning for his soft, dark eyes, while an extremely generous nose rode above a brush-like mustache and humble mouth.

"G'day. Grab a seat," Geneen said over her shoulder.

"Morning." Vanessa sat down. "Good morning," she said to the man sitting across the table from her.

"G'day," he replied.

"This is Joseph, Vanessa," Geneen turned around long enough to explain. "And Joseph, that's Vanessa."

They both nodded.

"What are you having this morning?" Geneen inquired.

"A couple of fried eggs and toast," Vanessa said.

"You got it," she replied.

Vanessa looked at Xavier, then at Joseph, who continued to eat a plate of eggs and vegetables without looking up.

Evin burst into the room carrying an intricately carved object shaped like a stretched vee. "Look what Joseph left on my bed, Ma."

"Nice boomerang." Geneen brought Xavier's plate to the table. She looked at Joseph. "Did you carve it yourself?"

"Yes." Joseph smiled at Evin.

"You've got to stop bringing him things," Geneen chastised Joseph. "His room is beginning to look like a crowded museum."

"No," Evin disagreed. "I keep my room straight." His man-child face tightened.

"Yes, you do." Geneen turned loving eyes on her son. "I can't argue with you there."

"You carved that?" Vanessa studied the well-crafted piece.

"Yes," Joseph reiterated.

"It's beautiful. May I see it, Evin?"

Evin hesitated before he handed the boomerang to Vanessa.

"This is great. I've never held a boomerang before." Vanessa turned it in her hands. "If I threw it would it actually return to me?"

"Not this one," Joseph replied. "This boomerang is for making music. We beat out the rhythm of the song with this kind, but it can be used for hunting too."

"Is carving something you do all the time?" Xavier asked.

"Not all the time. This is something special I did for Evin."

"He did it for me." Evin pointed to his chest. "Joseph and I are mates," he declared with pride.

Vanessa tried not to, but she found herself staring at Joseph. "You're an Aborigine."

Joseph nodded.

She looked down, embarrassed. "I don't mean to be rude. But it's like meeting someone who I've only read about in books. I'm truly honored."

"As you can see, we are real people just like you and anyone else. And your curiosity does not bother me. Many people come to Australia curious about us. Some of them very kind. Others not so kind," Joseph added. "I, and some of my friends, are members of the Aboriginal Cultural Foundation. We try to protect our people and our culture as much as we can."

"Do the majority of the Aborigines live in this area of the country?" Vanessa asked.

"Many tribes live in the west, some in the northwest. I am Arrernte. Our tribal lands are here in the heart of Australia. The land surrounding Alice Springs in all four directions is the Arrernte region."

"So you know this area, this land very well?" Vanessa persisted.

"The land and I are one. How can I not know my own body?" Joseph said quietly and calmly. "My people have been here since the Dreaming, the beginning."

Vanessa's eyes widened. "The Dreamtime?"

"The Dreaming . . . the Dreamtime . . . it is one and the same," Joseph replied.

Vanessa was itching to ask another question, but she held back. Still, there was a dawning that Joseph could make her search for her mother easier.

"Are you familiar with the Pintupi community?" Xavier asked.

"Of course," Joseph said as Geneen delivered Vanessa's plate.

"I'm trying to find one of their members."

"May I ask why?" Joseph turned an even gaze in Xavier's direction.

"Some Pintupi were involved in a business deal of mine that fell through. It involved some of their artwork."

"I do not get in the middle of anyone else's deals." Joseph's tone held finality. "Even if it were Arrernte I would still be hesitant."

The table fell silent. Vanessa looked at Xavier, who sat back in his chair, while Joseph began to eat again, focusing on his plate.

"Sounds like it's time for me to sit down and have a cup of coffee." Geneen descended into one of the chairs. "I might as well tell you now, I've been known to be nosey. Just can't help it. So I've got to ask what happened to the deal." Geneen looked at Xavier.

"That's what I intend to find out," Xavier replied. "A deal had been made where some Pintupi who live in Kintore would provide several pieces of art to be displayed in the States. Things were going along fine, then we hit a brick wall. I was told they changed their minds. I thought I might be able to save the project by coming here and talking to anyone who might listen." Xavier looked at Joseph, but from his body language, it appeared he had shut himself off from the conversation.

"Did they say why the Pintupi changed their minds?" Geneen questioned.

"I talked to a man in Alice Springs about it. He told me the Pintupi didn't believe our exhibit would honor the artwork in the spirit in which it was created. The spirit of the Dreamtime. Meaning getting people to realize these aren't just markings on a canvas. That some of the Aboriginal artwork reflects a belief that past, present, and future are not separate, but are happening at the same time. That there is a oneness to all things."

"That gets a little deep for me." Geneen looked wary. "Do you think they were right?"

"I'm not certain." Again Xavier looked at Joseph, who still kept his gaze focused on the table. "But my intention is to give the exhibit all the honor my knowledge and additional research would allow me to give."

"It is difficult for *Kardiya*, White people, to understand the Dreaming," Joseph said. "It is also difficult for people like you who have been cut off from their roots. Their homeland. In my language the Dreaming is called *Jakurrpa*. It is connected with the land, the earth." Joseph looked around the table.

Vanessa couldn't wait one more second. "I believe my mother came here in search of the Dreamtime as if it was a place in time." She hoped Joseph could shed some light on the situation.

"Like I said, it is difficult for foreigners to understand," Joseph repeated.

"Joseph, please help me understand." Vanessa pleaded with her eyes. "My mother never returned home. She came to Australia over two weeks ago and she never returned. I believe she thought the Dreamtime, the Dreaming, was like a window in time where she could meet my father, who passed away two years ago."

Joseph examined Vanessa's anguished face before he spoke. "The Dreaming is a time when the Ancestral Beings were born out of their own eternity."

Vanessa shook her head, confused.

"The Ancestral Beings have always been, but they made themselves known on the Earth during the Dreaming. Many emerged out of the very Earth herself. Through their adventures mountains and streams were born. The stars were thrown into the sky. The mulga and gum tree sprung from the Earth, and creatures such as the wallaby, possum, and the Aborigine came into being."

"You mean the Dreamtime is an Aboriginal creation myth." Vanessa looked incredulous.

"It may be a myth to you, but it is truth to my people."

Vanessa was stunned. "I can imagine how my mother must have felt when she realized what the Dreamtime really is. When it hit her that nothing was going to come from her expectations. Nothing could come of them because she never really understood the Dreamtime." She looked at the floor without seeing it. "How horrible that must have been. Travelling halfway around the world, hoping to reunite with my father and finding nothing." Vanessa spoke aloud, but it was as if she was talking to herself.

"I do not know about your mother," Joseph

said. "But do not underestimate the power in the Dreaming. There is so much power that there is much secrecy within Aboriginal society because of it."

Vanessa did not respond. She continued to look down at the floor.

"Are you okay?" Xavier touched her arm.

Vanessa looked at him as tears rolled down her face.

A heavy silence settled around the room.

"Where did your mother go, here in Australia?" Joseph asked.

Vanessa attempted to dry her eyes, but it was of little use. "She came to the Alice Springs area. That's why I'm here." She looked at Joseph's rich eyes through blurred vision. "I'm trying to find her. The last thing I heard she bought a ticket to tour the area around Ross River Homestead. But she never returned from the tour." Vanessa looked at the ceiling. "She wanted to visit some Aboriginal lands in the Western MacDonnell Range, but the tour company didn't have a tour scheduled for that day. I also understand she needed a pass. My mother didn't have one."

"Yes, you need a pass to visit Aboriginal lands," Joseph said, then added suggestively, "unless you know someone."

Vanessa looked at Joseph again. A spark of hope crept back into her desolate eyes.

Joseph stood up. "I am starting out for the Western MacDonnell Range this afternoon. If you want me to get you into some of the Aboriginal communities, meet me in Alice Springs. I will be at the Strehlow Research Centre at noon."

"We'll be there," Vanessa quickly answered, then looked at Xavier.

He nodded.

Joseph crossed to the door and opened it. He turned and looked at Xavier. "Kintore is a large Pintupi community. It is also in the West Mac-Donnell Range."

"Thank you." Xavier acknowledged the olive branch. "We'll see you in Alice Springs."

Joseph closed the door behind him.

"Good. So that worked out," Geneen commented with a self-satisfied look on her face. "We just had to open the door for Joseph. I knew he'd walk right through it." She walked over to the sink. "I've got to go to Alice Springs today myself. You probably rented your cars from Diane's Car Rental."

Vanessa and Xavier nodded affirmatively.

"Thought so." Geneen rung out the dish cloth. "I can take one of them back for you. That way you can ride together to Ross River Homestead. You see," she said, folding the cloth up neatly and started wiping, "the car rental company is my cousin's business. We do this all the time. Makes it convenient for customers, which puts more money in both our pockets."

Vanessa felt a real surge of hope. "You've got a deal."

twenty-one

As they stood outside his cleaners, Yan Laoshi listened as Vanessa began to describe her mother. Calmly, he put his hand up and stopped her. "No need to go any further. I remember your mother."

"You do?"

"Yes. I remember her because she came inside and asked me if I had a public phone to use. One to call back to America."

"I bet she was going to call me." Vanessa looked at Xavier, then back at the Chinese man. "Do you have a pay phone?"

"No." He shook his head as if the idea were preposterous. "And she did say something about wanting to call her daughter before she returned to Alice Springs."

"But that's just it," Vanessa protested. "My mother never returned to Alice Springs."

"I know," Yan Laoshi said.

"How do you know?" Vanessa asked with apprehension.

"I know she did not return to Alice Springs that day because she accepted offer for another tour. A tour to the Western MacDonnell Range."

"But your niece told me they didn't have a tour scheduled for that area that day."

"This is so. But two men with another company made her offer." Yan Laoshi looked disapproving.

Xavier stepped in. "Were you familiar with their company?"

"Company. Hah! They're no good. Most people around here know that."

Vanessa's eyes widened. "Then why didn't you stop her?"

"I could not. Had customer. By the time customer gone, your mother gone too." Yan Laoshi adjusted his glasses. "But also it is not my place to stop her. These men no good. I live here. Not leave and go anywhere. My family here too."

Frustrated and overflowing with concern, Vanessa looked at the ground. "I don't know why the Alice Springs police didn't know about this." She looked up at Yan Laoshi. "Did they talk to you?"

"I have been out of town. Just returned yesterday evening."

Vanessa turned anxious eyes on Xavier. "We've got to tell the police."

"Have you seen those men around here since you've been back?" Xavier pressed.

"No. No see them."

"Do you know the name of their company?" Vanessa asked.

"No." Yan Laoshi shook his head. "Not real company. Only take people from time to time. No real schedule."

"Thank you for your help," Vanessa said, but what Yan Laoshi had told her had only deepened her concerns. "We've got to get back to Alice Springs and let the police know."

"I understand," the Chinese man replied as they headed for the car.

The drive back to Alice Springs was heavy with quiet. Xavier wanted to ease Vanessa's worries about her mother, but the truth was he didn't want to give her false hope. He was also pointedly aware of how Vanessa kept her face averted. Why wouldn't she look at him? Whenever he looked her way, she made it a point to look out the window. Xavier had done all he could think of to try to help her, and now it felt as if she had turned away from him. Why?

He glanced at the exposed nape of her neck and the rich brown skin beneath it. Xavier tried to put Vanessa's fears before his own. Logically it was easy. He could fathom the upheaval she was experiencing surrounding her mother's disappearance. It would be devastatingly hard for anyone, and Xavier knew human reaction to tragedy was as individualized as the people involved. But still, something inside Xavier felt that if Vanessa truly cared, she would not react to him in such a fashion.

"It won't be long before we're there," Xavier said, needing to fill the silence and get out of his own head.

Vanessa remained quiet.

"Vanessa . . ." He glanced at her long enough to see harsh eyes turned in his direction. Xavier looked back at the road. "Why are you looking at me like that?"

She hesitated. "Don't ask me if you don't want to know."

"I asked," he said. "So I want to know."

"My mother may be dead, Xavier. Dead." There was a tremor beneath the word. "And this would not have happened if she had not come to Australia."

"It sounds like you blame me for that." Xavier's tone was cautious.

Vanessa looked out the window again.

"Answer me, Vanessa. Is that what you're thinking? If so, I feel you're just using me as a scapegoat."

She looked at him again. "Scapegoat for what?"

"For life being what it is. Life. Something you cannot control." He kept his eyes on the road. "Something that blows us here and there and makes us pray that we land standing on our feet. You can't control life, Vanessa. If you could you would be God." His angst at how quickly she changed her feelings toward him showed.

"I'm not trying to be God." She folded her arms across her solar plexus. "All I know is my mother would be at home in Columbus, Georgia, if you hadn't introduced her to your Australia. You can turn that into anything you want, but it's the truth," Vanessa retorted.

"You don't know that," Xavier rebutted. "You don't know what your mother might have done if she hadn't gone to Australia. You don't know what tomorrow will bring. None of us does. But some of us have the guts to accept what unfolds and make the best of it." Xavier pulled up in front of the Alice Springs police station. He turned full eyes on Vanessa. "And that goes for us as well. No matter what happens between. No matter how this plays out, I'm going to be okay." He had had enough of her wishy-washy ways.

Vanessa got out of the car. Xavier didn't follow her, and he didn't watch her enter the building. Vanessa had all but accused him of her mother's death. It was a hard pill to swallow, no matter her pain.

Five minutes later, when she re-entered the car, their eyes locked. There was hurt on both sides, and the rift, unlike the physical distance between them, was wide.

"It's almost twelve," Vanessa said, her voice strained. "I asked the police where the Strehlow Research Centre, where Joseph said to meet him, was located." She glanced down at a slip of paper. "It's on Larapinta Drive." She started to point.

"I know where it is." Xavier put the map that was in his lap back in the sunvisor. He started the car.

"Look, Xavier, I . . ." Vanessa's voice was soft, uncertain.

"You don't have to say anything," he replied. "I think you've said it all."

Vanessa looked at the hardness of his profile, and she felt the tears sting her eyes. Why had she said the things she had said to him? Why? She knew Xavier had not forced her mother to come to Australia. He had been only one of the tools her mother had used to make her journey. So was he right? Was she trying to hide from life? Too weak to face the harsh realities that some people face every day? The same people who needed the charities that she supported and claimed she believed in. Vanessa felt an isolating chill run through her body. Xavier had been her friend. Her lover. Her only ally, and now with a few harsh, pain-filled words, she had alienated him.

Again Vanessa turned her head toward the window, this time so he would not see her tears. For this time, Vanessa knew, she would not see the caring concern that Xavier had shown before—only disdain for a woman who could not accept her own pain without placing the blame on another.

twenty-two

Joseph was standing at the door of the Strehlow Research Centre when they arrived. The white band on his dark hat was a hint of style that was markedly absent from the rest of his clothing. When Xavier and Vanessa pulled up to the curb, he walked toward them in an unhurried manner. Xavier unlocked the passenger doors, but Joseph remained standing a few feet away from the car. After a few moments, Vanessa opened her door and talked to him across the top of the vehicle.

"Hello, Joseph."

"Hello."

"We're ready to go whenever you are," she informed him.

"I'm ready to go now." He looked at her with a steady gaze.

"Did you want to ride with us, or are you going to drive?" She looked for a car that might be his. Then Vanessa recalled she never saw an extra vehicle at Geneen's place.

"I don't have a car," Joseph replied.

"So how did you get from Geneen's house?"

"Walked."

"Walked," Vanessa repeated with disbelief.

"I prefer it that way. When the distances are very far I have other ways of getting around."

Vanessa recovered from her surprise. "So you plan to ride with us?"

"Yes. At least part of the way." He examined the Rodeo with his eyes. "But I think for your sakes, this vehicle will not do."

"It's a four-wheel drive." Xavier stuck his head out of the window. "Where we're going is too rough for a four-wheel drive?"

"No," Joseph replied. "But Aboriginal land, this land, is very unpredictable. During the best of times it could take twelve hours to get to Kintore, and during the worst . . . I cannot say. Sometimes when foreigners and Australian *Kardiya* travel in Western Australia, they travel in caravans with beds and stoves inside."

"RVs?" Vanessa questioned.

"It's like having a room or a house on wheels." Joseph gave a further description.

"Yes. That's what we call a recreational vehicle," Vanessa replied.

"I think it would be best if you rented one of those," Joseph advised. "That way you will have a place to sleep and a roof over your head at all times."

"How many days do you think we will be gone?" Xavier asked.

"Perhaps two days, two nights if everything goes smoothly. But in Aboriginal land—"

"You never know," Xavier and Vanessa said in unity.

"Now you are beginning to understand."

"So we will need enough room for three," Vanessa said.

"Only during the day. At night I will be welcomed into one of the homes, I am sure. I am like my nomadic ancestors. I travel about. I have many places that welcome me."

"Now where can we rent an RV?" Xavier asked.

"There is a place up the street." Joseph pointed.

"We'll have to drop by the hotel and pick up some things before I turn this vehicle in," Xavier replied. "Do you want to ride with us?"

"I will walk and meet you at the place where you will get the RV." Joseph backed away from the vehicle.

"Okay." Vanessa climbed back inside. They both looked in the side mirrors. Joseph could be seen trailing far behind at a leisurely pace.

By the time they turned in the four-wheel drive and arrived at the rental office, Joseph was sitting on a bench outside. In a matter of minutes Vanessa and Xavier had chosen an RV.

"Who will be the primary driver?" the employee asked as he filled out the paperwork.

Before Xavier could respond, Vanessa said, "I will."

The man looked from Xavier to Vanessa. "Are you certain? You've rented a mighty big vehicle. Perhaps you should let your husband drive."

"He is not my husband." Vanessa dashed the man's assumption. "And I am capable of driving."

The man looked at Xavier as if he was waiting for him to intervene, but Xavier remained silent. "If that's the way you want it." He placed Vanessa's name on the primary driver's line and Xavier as the secondary. After both signatures were obtained and credit card imprints taken, the man handed the keys to another employee. Moments later the RV was brought out front. Vanessa climbed into the driver's seat. Xavier climbed in the passenger side, while Joseph took a seat deeper inside.

"I have never seen a woman drive one of these before," Joseph commented as Vanessa adjusted her seat and the mirrors. "You are an expert at this?"

"No. It's my first time," Vanessa replied.

Joseph looked at Xavier, and his heavy brow descended even lower. Xavier, on the other hand, sunk down into the corduroy seat and closed his eyes.

"Closing your eyes—is this a good thing to do under the circumstances?" Joseph inquired.

"As good as any," Xavier said without moving a muscle.

Several jerks and stops later, Vanessa backed the RV up, then finally turned it onto the road. By that time sweat was pouring from her brow and Joseph was holding on to the back of her seat for dear life. Xavier was the only one who appeared cool and calm. Never once did he open his eyes. Never once did he reach out to steady himself.

"And what is your name again?" Joseph asked.

"Vanessa Bradley."

"Not you. I mean this one who remains as undisturbed as a lizard sleeping safely under the shade of a rock."

Xavier opened his eyes slightly. "Xavier Johnson."

"Xavier Johnson," Joseph repeated as he nodded his head. "And you, Vanessa Bradley, as active as an emu." He nodded his head again. "The lizard is cool and slow. The emu warm and quick. If you were Aborigine I would give you those animals as totems. They are a good match for one another. There is balance there. The makings for a good, long relationship." Joseph paused, and Vanessa stole a glance at Xavier, who appeared to be resting comfortably. "So something good has come out of this experience. The Ancestors have given you totems for your journey, and me, understanding as to why I am in this vehicle instead of walking safely on my Mother The Earth."

Joseph settled back in his seat and Vanessa settled in for the long haul, refusing to think about

emus and lizards and what had happened last
night. She didn't know why she had insisted on
driving. Maybe it had had something to do with
how quickly Xavier had abandoned her. In her
mind that's exactly how it added up. He knew the
possibility of what she might be facing, the possibility of her mother's death, and still, when she'd
struck out at her weakest moment from the sheer
fear and pain of it all . . . he had let go without a
second thought. Not a comforting word did he
provide. Not the slightest touch.

Not that she was right. In Vanessa's heart of
hearts she knew the things she had accused him
of were not true. Yet she believed that when you
truly cared for someone you held on to them and
comforted them in their time of need. Xavier had
answered her anguished plea not with love but
with a sword that had easily severed the embryonic tie they had recently established. Now
Vanessa realized she wanted to prove to him and
to herself that she did not need that tie that she
had held on to so tightly since arriving in Australia. If it were strong and true it would have
been her rock, but distorted and weak, that same
connection could be a strong source for hurt and
doubt.

Paramount in Vanessa's mind was the knowledge that if her worst fears were realized when it
came to her mother, she would face a profound
wound. A wound created by her mother's death
and the anguish over things she had never had

the courage to say but had always felt in her heart. No, she would not have room for false relationships. Vanessa had to know that she was capable of weathering the storm alone.

She handled the RV with ease as they travelled westward on Larapinta Drive toward the Western MacDonnell Ranges. Vanessa didn't know if Xavier actually slept, but from what she could tell his eyes remained closed for the first hour of the trip.

Vanessa feasted on the landscape, which was uniquely beautiful, with its vast endless view of sandhills. She had never seen a land that compared to this, and she was grateful for the mental reprieve from her worries. From time to time Joseph pointed out mulga, gum, and acacia trees, and grasses such as spinifex and native. On a couple of occasions Vanessa looked at Xavier, wanting him to share in the awe of the moment. But he remained as still as stone beside her, and she remembered they were no longer on such friendly terms. It was a loss, and she felt it.

For quite a distance Larapinta Drive was paved and driving was easy. But once they passed Glen Helen Gorge, the sealed road turned to dirt, and controlling the huge vehicle became much more taxing. Still Vanessa drove on, but her insecurity about her ability to handle the RV grew as the road became tougher to navigate. It wasn't long before she was gripping the steering wheel so tightly that her hands would soon blister. At a

particularly trying moment she glanced at Xavier
and was glad to see his hawklike eyes on the
road, although he did not break his silence.

"Vanessa," Joseph said, "I think I should warn
you, another gorge is around the bend and the
road is very narrow."

"All right." She sat up straight and prepared
for what was ahead. The truth was that if she
could have, she would have turned the RV over
to Xavier's capable hands. But she knew the road
was too narrow to stop without being in danger
from oncoming traffic. Not that there had been a
lot of other vehicles, but the danger existed nevertheless.

When the RV started travelling alongside the
gorge, Vanessa began to sweat. Although the
chasm was narrow, it was so deep that the bottom
could not be seen. Yet that wasn't Vanessa's
biggest challenge. It was the extreme narrowness
of the road.

Xavier saw Vanessa's rich brown face turn
somewhat ashen, and he totally understood. The
road had barely been made for cars, and certainly
not for RVs.

"You're going to be fine," Xavier said in a voice
that was low and comforting. "This gorge can't
go on forever."

"You're right," Vanessa repeated, fortifying
herself. "I'll just stay close to the cliff and this
should be over soon."

"Real soon," Xavier assured as he saw
Vanessa's arms tremble. "You've proven yourself

to be quite the driver." He reached out gently and laid his hand on her back, then glanced at the rain clouds that were forming overhead.

"How much further do we have to go, Joseph, before we reach a resting point?" Xavier inquired.

"Not far," he replied, but his eyes told a different tale. "Haasts Bluff is Aboriginal land. We can rest there."

"Haasts Bluff. Sounds like the kind of place where we'll both get lucky, Nessa," Xavier continued in the same comforting tone.

The nickname was warm and familiar. It reminded Vanessa of home and her mother, and the reason she was in Australia driving across its austere land.

"My mother used to call me Nessa."

"Did she?" Xavier paused, trying to gauge whether he had pressed the wrong button with his serendipitous selection of names. "I like it. It suits you."

"Now when I look back, my mother had been right about many things I never gave her credit for." Her eyes remained glued to the road. "I wish I could let her know that. I wish I could take back some of the cruel things I said."

"Sometimes we all say things we don't mean," Xavier said, and they both knew he was not only speaking of Vanessa's conversation with her mother but also the rugged exchange they had shared.

"But through the years I've hurt her, Xavier. I

know I hurt her." One of Vanessa's hands went up to her face, and the RV jerked.

"Don't think of that now, Vanessa. You've got to keep your hands on the wheel and think of the joy you're going to feel when you see your mother again," he added softly.

"Do you really believe that?" Vanessa reached out to Xavier for hope.

Xavier dug down within himself until he could answer truthfully. "Yes. I do," he replied, then prayed his soul-searching had given him the right answer.

twenty-three

"There's a place to pull over." Xavier pointed as raindrops began to hit the windshield. "If you don't mind, I'll take over from there."

Vanessa's muscles in her arms and shoulders had been stressed to the limit, and it was difficult to relax as she slowed the RV down to pull over. With tired eyes she looked at Xavier and turned off the ignition without protest.

Shaken and exhausted, Vanessa climbed out of the vehicle and into the rain. Halfway to the other side she met Xavier. Water trickled down their faces as they stood in the elements together.

Vanessa was the first to reach out. She placed her hand on Xavier's face. A face that looked down at hers tenderly.

"What am I going to do with you?" Xavier said.

"Care. I hope," Vanessa answered softly.

Xavier's eyes narrowed with emotion.

Vanessa continued, "And whatever I find out about my mother, I want you to know, I know it's not your fault."

Xavier removed a clinging wet braid from her face. "And I want you to know I'll be here for you no matter what." He pulled her to him and rested his cheek on her wet hair. "But we better go inside now."

Vanessa raised onto her toes and kissed him. "Thank you," she said, then ran for the passenger's side.

When they were back inside, Joseph's knowing eyes watched as Xavier put the vehicle into gear and pulled onto the road again. "Things are better between you now."

"I think they are better," Xavier replied.

Vanessa gave a slight smile and leaned her head against the back of the high seat.

"Good," Joseph said. "For you two and for me. Now that Xavier is behind the wheel, I can finally rest."

Xavier smiled at Joseph's candor, but when he looked at Vanessa her eyes were already closed. It was obvious the drive had taken a lot out of her, but Xavier knew it wasn't the only reason she was tired. The uncertainty of what was to come had taken the biggest toll.

"Now Joseph," he said quietly, "how much further is it to Haasts Bluff?"

"Maybe one more hour at the most." Joseph

looked at Vanessa, whose breathing had deepened. "She sleeps now."

"Yes," Xavier replied.

"You told her you see her feeling joy when she sees her mother again. Did you speak from the heart?"

Xavier recalled the silent prayer he'd made at the moment. "Yes. I did."

"Good," Joseph replied. "I have chosen the right animal totem for you. You have the gift that lizard gives. The gift of the Dreaming. Being able to feel the past, present, and future. Now I too think Vanessa will feel joy at seeing her mother again."

Xavier looked at Joseph through the rearview mirror but remained silent.

"It has not been long since you two have been together."

"You're right. I've only known Vanessa a short time. Coming to Australia has actually brought us together."

"Very short time. Your relationship is still undergoing the trial of basic trust."

"You could say that. But I don't know how much of a relationship we really have."

"You are together," Joseph said. "And there are feelings. Maybe you don't know what to make of your feelings. But they do exist."

Xavier nodded. "Here in this country, they do. Maybe it is the situation that's the glue. Maybe when everyday life confronts us again, it will all fall apart."

"Maybe this. Maybe that," Joseph said with no expression. "Thinking can be tiring. Feeling is so much easier. She is like the emu. You may not know what Vanessa is going to do. Where she is going to go. But the emu is a nonflying bird who can easily be captured."

Xavier smiled slightly. "I'm going to remember that. It may come in handy one day."

Joseph sat back again.

They drove in silence for awhile before Xavier asked, "Have you ever heard of a Pintupi named Kaapa?"

Joseph positioned himself between the front seats. "What is his skin name?"

"Skin name?" Xavier repeated.

"In Aboriginal life what you call the family name, we call the skin name."

"I see," Xavier replied. "I was only given the one name, Kaapa."

"M-m. Perhaps he is a *courie*—an Aboriginal who lives in the big city and has become disconnected from the land. That is very difficult to do, but it happens."

"If that's the case, my chances of meeting him here on Aboriginal land are not very good?"

"Maybe not," Joseph replied. "But there will be other Pintupi. You are bound to find someone who knows of your deal, and why it became broken."

"I simply hope I can fix it," Xavier said.

"Is money the reason this deal is so important to you?"

"There's money involved, but I won't get any of it," Xavier replied. "Plain and simple, I want to share the richness of Aboriginal art and culture with the people back home."

"And why is that?" Joseph's expression turned serious. "We are not some exhibit in a museum. We are human beings like everyone else. Sometimes I think foreigners forget that."

"You have a point, and I understand," Xavier said. "But your culture is the oldest continuous culture on the planet. You have survived, and through that survival I believe you have accumulated priceless knowledge. Knowledge that we all could benefit from."

"I am listening," Joseph replied.

"For example, you see all aspects of life as one, and you honor it as so. To your people all relationships are a part of the whole. Everyone and everything being equal, and if one part of the circle suffers, the entire circle suffers. It would be good if we could take that understanding to heart in America, throughout the world."

Joseph smiled. "You have a good understanding of the Aboriginal mind and heart, Xavier."

"I've tried to grasp it, but like Australia, your views of life are so vast it is extremely difficult."

"But it is because of your heart that I will see what I can do to help you repair your deal with the Pintupi," Joseph said.

"I appreciate it, Joseph. I feel I'm going to need all the help I can get."

The sun was beginning to go down when they

pulled up to the settlement near Haasts Bluff. Xavier shut off the RV and stretched.

"You wait inside," Joseph advised. "I will have to get permission for you to be here."

Vanessa woke up when Joseph opened and closed the door. "Are we there?" she asked groggily.

"Just pulled up." Xavier rolled down the window. "Joseph says he's got to clear the way for us."

Joseph's feet had barely touched the ground before several Aboriginal men were approaching the vehicle. Xavier and Vanessa didn't understand the things that were being said, but there was an obvious language barrier, and Joseph didn't appear to be on the winning end of it.

"Long Jack," Joseph called when a younger man penetrated the animated group.

He smiled widely. "Joseph. Good to see you."

Another group discussion broke out, disrupting the reunion. Finally, Long Jack explained, "These men are visiting. They have stopped over on their way to the *corroboree* at the foot of Mount Lieble tomorrow night. Several tribes will song and dance there. These men did not recognize the famous Joseph." He smiled again. "Especially not with this big caravan. They are asking me if it is yours."

"You know me, Long Jack," Joseph replied. "I do not own a car. I certainly do not have one of these. It is being rented by two friends of mine."

"*Yapa?*"

"No, they are not of the people. They come from United States of America."

Long Jack looked wary.

"But they have good hearts. I have examined them," Joseph reassured him.

After a moment of hesitation Long Jack's expression changed. "I have known you for many years. I trust your judgement, Joseph. If you say their hearts are good, I believe you. They are welcome to park on Loritja land."

"Thank you," Joseph replied.

"And you can share my house as usual," Long Jack added. "If you are hungry there is a community pot of food, and your friends are welcome to share it if they like."

"I will tell them." Joseph patted Long Jack's arm. "And thank you again, my friend."

"It is as it should be," Long Jack replied before slipping into another language at the urging of his comrades.

twenty-four

$\mathcal{V}$anessa sat beside Xavier. She looked at the group, eating and talking around a large, black pot perched on top of a wood-burning fire. Although she couldn't understand what was being said, there was no doubt in Vanessa's mind that she and Xavier were the focus of much of the conversation.

She dipped her spoon into the stewlike dish that was being passed around in plastic containers and bowls. The taste was quite foreign. Not bad. Just different.

"Do you like it?" Joseph asked.

"It's fine," Vanessa replied gingerly.

"What kind of answer is that?" Joseph said.

Vanessa looked embarrassed. "I mean . . . it's different. But it's good." Her eyes gleamed honestly.

Joseph nodded, then filled his mouth again.

"What's in it?" Xavier inquired.

Joseph pushed the contents of his bowl around with a bent spoon. "Goanna. Bush tomatoes. Onions and potatoes."

"What's goanna?" Vanessa placed a slice of potato in her mouth.

"A kind of lizard," Joseph replied.

Her mouth dropped open slightly before she secretly nudged Xavier. "I'm going to get you for asking that question," she said beneath her breath.

"If that's the only way it'll happen, I'm glad I asked," was Xavier's silky reply.

Surprised, she looked into his eyes. The desire there had nothing to do with the food.

Vanessa broke the connection when a repetitive noise, which sounded like a boisterous intake of breath, sounded nearby.

"It is nothing to worry about," Joseph pointed. "That man is playing a didjeridoo. It has been a part of Aboriginal culture since the Dreamtime."

Vanessa watched the man sitting comfortably and blowing on a long, wooden pipelike object that rested over his extended leg. Some people nearby bobbed to the unique sound. Others continued to eat as if they were oblivious to it.

In Vanessa's opinion, there appeared to be more men than women at Haasts Bluff. She wondered if that was so, or if the women were inside the small, modest homes that sprinkled the area. "I don't see many women."

"They are here," Joseph replied. "But are probably eating and talking together in some of the houses."

"Is that customary?" Xavier asked.

"Some of our tribal laws call for the separation of men and women during sacred ceremonial dances. And at times you see this played out in other ways."

"I'm not breaking any laws by being here, am I?" Vanessa asked, suddenly feeling uncomfortable.

"No. You would be told if you were," Joseph replied.

Vanessa scooped up the last morsel of food left in her bowl. She closed her eyes as she took her first bite of goanna. She expected it to be chewy, perhaps even tough, but the goanna was surprisingly tender. "I had hoped to ask a few questions about my mother tonight." She looked at the men, who continued to talk among themselves almost as if she and Xavier weren't there.

"I know you are anxious, but it is late," Joseph replied. "And some of the men are preparing to dance." He nodded toward a man striking two boomerangs together.

"There's going to be a performance?" Vanessa asked.

"We do not think of it as such. Dancing and singing are a part of Aboriginal life. It is our way of honoring the Ancestors. They gave us our dances to be close to them."

"So it is like a prayer in motion," Xavier said.

"Perhaps that is one way for you to understand it," Joseph replied.

Vanessa couldn't help pressing the issue. "So this is not a good time."

"I think it would be better if you asked your questions tomorrow," Joseph concluded.

Vanessa didn't want to wait, but she knew she should accept Joseph's advice. "If you think I should." She clasped her hands in her lap.

"I do," Joseph said.

"Then I will wait until morning," Vanessa announced with resignation.

By that time a small group of men had gathered on the sideline, and they began to dance in unison. Intermittently, they would separate from the group and execute an array of stomps and jerks, spraying sand into the air. Once in a while a flickering flame would illuminate one of their faces, highlighting their serious expressions. A few others joined them. It was like watching a travelling herd. Each man unique, but always a part of the whole.

Vanessa watched quietly with Xavier's body pressed against her side. She was fascinated by the tribal dancers, but her mind kept straying to her mother. It was so hard not to disobey Joseph's advice. But the truth was, very few of the Aborigines spoke English, and communicating with them would have been nearly impossible without Joseph's assistance.

Vanessa felt a warmness descend on her hand. Xavier had covered it with his own, as if he was able to read her thoughts and could feel her frustration.

"Tomorrow is not far away," he said softly. "And you will be that much closer to finding out the truth." Xavier gently squeezed her hand.

Vanessa allowed herself to lean against him, but in a manner that would not call attention. As she absorbed strength from Xavier's body, Vanessa realized how tired she actually was. Once again she was thankful for Xavier's presence, and she wondered how she would have fared without him.

"I think I'm going to go to bed now," she announced to Xavier and Joseph.

"I will see you in the morning," Joseph replied as Vanessa got up.

"I'll be in later," Xavier said, following her every movement with his eyes.

Vanessa could feel Xavier's eyes on her as she walked behind the circle of men and entered the RV. Quickly, she stripped off her clothes and bathed in the small shower, appreciative of every drop of water that cleansed her body of the sand that pervaded the land.

Afterward she dug in her bag and slipped on a thin nightshirt. It felt good against her skin as she climbed in under the sheets. Of course, Xavier was not far from her mind. Vanessa longed for him, but she was exhausted, and although she tried to stay awake and listen for his entry, it wasn't long before she was deep asleep.

When Xavier entered the RV he walked over to

the bed and looked down at Vanessa. She lay on her stomach with her arms near her head, her braids covering the pillow. The baby blue of her nightshirt complimented her skin, and he reached out and touched her ever so gently.

It didn't take long for Xavier to shower, and when he climbed into the bed the scent of Vanessa's soap rose from the linen. She looked so peaceful. He was glad she had finally found a respite from her worries. As softly as he could, Xavier placed a featherlike kiss on her lips, but no matter his intent, Vanessa's eyes opened slowly.

"You're here," she said softly.

"Of course I am."

She placed her arms around his neck and snuggled close. "I'm so glad."

Xavier could feel his body react to her touch. It didn't take much. Just the thought of her body warmed him. He positioned himself so Vanessa would not feel his desire. "You go back to sleep now. It's the only source of peace that you have."

Vanessa rested her head near his shoulder. "I was dreaming," she said. "There was so much sand, and I was walking alone. But no matter how far I walked, I was always alone." Her breath warmed his neck as she spoke.

"You are not alone, Vanessa." He tightened his arms around her.

She remained quiet, then said, "But the irony of it is, I have always prided myself on being independent. Declaring I didn't need anybody else. That I would never want to depend on someone

the way my mother depended on my father. Now
I know co-dependence doesn't mean you are
weak. It means you have formed a unit with another human being, and that unit has a meaningful life of its own."

"You learned that from your dream?" he asked
softly.

"No. From being with you," Vanessa declared.

Their mouths found each other easily, and the
kiss was slow and drunken. It was not the ex-
ploratory kiss of old, but an acceptance of what
they had discovered. Vanessa's body molded to
Xavier's, and as he held her against him he could
feel her heart beat. "You feel so good," he said
above her head.

"Don't let me go, Xavier. Never let me go."

They kissed again, and Xavier's hands explored her back, her hips. He held her so tight
that he stopped himself for fear that he might
hurt her. "I want you so badly, Vanessa," he said,
his words ragged, whispery.

She looked into his desire-filled eyes. "I am
yours, Xavier." Vanessa kissed his mouth and the
tender area near the base of his throat.

"But I don't want to place my need before what
is good for you," he said, aching for her. "You
need your rest."

"You are good for me, Xavier," Vanessa reassured him. "You have placed my needs before
your own, and I will be forever grateful."

"I wish I had the power to turn back the clock
before all this happened." He nuzzled the tender

skin above her breasts. "I wish I could relieve the pain, if for only a moment."

"And that is what you are doing now," Vanessa replied. "Every kiss nullifies my pain. Every time I look in your eyes and see how much you want me, for that moment I forget."

"I will bring you peace, if only for a moment." Xavier held her gaze as he descended, planting a path of warm kisses from Vanessa's breasts to her abdomen. When his mouth lingered at the top of her triangular garden, and he glistened the hair with the tip of his tongue, the spark in his eyes fanned hers. Xavier knew that Vanessa anticipated what was to come, and slowly, deliberately, he explored her there, until his tongue parted her center and reveled in its softness. Never once did Xavier break his gaze as he watched Vanessa's face first light with passion, then plunge into sheer ecstasy.

Moments later, when Vanessa opened her eyes, Xavier's were there to meet her, and she whispered, "I love you, Xavier."

He brought his face parallel with hers, and as he entered her he declared, "I love you, too, my Nessa."

All the pleasure in the world began with his words, and they gave themselves to each other without reservation. Each stroke a promise. Each kiss a pact.

When Xavier knew he could no longer hold back his release, he sought Vanessa's gaze again. "We will never forget this night."

"Never," Vanessa echoed as her body pulsed with the impending release.

"I have never loved a woman the way I love you, Vanessa," he swore as her body arched with his words.

"I know I have never loved at all until you, Xavier."

Their frenzied movements accelerated, and Xavier's face was mere inches away. "God, this is heaven," he said, his gaze blurring with ecstasy.

"And you have taken me there," Vanessa moaned as they plunged together, their bodies flowing like one.

twenty-five

When Vanessa opened her eyes the following morning, it was barely light outside, but she was greeted by Xavier's rich, dark stare.

"Welcome," he said.

Vanessa examined his nearly perfect features. Looking at Xavier was like seeing a Tyson Beckwith photograph filled with life. "Did you sleep at all?"

"I slept wonderfully," he replied.

"Good." Her lips turned up slightly. "Now . . . welcome to what?"

"Welcome to my world." He pulled the sheet over their heads. The pale yellow screen created a soft enclosure and a feeling that they were truly alone in the world.

"I never would have guessed that you were so

romantic." Vanessa's eyes sparkled with the sheer joy of the moment.

"Is that all I am?" He manipulated the tip of one of her breasts between his thumb and index finger.

"Absolutely not." She reciprocated by reaching out and stroking him.

"Well, aren't we aggressive this morning," Xavier teased. "Be careful, you may rouse the tiger in me."

"I think I can handle it. But just in case you get too far out of hand I've always got my whip." She tapped his face lightly.

They tousled, and Xavier literally came out on top. That position was all it took for them to make love again. Afterward, when they lay in each other's arms, Xavier said, "We said a lot of things and made a lot of promises last night."

"We did, didn't we?" Vanessa's breaths were still labored.

"For you, was it just the moment?" His dark lashes descended, hiding his eyes.

"Of course not." Vanessa was surprised by the question.

"Good." He looked at her intently. "Because there's something I want to tell you." Xavier thought of his father. "Something that—"

A knock sounded at the door.

"Just a moment," Xavier called, picking up his watch.

"What time is it?" Vanessa pulled the sheet up to her neck.

"It's six-thirty." Xavier put on his pants and went to the door. Joseph was standing outside.

"I know it's early, but I didn't think Vanessa would want me to wait any longer. I believe a couple of Wailpri men have word of her mother."

Xavier turned toward Vanessa. "Joseph thinks there are some men here who know about your mother."

"What?" Vanessa clenched the sheet. "Tell him I'll be right out."

"We'll join you in a moment," Xavier relayed.

"I'll be over by the community cooking pot," Joseph replied.

By the time Xavier closed the door, Vanessa was out of bed and at the shower. She was in and out in minutes, and as Xavier was completing his shower Vanessa was closing the door to the RV.

At a run, she crossed the yard. "You've talked to someone who knows about my mother?" she asked Joseph.

"I think so. Last night after you and Xavier went into the RV, I heard bits and pieces of a short conversation between two men who had just arrived. I don't speak their language, but I caught a couple of key words. Black foreigner. And that it was a woman."

"Where are these men?" Vanessa asked, eagerly.

"They joined an early hunting party. They come from a small settlement near Kintore. These men still enjoy hunting kangaroo and goanna, as our previous generations did."

"What's going on?" Xavier asked as he joined them.

"Joseph overheard two men talking about a foreign Black woman. He thinks it may have been my mother."

"Are they willing to talk about it?" Xavier pressed.

"I'm sure that can be arranged, but they must return from the hunt first," Joseph explained. "In the meantime, I will see if Long Jack will be the go-between. I am not familiar with the Wailpri language."

Anxiously, Vanessa watched Joseph walk away. She was surprised at the large number of people milling around so early in the morning. This time the women were very present, dealing with children and performing morning tasks. Vanessa noticed several beat-up trucks parked on the property, and a group of men busy painting their faces and bodies. One of them looked up and pointed toward the east. Four men were approaching, carrying a trussed-up kangaroo.

"That must be them," she said to Xavier. Vanessa didn't know if she should approach the men or wait for Joseph.

A staying touch from Xavier helped her decide. "Joseph will be here in a minute. There is no way you can communicate with them, Vanessa. You really don't have a choice."

They watched as the men stopped with the animal and untied it. One of them appeared to say a prayer before they began to skin the beast.

Vanessa and Xavier were so caught up in watching the hunters that they did not hear Joseph and Long Jack approach.

"Long Jack has agreed to help with the conversation," Joseph said from behind them.

"Thank you." Vanessa reached out her hand. Long Jack shook it enthusiastically.

Together they walked over to the hunters. Although her mother's plight was uppermost in her mind, Vanessa could not ignore the partially skinned kangaroo and blood on one of the men's hands.

Long Jack started the conversation. It was obvious Joseph had made him aware of the situation, and as he explained it to the Wailpri, several times they nodded their heads in acknowledgment. Finally, Long Jack turned to Vanessa.

"There is a foreign Black woman at their settlement."

"Now?" Vanessa's eyes widened.

"Yes."

"Is she okay?" Xavier put his arm around Vanessa as she asked the difficult question.

"She is weak, but she is alive," Long Jack replied.

"Thank God." Vanessa clasped her hands together and brought them up to her face. She looked over them. "How did she get there?"

Long Jack posed the question, then translated the answer. "She was brought there by two of the men. They had been hunting. She was near death. They found her lying at the foot of a sacred place of the Rainbow Snake. They believe he kept her alive until they arrived."

"Where is their community? Can we go there now?" Vanessa could feel Xavier squeezing her shoulder as she rushed through the questions.

"It is about four hours away," Joseph spoke up, and several of the men began to speak again, including the ones still working on the kangaroo.

"They say most of their people will be at Mount Lieble for the ceremonies tonight. They do not know if you should go to their community. They feel you should wait at the ceremonial place. Their leaders will be there to direct you," Long Jack said after listening to the jumbled exchange.

Vanessa looked disheartened.

"Mount Lieble is not far away from this particular Wailpri community," Long Jack assured her.

Vanessa walked over to the Wailpri hunters. "Thank you so much," she said with her words, her eyes, and her heart. Although she knew they did not understand her language, their shy nods and gestures indicated they understood her heart.

"And so you have good news," Joseph said when Vanessa joined them again.

"Excellent news," Vanessa replied and threw her arms around Xavier's neck.

"I'm so happy for you, Nessa," he whispered in her ear.

Vanessa looked at Long Jack and Joseph. "How soon can we go to Mount Lieble?"

"The trucks will go in a couple of hours," Long Jack replied. "In the meantime, there is food to eat and preparations to make before we go. I will send you some plums and *akatjirri*, bush raisins."

"We'll be glad to have them," Xavier said as Joseph and Long Jack walked away.

"She's alive, Xavier." Vanessa hugged him again.

"Yes, she is. That's incredible. I wonder how she ended up alone in the outback like that?"

"I don't know." Vanessa's brow furrowed. "It's just a miracle that those hunters came along when they did."

"All kinds of miracles seem to happen in Australia, don't they?"

His eyes were so serious that Vanessa's heart fluttered. "It seems like I am going to be able to leave Australia with what I came for. What about you?"

Xavier smiled. "I've got a few leads cooking. I hope to find out something when we get to Kintore. But one thing's for sure, I'll be leaving here with more than I anticipated."

Vanessa could feel her body react. There was an ache that throbbed ever so slightly. "Do you think we'll have time to rest in the RV before they pull out?" she asked, her eyes hazy with longing.

"We'll make time," Xavier said. "I'll get the fruit. And I don't know about resting, but you wait inside the RV, and I'll expect you to provide the rest of the morning meal." Shielding Vanessa from prying eyes, Xavier touched her.

Her knees went weak. "Xavier, what am I going to do with you?" She looked around to make sure no one had seen the intimate contact.

"Do you want me to tell you what I want you to do?" He took her hand and started to lead her toward the vehicle.

"Tell me," she said as he opened the RV door.

"I want you to lie on the bed without a stitch on and wait for me. I want you to think about what I'm going to do to you." He looked in her eyes, then let his gaze rest on her breasts and between her legs. "So by the time I'm there, every part of you will be moist and ready. Can you do that?" His silky words were an erotic caress.

Vanessa swallowed, and she nodded. "I'll be waiting."

"That's my Nessa," he replied.

twenty-six

When the last truck pulled off the road, Xavier pulled off behind it. It had been a slow drive following the vehicles loaded with passengers in their beds. Vanessa had established a waving game with several of the golden-haired children. Their wide eyes and shy grins had endeared the Aboriginal people to Vanessa forever.

By the time they arrived at Mount Lieble the ceremonial site was buzzing with activity. Clumps of men body painting one another were everywhere, along with others who were touching up shields, blankets, and gourds. The women, on the other hand, were busy sorting seeds, grasses, and other foods. Several women dropped vegetables into two large pots perched over fires. Some of their faces were painted, but they were not nearly as colorful as the men.

Xavier and Vanessa climbed out of the RV and went to look for Joseph, who had ridden in one of the trucks. As they passed, curious eyes watched them, and a wave of various languages followed. One man came up and began to talk rapidly. Xavier made gestures indicating they did not understand, but it didn't halt the man's animated chatter. Soon Vanessa and Xavier were surrounded by a group of staring men, some with their bodies and faces elaborately painted with animals, lines and dots. The features of others had been molded by time, their hair varying shades of white, their eyes yellowed.

Long Jack joined the circle. "You have made quite an impression."

Vanessa breathed a sigh of relief. Although she did not feel threatened, it was an unusual feeling to be in the midst of so many whose skin color was similar, but whose culture was so different. It made her aware of how much culture meant and that skin color was a tie, yet people who looked similar could still be worlds apart.

"I suggest you stay with my people until everyone understands why you are here," Long Jack said. "Some of the *tjingari*, ceremonies and song, are secret sacred, and they are not to be seen by those who the Ancestor Beings have not chosen to have the knowledge. So you must be careful," he stressed. "There will be performances held here in the center, but there will be others that you should not walk into by mistake."

Vanessa slipped her hand into Xavier's. "We understand."

"So." Joseph's familiar voice was a welcome sound. "Long Jack has been laying down the law for you."

"Pretty much." Xavier looked at Vanessa. "I was somewhat aware of these things, but I don't know about Vanessa."

"It does sound a little daunting." She attempted to smile as they followed Joseph and Long Jack to an area chosen by the Haasts Bluff community.

"It's not meant to be," Long Jack replied. "The secret sacred ceremonies reveal the Dreamtime journeys of the Ancestor Beings. There is much power in that, and it must be guarded carefully."

"Have the people from the Wailpri community where my mother is staying arrived?"

Joseph and Long Jack looked around the huge circle that was still forming. "I do not see them," Joseph replied.

"I do not," Long Jack sanctioned.

"How can you tell with so many people here?" Vanessa figured there were over a hundred and fifty.

"Each tribe, each community, has its totems born out of the Dreaming," Joseph explained. "Dingo. Black swan. Carpet snake. Cloud. There are so many. It is easy to recognize the totems by the way our people paint their bodies, shields, and blankets. The Lace Lizard is not here, therefore that Wailpri community is not here."

"The paintings on their faces and bodies remind me of the artwork that's targeted for the museum deal," Xavier said to Vanessa.

"Really," she replied, feeling a tug on her pants leg. One of the children that had waved at her from the truck was standing by her side. He held out a handful of *akatjirri*. There was sand on his arms and legs, and Vanessa was sure there was sand in the bush raisins as well, but she smiled and put them in her mouth anyway.

"Come with us, Xavier," Joseph invited, "and see some of the hunting tools that our men use."

"I'd find that quite interesting," he replied.

"Vanessa," Joseph continued. "I see you have a friend, so you wait here while we take Xavier with us."

"Okay," Vanessa said, knowing she was being excluded from the all-male excursion. She sat down near a small knarled tree. Her newfound friend sat down beside her. In a matter of minutes they were joined by several other children, all with shy smiles and beguiling eyes.

Xavier, Joseph, and Long Jack joined a group of men who appeared to be in a leisurely competition. Xavier watched one man spin and then jerk an elongated object. His demonstration was followed by another, and then another.

"Are they about to compete?" Xavier asked.

Joseph smiled. "If you were to ask some of

these men that question and try to explain it even in their own language, they would not understand."

"Why not?"

"Because in Aboriginal culture there is no such thing as competition. You do your best for the whole, and then the whole is the best it can be."

"So what are they doing?" Xavier inquired.

"They are celebrating what they have made. Demonstrating the finery of each *woomera*, spear thrower."

Xavier's gaze fell on a stack of spears. "That's amazing. Each one of the spears look almost the same, yet I know they must have been handmade."

"Yes, they were," Long Jack confirmed. "They are made from a branch of the spear bush. First the branch is heated in hot sand and ash. Afterwards we straighten it with our hands."

Xavier looked at the hands of the men around him. Some of them were as dark and tough-looking as shoe leather. His hands, in comparison, looked very feminine. "That's an interesting-looking belt that man has on." Xavier nodded toward an elderly man sitting quietly alone.

Joseph and Long Jack bowed toward the old man, then exchanged some words Xavier did not understand. Finally, Long Jack said softly, "He is known as a *mekigar*, a medicine man. Not many of them left like him with the secrets. It is a part of Aboriginal culture that is dying away."

"What a shame," Xavier said, then he bowed slightly to the older man before he started to turn away.

"This belt is hair," the *mekigar* suddenly said. "In past it have other purpose."

Xavier stopped to listen.

"Now I wear to remember past." The medicine man's English was much more broken than Joseph's or Long Jack's.

"Thank you for explaining it to me," Xavier said.

"Why foreigner like you here?" His voice was surprisingly strong.

Xavier looked at Joseph, whose eyes held reverence for the medicine man. His nod encouraged Xavier to speak.

"I came here on business, and with a friend"—Xavier paused at the inadequate term—"to help her find her mother."

"You come from where?"

"From the United States."

"In the far past no man come from there to my people land."

Xavier nodded, not knowing what to say. There was such a presence about the *mekigar* that Xavier wasn't certain how to address him.

"You have business with *Kardiya*?"

Xavier looked at Joseph.

"Australian White people," Joseph translated.

"Some," Xavier replied. "But they were the go-between for me and some people from the Pintupi community."

"I am Pintupi." His broad back appeared to straighten. "What business did you have with my tribe?"

With the serendipitous meeting Xavier was on instant alert. "I expected to show several paintings from your tribe in my homeland. But somehow things went wrong."

The *mekigar* studied Xavier before he said, "How?"

"I don't know. I am looking for a man named Kaapa, who might shed some light on the situation."

"What Kaapa have to do with this?"

Xavier's eyes narrowed. "You know him?"

The *mekigar* did not answer.

Joseph leaned forward. "You should let him ask the questions."

Xavier nodded, then continued, "I'm told he was the contact for the Pintupi."

"Kaapa no contact for anyone." The older man's eyes narrowed. "He cannot contact his own spirit."

Xavier looked confused, but he waited for the medicine man to explain.

"Kaapa is my nephew, but he is lost to the alcohol. He try to be both Aboriginal and *Kardiya*. It split him in two." He spread his hands apart.

"I was told Kaapa was the person who said there was no more deal. That he was responsible for breaking it off."

"Kaapa no do that. I did." The *mekigar* waited as if he wanted to see Xavier's expression. When

Xavier remained openly patient, he continued, "Because we live as Aborigines, they think we do not understand. They offer us big money in the beginning, but in the end, the money so small." He placed his thumb near his index finger. "So small that it was an insult to the Ancestor Beings. I say this is not honoring the Dreamings. It is the message of the Dreaming, which all who see with their heart would understand from looking at these paintings. They are powerful messages. They are the messages of the Ancestor Beings. The messages of our lives." The *mekigar* looked dissatisfied. "I know that deal is not honoring the Dreamtime."

"But I can assure you, there was a large amount of money offered and I never knew of any other offer."

"This is not what Kaapa say before he stay away from Pintupi land. That day he come with his body full of alcohol. He say with tears in his eyes the small money they offer. I tell him no, we will not sell our culture, our beliefs, ourselves for so little. Kaapa plead with me. I don't change my mind. Then he cry for the Dreamtime. He cry for the Ancestor Beings. He cry for his people and himself." He paused. "I not see him after that." A sadness entered his wizened eyes.

"What if I told you that I made sure, because of my respect for your people and your rich culture, that the offer was very honorable."

The *mekigar* studied Xavier quietly, but he did not speak.

Xavier turned to Joseph and Long Jack. "What if I told you I will *make* sure that the money that I promised to your people in the beginning will be delivered to you by someone that you know and trust. Would you deliver the money to the *Mekigar*?"

With their heads hung in respect, both men answered yes. Joseph added, "We will accept it on behalf of the Aboriginal Cultural Foundation."

Finally, the *mekigar* replied, "I will say I believe you. I say this because I can see into your heart. It is well intended for your country and for my people." He studied Xavier's face before he continued. "And I will also say, Kaapa has truly cut himself off from the Dreaming. Cut himself off from what makes my people know who they are. That they have been, are and always will be part of the Ancestor Beings . . . part of the Dreamtime," he added poignantly. "Being cut off from the Dreaming is worse than death for an Aborigine. I feel sorry for my nephew."

Xavier didn't let out the breath he'd been holding until he was safely out of the *mekigar's* eyeshot and eyesight. Then again, perhaps the *mekigar* had still been able to feel Xavier's incredible relief.

twenty-seven

Vanessa was busy cutting up onions under the approving looks of several women when Xavier returned. "There you are," she said. "To pass the time away, I thought I might as well make myself useful." She smiled at a small girl not far away who was poking at an edible root with a digging stick. "How was your tour?"

"Very productive. Somehow . . . with incredible luck I think I may have talked to the right man."

"Who?" She dropped bits of onion into the pot. "The man you call Kaapa?"

"No. It appears Kaapa was a contact for the Pintupi, but he doesn't really have any power. You see the man sitting alone over there?" He indicated the *mekigar* without pointing disrespectfully. "He is the spokesperson for the Pintupi."

Vanessa studied the man carefully. "And he told you the deal was on again?"

"Not quite. I have to make good on our initial monetary offer, but after that I think the exhibit will be coming to Columbus," Xavier said with a hint of excitement.

Vanessa was glad for Xavier, so she continued to indulge him. "So the original deal was completely dead?"

"Yes, it was." Xavier's brow furrowed. "With some help."

"What do you mean?" Vanessa asked, genuinely interested.

"I think somebody was skimming money off the top. And I think they got a little too greedy and ended up offering the Pintupi a pittance." Xavier folded his arms. "The medicine man took it as an insult. He believes whoever did it didn't think it would make any difference to the Pintupi because they know very little about business. At least as the Western world conducts it."

"Well obviously if he told you all that, that isn't so." Vanessa made a disconcerting face.

Xavier looked around. "I can't say that the Pintupi, who haven't been a part of the mainstream culture, do have a good grasp of Western business acumen. They were among the last Aborigines to come in from the desert, and to start living in communities like Haasts Bluff and Kintore. But I believe the Pintupi, like the others, do know when what they believe in is not being respected.

When it's being cheapened and used to fatten the pockets of people other than Aborigines."

"Wow." Vanessa surveyed the people painted in their ceremonial colors, some wearing ceremonial clothes. It would be easy for a Western mind to rate their culture as primitive and below Western understandings. It occurred to her that Westerners would never think, just perhaps, that a culture that has been around for nearly forty thousand years, may have much to teach a people who have known civilization for only a fraction of that time.

Her wandering gaze landed on Joseph and Long Jack. They were talking with a man who had a lizard with a frilly fin painted on his chest. She noted there were several others, and in her gut Vanessa knew this was the Wailpri community that had taken in her mother. The knife and the onion slipped from her hands onto the ground.

"What is it?" Xavier looked where Vanessa had focused, but she was already in motion.

"The Aborigines who found my mother are here." Her voice projected behind her as she shot across the clearing.

Vanessa's abrupt appearance surprised the Wailpri. Long Jack tried to talk to Vanessa and the Wailpris at the same time. It was impossible.

"Are these the people who found my mother?" She clenched Joseph's arm.

The leader looked at her with wary eyes.

"Yes," Joseph replied. Then he was bombarded

by several Wailpri, although he did not understand their language. Vanessa could tell Long Jack was trying to explain, but she had waited long enough to obtain permission to go get her mother, and she wasn't about to wait any longer.

"What are they saying?" Vanessa insisted. "When can we go to their reservation? Is my mother still there?"

Long Jack tried to translate as quickly as he could. "They are saying, no, don't go to the community."

Vanessa's heart stopped. "Why? Why not?" she heard herself ask as Xavier put a comforting hand on her shoulder.

"Because—" Long Jack began.

"Nessa!" a weak, but familiar, voice called.

Vanessa turned, and she saw her mother, supported between two Wailpri women, coming toward her. "Mama!" All the joy and relief echoed in the endearing name.

"Nessa! My God, it's you." Jackie's voice broke during her feeble yell.

Vanessa ran to her mother and put her arms around her. Jackie was much thinner than when she had left. Vanessa hugged her and held on to her, rocking Jackie like a little child. "Oh, Mama. I didn't know if I'd ever be able to do this again." Vanessa could feel her mother's shoulders quake, and she knew she was crying. Vanessa began to cry too, but she leaned back and wiped her mother's tears.

"How did you get here?" Jackie managed to say.

"I came here to find you."

"You came all this way to find me?"

Vanessa nodded. Her mother's mouth trembled with emotion, and they were in each other's arms again. Somewhere nearby someone struck up a rhythmic drumming sound as if to celebrate the defining moment. "Thank you. Thank you," Vanessa said to the women who remained at her mother's side, and to the men of the Wailpri community. "I will never be able to thank you enough."

They smiled knowingly. Vanessa placed her arm around Jackie's shoulders and walked toward Xavier, who was standing beside Joseph and Long Jack. His relief over their reunion was apparent.

"Mama, you remember Xavier Johnson, don't you?"

Jackie swallowed first, as if it was difficult to speak. "How could I forget?" she answered softly.

Xavier took her trembling hands in his. "Mrs. Bradley, it's really good to see you again."

"You too," Jackie replied.

"And we couldn't have made it here without Joseph or Long Jack's help," Vanessa said, singling them out.

"Thank you." Jackie's words of gratitude were difficult to hear.

"They told me," Long Jack said, pointing to some of the Wailpri men, "that they didn't think you were strong enough to come, but you would not stay." He spoke above the burgeoning group.

"No." Jackie's eyes filled with water again. "I could not stay. I had to try to start back home." Weakly, she leaned against Vanessa.

There were more lines in Jackie's face and a hint of fear in her eyes. "Let me take you to our RV, Mama. You can rest comfortably there."

Jackie nodded, but even her first steps seemed to take more energy than she had.

"Let me," Xavier said, and he picked Jackie up and carried her.

They walked to the RV with a group of Aborigines behind them. Vanessa opened the door to the RV and watched as Xavier gently placed Jackie on the bed. Afterward Vanessa went to the sink and wet a towel to wash her mother's face, hands, and feet.

"Wait," Jackie said as Vanessa wiped her cheek with the warm cloth. "This is a special mark, here." She pointed to an almost faded symbol on her forehead. "I want to keep it as long as I can," she managed to say.

"Whatever you want, Mama," Vanessa replied. She cleaned her mother's face as best she could, then her hands, and tenderly she washed her feet, which were blistered and sore. Vanessa had tears in her eyes when she turned away and looked at Xavier. She was glad Jackie's eyes were closed. Vanessa did not want her mother to see her anguished relief.

Vanessa looked over her shoulder when she

heard a soft tapping on the RV door. Xavier immediately opened it. An Aboriginal woman was standing outside. She held something in her hands and motioned as if she were asking to come in.

"Please come in," Vanessa said, but the woman simply strained her neck to get a better look at Jackie.

Jackie opened her eyes again. She adjusted her head in order to see out the door. Her eyes softened when she saw the woman. "Come in," Jackie said softly. She slowly lifted her arm and beckoned. Timidly, the woman obeyed. She walked over to the bed and offered Jackie a plastic cup containing a murky liquid.

"Do I have to?" Jackie looked at the drink and sighed. "I guess you think I haven't had enough of this, huh?"

The woman placed the cup up to Jackie's mouth.

"Okay. I'll drink it, but not now." With a shaky hand Jackie took the drink. "Give me a few minutes."

The woman appeared to understand. She placed the cup on a small ledge next to the bed. Next she pulled out a foul, sticky substance wrapped in what looked like Saran Wrap.

"Nessa, I think you might want to get a towel or something. I don't think you want whatever that is on your bed. But it's good stuff. My feet are much better than they were a couple of days ago."

Hurriedly, Vanessa did as she was told, and she watched as the woman tenderly applied the balm to her mother's sores. When the Wailpri woman was done, she went to the door so Xavier could let her out. Vanessa wanted to hug her, but she didn't know how the woman would accept that, so she stood beside her, touched her own heart, then extended her hand toward the woman's heart. The Aborigine woman smiled shyly, looked back at Jackie, and left.

"As you can see, they have taken very good care of me." Jackie attempted a smile.

"And I thank God for that," Vanessa replied.

"I thank him every time I think about it," Jackie said in raspy tones. "Because, for as sure as I'm lying here"—she looked from Vanessa to Xavier—"I had been left in the desert to die."

twenty-eight

"*W*hy?" The word wretched from Vanessa's throat.

"The two men who ran the tour were no good, that's why," Jackie explained. "I left my bag in their vehicle at one of the stops and they robbed me." A single tear worked its way out of the corner of Jackie's eye. "Earlier that day, they had told me the price was all-inclusive, and that I had already paid for everything." She swallowed. "So I guess they didn't expect me to find out my money was gone until after they had dropped me off. By then they would have been far gone. But I was looking for some film to put in my camera." She stopped to catch her breath. "And I noticed the rubber band that had been around my wallet was gone. I hadn't bought a new wallet for sentimental reasons. Your father had bought that wallet for me." Jackie looked at Vanessa. "I tell you I was so mad I confronted them about it. I should have waited until we got to the next site where they said they would be picking up a couple more people. But you know me and my mouth, Nessa, I couldn't." Jackie closed her eyes for a second. "As one of them was reassuring me they hadn't taken it, the other drove off the road a good distance. They talked to me really bad, and when he finally stopped they pushed me out of the car and left me out there."

"Oh no," Vanessa said, horrified.

"It's a good thing they didn't hurt you in any other way," Xavier said softly.

"I'm thankful for that," Jackie replied, sounding exhausted again.

"I think we need to let you rest, Mama," Vanessa said, stunned by her mother's account.

Jackie closed her eyes. "I'm not going to lie, I could use some sleep."

"We'll be right outside," Vanessa assured her. "And we'll start back for Alice Springs right away."

Jackie's eyes opened slowly. "Don't do that. Not until I thank the people who have kept me alive. I've got to do that. I want to be able to say good-bye to them too." Jackie held her daughter's gaze, and Vanessa indicated she understood. "Do you think your Aboriginal friends would help me?"

"I'll ask them," Vanessa replied.

When Vanessa and Xavier resurfaced outside, many of the tribes had completed the important painting aspect of the ceremony. Now they appeared to be waiting for the dancing to begin. Vanessa and Xavier sat in the vicinity of the Haasts Bluff community, which was in close proximity to the RV. Vanessa watched while Long Jack's face and body were painted, whereas Joseph, who sat with another community, had chosen face paint only.

Vanessa was aware of what was going on around her, but her thoughts were still with her mother. The full impact of her mother's story was hitting her. "My mother was very, very, very lucky, Xavier," she said without looking at him.

He squeezed her hand. "Your mother *is* very lucky. And so are you. You've got her back now." Xavier placed her hand against his lips and kissed it. "To have a loving parent who is alive and well is a gift."

Together they watched several elderly Aboriginal men come to the middle of the gathering. Each one spoke briefly. Vanessa guessed each dialect was quite different, although to her untrained ears they all seemed alike. It wasn't long before the first group of dancers began to stomp, twitch, and bob to music created on didjeridoos, boomerangs, and various clacking sticks.

Vanessa and Xavier watched with fascination as one group after another performed elaborate, choreographed dances. Their bodies moved in ways Vanessa had never seen, their faces expressing the seriousness of it all.

At one point Vanessa said, "I get the feeling

these are very special dances. There's something about their faces. The sincerity."

"You're absolutely right," Xavier replied. "These dancers are reenacting tales from the Dreamtime. Adventures of the Aboriginal creator gods that resulted in the world around us. How the mountains were formed, or the rivers," he explained. "The dances that Long Jack said were secret sacred reveal the power of the Dreamtime, and they pass that power on to those who see the dance, as well as to the dancers, who the Aborigines believe are taken over by Ancestor Beings like the Rainbow Snake."

Vanessa watched a group of women take center circle. "The women and the men don't dance together?"

"Normally not. Sometimes you'll see the younger ones mixing, but normally not."

Vanessa shook her head with awe. "The way they move their bodies."

"The Aborigines say they *become* the emu or the cockatoo, or whatever the dance calls for."

As the evening progressed, wood for a large fire was gathered and stacked. Vanessa guessed it would be lit once the sun started to descend. They watched as Long Jack and the men from the Haasts Bluff community danced. The change in Long Jack when he began to move to his Aboriginal music was touching. Mesmerized, Vanessa watched, and more than ever it was very obvious how little she understood about Long Jack's culture and what made him who he was.

During the ceremony the RV door slowly opened, and Vanessa rushed over to help her mother down the stairs.

"Are you feeling better now?" she asked as she doubled up a blanket for Jackie to sit on.

"I feel better. It's probably a combination of things." Jackie studied her daughter's face. "Seeing you again and being able to talk to somebody." Her smile was genuine this time. Jackie looked at the dancers. "My, my, my. Dancing is as much a part of these people's lives as breathing."

"Do you think so?"

"There was dancing every day in the place where they took care of me. When I finally gained consciousness, I would hear music on and off every day. And once or twice when I had the strength, I looked out my window, and there they were . . . dancing."

"How long were you unconscious?" Xavier inquired.

"I'm not sure." Jackie looked down at her hands. "I think the heat is what did it. I remember walking, and walking, and finally ending up at this sandhill. It seemed so big. And I just couldn't figure out how to get around it. I didn't have the energy." She appeared tired just remembering. "I guess my thoughts and everything were affected by the heat."

"That must have been where they found you," Vanessa said. "Long Jack told us you were found at a sacred spot." She looked at Xavier to explain further.

"You see, the Wailpri believe that during the Rainbow Snake's Dreamtime journeys, there were special circumstances surrounding the creation of that sandhill."

"The Dreamtime." Jackie got quiet and wrapped her thin arms around her body. Moments later her expression changed as if her mind had begun to drift.

"Mama, are you all right?" Vanessa put her arms around her.

Jackie looked at her, a little startled. "I'm fine." Her eyes filled with emotion before she patted Vanessa's face. "You know, I almost got what I wanted," she said softly.

"And what was that?" Vanessa replied.

"I got to see your father, but I didn't get to stay with him."

For a brief second pity surfaced in Vanessa's eyes, but it quickly turned to acceptance. Considering what her mother had gone through, she was entitled to her hallucinations. "You saw Daddy?"

"I did see him, Nessa." Her mother's expression was soft but serious. "I know you're probably thinking your poor mother had temporarily lost her mind from the sun or even the stress. But I tell you, I saw him. He was the one who told me to go to *that* sandhill. There were many, many sandhills, and I was so confused. I could have walked in any direction. The land was so strange-looking, yet it looked the same no matter where I looked. And I tell you, that really frightened me because there was nothing to go by. No landmarks or anything.

So I lay down right out in the open, and just told God, if I'm going to die, just let me die. And just when that fear was about to take my mind, I heard William call my name." She looked from Vanessa to Xavier with awe. "I could see him at the end of this long tunnel, and behind him was nothing but the most beautiful, peaceful light I have ever seen. God, I was so happy to see him, and somehow I found the strength to run toward him. And then we were there standing together. He hugged me and I remembered how good it felt, and how much I missed that." A single tear wet her cheek. "And you know what?"

"What?" Vanessa asked, taking in the sincerity that emanated from her mother's face.

"Bill didn't have to hear me say what I was feeling. Somehow he knew it, and he simply told me not to worry. He told me we'd have plenty of opportunities to be together again after this lifetime. He said we had been together in many before this." She paused. "And he said when the time is right for me to be with him, then I'll be with him. But not a minute before."

Vanessa didn't know what to make of her mother's account, but she remained silent and continued to listen.

"He told me I had to go back. That there were some other things that I had to do that were important. Not on a global scale, but in the lives of the people who I love, like you." She smiled at Vanessa. "And those who are important to you." Jackie collected her thoughts. "Your father told me when I was back in the desert to walk directly toward the sun, and if I just kept going I'd come to a large sandhill, and things would get better from there. We hugged and kissed one last time, and the next thing I knew I was lying on the desert floor. I remembered your father's directions. I followed them. And that's where they found me."

"And you think the Dreamtime did that for you?" Vanessa sought clarity.

"I call it the Dreamtime. I don't know if it's exactly the same thing that these people believe." Jackie looked around. "Some might call it a near death experience. All I know is it was like being in a dream, but the dream itself was more real than any reality I have ever known. So to me it was the Dreamtime. And if I hadn't come here to Australia and gone through all I did, I may never have seen your father again, not before I crossed over, and for that I'm grateful."

Vanessa looked at her mother. "And I understand that."

Jackie held her gaze. "Do you really?"

"I think so," Vanessa replied softly.

"I think the experience you had can be included in what the Aborigines believe," Xavier said.

"You don't say." Jackie looked for him to explain.

"It's all about creation. You connected with a timeless time. And the Aborigines believe the Dreaming is perpetual. That the energies of the Ancestor Beings never die. That there are ways of connecting with that timelessness. It seems as if that is what you've done, Mrs. Bradley."

Jackie smiled. "Thank you for that, Xavier." She leaned over and touched his arm. "I thank you from the bottom of my heart."

The dancing came to a halt, and some young boys began to strategically stack the firewood in the middle of the gathering.

Xavier wanted to ask Jackie about the piece of paper in his wallet, the note included with the poem. But he looked at Vanessa and her mother, and he thought about all that Jackie had been through, and he knew it was not the right time. "I'm going to speak to Joseph," Xavier announced. "I'll find out if this is a good time for you to speak to the Wailpri," he said to Jackie.

"I'd appreciate that," Jackie replied.

Jackie and Vanessa watched Xavier stride across the opening.

"How did the two of you finally get together?" Jackie asked.

"Actually, after all your hard work back home," Vanessa sighed, "without knowing it, you ended up bringing us together anyway."

Jackie looked surprised. "Really?"

"With some intervention from destiny." Vanessa couldn't help but think of Dellia. "You remember the deal involving the Aboriginal exhibit?"

"Yes."

"Well, it ran into some trouble. This was around the time that I was expecting you to return home. So in the end, Xavier decided to make a trip over here, and he offered to help me find you. He's been at my side from the very beginning, Mama, almost to the detriment of his own interests."

Jackie balled up a scrawny fist. "I knew he would be good for you."

"Well, I have to say you were more than right."

They watched Xavier and Joseph speak to Long Jack, and moments later they were all headed back across the sand, along with a small band of Wailpris.

"I'll be glad to interpret for you," Long Jack said after they sat down in front of them.

"Thank you." Jackie faced the woman who had come to the RV, another who carried a covered plate, along with the two hunters who had actually found her. "Would you start by telling them how much I appreciate the help that they have given me?"

Long Jack immediately launched into interpreting. Expressive eyes took it all in. Finally, Long Jack replied, "They say the Rainbow Snake had protected you. It was the way of the Dreaming, and their honor to do the rest."

"Tell them I will never forget them, and what they have done." Jackie looked at the Wailpri as she spoke.

Long Jack interpreted.

"And also tell them, I received a gift while I was in the desert. One I've wanted for a long time. Tell them I am thankful to Australia and the Dreamtime for that."

Once again Long Jack did the interpreting. They all smiled, and the woman holding the plate spoke a few shy words. Long Jack translated, "She said the first day when she was helping you to heal, Koel, the black cuckoo, came to show herself. She felt this was a good sign, for Koel is brave, and she knew you would be fine. She tells you this now to let you know who is your totem. She wants you to take this knowledge home with you, knowing you will always have Koel's magic."

"Thank you," Jackie said. "I will always remember."

The woman sat the plate between them. She uncovered it and revealed several large, cooked, grub worms.

"This is one of our delicacies," Joseph explained. "She offers this food to you because it is the best." He wanted them to know it was a great honor.

Jackie looked at Vanessa, and Vanessa looked at Xavier. Each one of them picked up an embryonic moth.

"Welcome to the world of travel, Nessa," Jackie said before she popped the larva into her mouth.

"Thanks, Ma," Vanessa replied, then swallowed hard before she and Xavier followed suit.

twenty-nine

"This is Geneen's telephone number," Joseph said. "You can be certain I will get the message there. I always go back to visit Evin. And calling me there will be easiest for you. You will not run into any language barriers." Joseph handed Xavier a slip of paper.

"Joseph, always the man on the move," Xavier replied. "I appreciate your helping me out."

"I have to keep the spirit of the *yapa* in me alive," Joseph said.

"What does that mean, Joseph?" Vanessa inquired.

"The spirit of the Aboriginal hunter, accustomed to a life of endless travel."

"You are still the nomad," Long Jack acknowledged. "And that is why so many homes are open

to you, because of that spirit. It is in all our hearts.
You honor the *yapa* in all of us."

Joseph accepted the compliment with a humble look.

"I think we need to go," Vanessa said. "Mama,
you're looking tired again."

Jackie sighed. "I'm beginning to feel it."

Xavier helped Jackie to her feet. "You'll be
hearing from me," he said as he shook hands with
Joseph and Long Jack. "I want the Pintupi medicine man to know I do honor their artwork in the
spirit of the Dreamtime. I'll do everything I can to
make sure he gets every cent that was promised."

"And we will make sure, as part of the Aboriginal Cultural Foundation, that the Pintupi get
their money."

Everyone waved before Joseph and Long Jack
went back to their places. The last thing Vanessa
saw as she entered the RV were flames licking upward from a roaring fire, and Aboriginal dancers
entering the center, ready to honor the Dreamtime.

"You can lay back down, Mama," Vanessa suggested as Xavier closed the door.

"Are you sure? Where are you, and where is
Xavier, going to rest?" They all noted the obvious
separation. No matter what, Jackie was still holding on to her old-fashioned values.

"I plan to drive straight through to Alice
Springs tonight," Xavier said. "But even if I take a
little break, I can always kick back at the wheel,"

he reassured her. "There's a small bed in the rear where you can sleep, Vanessa."

Their eyes locked. Since they'd rented the RV, it would be the first time Vanessa would sleep alone, without Xavier.

"I think I'll keep you company for as long as I can," she replied.

Knowingly, Jackie looked at both their faces before she took off her sandals and crawled into bed.

Xavier and Vanessa settled into the front seats of the RV. He turned the vehicle on and pulled out. Minutes down the road, despite the beaming headlights, the darkness of the outback was powerful. It was like driving into a void.

"It's over seven hours to Alice Springs," Vanessa said.

"That's about what I guessed," Xavier replied.

"And it's so dark out here." She looked at the tip of the lights that dropped off into pure blackness. "If you get tired you should pull over and rest. You can have the bed in the back. You're the one who's driving. Don't worry about me."

"There's no way I'm going to be able to lie down in here without you by my side," he said softly, glancing at her. "Too many vivid memories. You know the old saying, 'An idle brain is the devil's workshop'? Although I wouldn't call what I'm thinking *evil* by a long shot."

Vanessa's body responded as Xavier talked.

"If I stop for one moment I'm not going to be

able to think of anything outside of making love to you." His voice was silky. "So I'm going to get on down this road, and I'm not going to stop until I'm in Alice Springs and you're in your room, along with your mother, and I'm in mine."

"If you insist," Vanessa breathed.

"I do. I don't want to do anything to disrespect Ms. Jackie."

"Speaking of my mother, I really want to thank you. You went out of your way to help me find her, and I'll never forget this. Never," Vanessa said dramatically.

"You needed me, and I was glad to be there." He glanced at her again. "So I plan to stay on the good foot. I don't want to do anything to upset the apple cart. Your mother has been through enough already. But I've got another reason. I care an awful lot for her daughter, and I want your mother in my corner." *If I ever want to make things more permanent*, Xavier thought. *That is, once I know you can accept my father and all the possibilities that go with him.*

Vanessa smiled at Xavier lovingly. "I'm sure after all you've done, you've got nothing to worry about." She leaned her head back against the headrest and settled in for the long haul.

When they entered the Plaza Hotel Alice Springs, the same clerk Vanessa had spoken to the very first time on the telephone was on duty.

He looked at Jackie. "Mrs. Bradley! They found you!"

"We most certainly did," Vanessa replied.

"I can't believe it." The clerk didn't seem to know who to look at first. "What happened?" He leaned on the counter, preparing to hear the details.

"It's too long a story to tell tonight," Vanessa replied. "We're all very tired, but if you would call the police station and let them know that my mother will be in tomorrow to file a criminal report, that would help a lot."

"I definitely will." The clerk stood up and straightened his uniform. "But I can't wait to tell Mr. Dalton that you found her," he continued in a very excited fashion. "When do you plan to fly back?"

"We're going to see if we can fly standby some time tomorrow," Vanessa replied.

"I want to get back home as quickly as I can," Jackie said. "I want my regular doctor to check me over. Although I feel okay, I just want to make sure everything is all right." She tried to look confident.

"Sounds like a good idea," the clerk said, then added, "you all have a good night."

"I'm going to stay in the room with my daughter tonight, and it'll be the best night I've had in what feels like a long time," Jackie replied.

They proceeded toward the elevator.

The clerk waved a piece of paper. "I'm sorry, Mr. Johnson. I forgot. You have a message."

Xavier went back to get it, then rejoined Vanessa and her mother. He read the message as they entered the elevator.

"Important?" Vanessa asked.

"It's from the guy I had been looking for, Kaapa."

"It is? Now everything is falling into place." The elevator door opened and Vanessa guided her sleepy mother out. "You'll have some good news to share with him."

"I'm not so sure." Xavier looked pensive. "I don't know how wrapped up Kaapa is on the bad end of this." He paused. "On the other hand, talking to him could be very useful in the long run."

They reached their hotel rooms. Vanessa unlocked her door, and Jackie went inside. "Are you going to call him tonight?"

"No, I'm tired. I'll wait to call him in the morning."

"Good," Vanessa said. "That's a good idea because you're a growing boy. You need your rest." Vanessa's eyes were full of longing as she held on to the door.

Slowly, Xavier walked toward her. "Now this is a good idea." He bent down and kissed her tenderly.

"Why did you do that?" Vanessa said softly. "Now I won't be able to sleep a wink."

"Just what I wanted to hear." Xavier walked back to his door, and they entered their rooms at the same time.

thirty

The telephone rang. Xavier shielded his eyes as he picked it up.

"Good morning."

"Good morning to you," he replied.

"Don't tell me you're still asleep."

"Nope. Just lying here thinking of you and wondering if I should do a quick fix of the situation," he said suggestively, "or deal with my desire once we get back to Columbus."

Vanessa cut her eyes at her mother, who was heading into the bathroom. She spoke softly. "Don't you dare. I want to take care of that."

"M-m-m." He made a sound deep in his throat. "Will it be worth the wait?"

"On my honor," Vanessa said, catching her reflection in the mirror. She couldn't believe the fire in her own eyes.

"Okay, now that one of my morning activities has been scrapped, what do you have planned for me to do today?"

"I promised Mama I'd get her film developed this morning. She's going to stay in the room and rest until I get back. And then we'll go to the police station afterward. You want to come to the camera shop with me?"

"Sure," Xavier said. "First, let me give Kaapa a call. I hope I can set something up with him before we get out of here."

"All right. I'll meet you downstairs in the restaurant. There's a pharmacy and camera shop next door. I'll drop the film off before we have breakfast so it can be ready by the time we're done."

"See you then," Xavier replied.

A half hour later they'd filled themselves on an all-American breakfast: bacon, eggs, and toast. Vanessa was in an extremely chatty mood, and Xavier was content to let her talk.

"And then I remember going up to the cutest boy in my first-grade class and just staring at him," she said as Xavier paid their bill. "He was the cutest thing I had ever seen. But he looked at me as if I was chopped liver. My first rejection." She hooked her arm through his.

"And you were shy with boys from that moment on," Xavier commented as they left the restaurant.

"Somewhat," Vanessa replied, pulling open the

door to the camera shop. She placed her ticket for the pictures on the counter.

"So how long was it before you had your first real boyfriend?"

She counted on her fingers. "Nine years later. I was fifteen and totally in love, but he ended up breaking my heart and my ability to trust."

"But they say you can't really be in love at that age."

"They lied," Vanessa quipped as the clerk handed over her freshly developed pictures. "Thank you." She accepted two packs of doubles and started to rifle through them. "I think some people are capable of loving early as well as quickly. I'm one of those people." Her dark eyes turned serious when she looked at him again.

He pecked her on the lips. "And I'm glad you are."

"These are some wonderful pictures." Vanessa turned so Xavier could see them. "Look at that." She continued to flip, then stopped abruptly. "Xavier! Look!" She extracted the photo. "Do you think these are the two men who left Mama in the desert?" Vanessa stared at a photo taken of the Ross River Homestead restaurant. The men were standing by a car parked outside. The car had a generic tour company sign inside the dashboard.

"There's one way to find out," Xavier said. "Let's ask your mother."

They wasted no time in returning to the hotel. If her hunch was right, Vanessa wondered how her mother would react to seeing a photo of the men who had all but murdered her.

"Mama?" Vanessa tapped on the door before entering. "Are you dressed? I've got Xavier with me."

"Yes. I'm dressed. Come on in."

Jackie was sitting on the side of the bed. She took one look at Vanessa's face and said, "What is it?"

"I think there's a picture in here with those two men in it."

"What?" Jackie looked confused, almost frightened.

"This one." Vanessa sat down beside her and handed her the photograph. "You took a picture of the restaurant, but—"

"Yes! That's them. I had no idea they were in this picture."

"You planned to go to the police this morning anyway. Now you've got some evidence too," Xavier said.

Jackie narrowed her eyes. "If I could get my hands on them . . . I would wring their necks."

"Let's hope the Australian police have something similar in mind when they catch up with them," Vanessa said.

Jackie stood up. "I'm ready to go to the police station right now."

"Why don't you two go ahead," Xavier said. "I've set up a meeting with Kaapa at the little deli next door, and it's too late to call him back. Hopefully, we'll finish all of our business around the same time, and we can go to the airport."

"I can't wait to show the police a picture of those jokers," Jackie spat between clenched teeth.

Vanessa knew her mother was feeling better. She sounded like her old self again. "I think we should check out of the hotel first, and leave our bags downstairs," Vanessa suggested. "That way all of our business here will be taken care of."

"I'll take your bags along with mine, Mrs. Bradley." Xavier picked up the two suitcases. "It will make it a little easier on you."

"You are such a gem," Jackie crooned.

"Schmooz. Schmooz," Vanessa chanted, to which Xavier raised a strategic eyebrow.

The checkout process was smooth and quick. Afterward Xavier waited for Vanessa and Jackie to secure a cab.

"We'll be back as soon as we can," Vanessa said while Xavier stood on the curb.

"I'll either be at the deli or waiting for you here in the lobby," he replied before the cabbie drove away.

Xavier sat on the same bar stool that he had sat on when he'd met Phillip Ramsey. Several minutes later a fair-skinned young man sat beside him. "Are you Xavier Johnson?"

"I am." Xavier noticed another young, hefty man leaning against a nearby wall.

"I'm Kaapa." He threw his head back in a jaunty fashion.

Xavier eyed him suspiciously. "I don't mean to be rude, but I thought you were an Aborigine?"

Kaapa seemed offended. "I am. Do we all have to look a certain way?"

Xavier paused. "Like I said, I wasn't trying to be rude."

"Just like your people in America, my blood's all mixed up. My father is White and my mother is Pintupi."

Xavier nodded slowly. "I see."

"Anyway, I don't see what my parentage has to do with this business deal. So who told you?" But before Xavier could respond, Kaapa had answered his own question. "Phillip Ramsey? David Paige?"

"What difference does it make?" Xavier replied.

"Exactly." Kaapa's eyes nearly turned red with anger. "They always want to make sure people know I'm part Aborigine. Separate themselves from the likes of me."

Xavier looked down. "Why did you call me?"

"I heard you wanted to renew the Pintupi art deal."

"From what Mr. Paige told me, that's no longer possible." Xavier wanted to see where Kaapa was coming from.

Kaapa looked ticked off. "It's possible. All it takes is more money."

"So the Pintupi artists pulled out because there wasn't enough money?" Xavier's eyes narrowed.

"That's exactly right," Kaapa replied.

"Or did they pull out because someone had stolen the majority of the money, then offered them what was left over?"

Kaapa cleared his throat. "That's also possible."

"Don't you feel bad about stealing from your own people, Kaapa?"

Kaapa laughed, but the muscle started to grind in his jaw. "Considering all the money that was on that table, I wouldn't call what I got stealing. Being given some crumbs, yes."

Xavier's eyes became hooded. "So now you're looking for more."

"If there is more. You and I can cut a deal similar to the ones the big boys cut. You could walk away happy, and I can walk away happy. Then the artists would be satisfied and you would get your paintings."

Xavier looked down at his hands. "I'm going to walk away happy anyway. I make enough money. I don't need to steal from people who deserve it." He looked up and challenged Kaapa with his eyes. "But there's one thing you can be sure of. I'm going to make sure everybody who had a hand in these dirty dealings gets what's coming to him."

Kaapa shook his head as his confidence slipped a few notches. "Look, I'm nothing but a small potato in this thing. If you want to get the big boys you need to look higher than me. And from what

I understand, you also need to look at some of the people on your side of the globe. Those who didn't want to see this project get off the ground."

Xavier stiffened. "Like who?"

"I'll tell you all the names you want if we cut a deal. If not . . ." Kaapa shrugged, recovering some of his attitude.

Xavier remained cool, although he wanted to press the issue. He was certain he'd be able to find out with or without Kaapa's help. "No matter what anybody else did, Kaapa, you betrayed your own, so what does that make you? You need to go back and beg your uncle and your people's forgiveness. They are worth much more than any money you'll ever get." Xavier looked down his nose at Kaapa. "So your offer to cut another deal has been turned down." He got off the stool, but before Xavier could turn around, the other young man had his arm around his shoulder, and there was a sharp object poking into his side.

Kaapa looked alarmed. "What are you doing?" he asked the guy.

"You heard what the old man said, he's got lots of money. And I don't plan to leave here without something."

Kaapa looked as if he wanted to protest.

"If you don't have the stomach for this go back and get in the car," the angry young man commanded. Then he smiled at Xavier as he tightened his hold. From all appearances it looked as if they were old friends. "Now let's go up to your hotel room and see what you can come up with," the man said as they entered the lobby.

"There's nothing up there." Xavier's tone was cool as steel, but the man laughed and put pressure on the knife, breaking Xavier's skin.

"Don't play with me."

They started across the lobby. When they reached the elevator, Xavier pressed the Up button. The doors opened, and they stepped inside together.

Vanessa and Jackie got out of the cab in front of the Plaza Hotel Alice Springs as Xavier and the young man entered the hotel.

"What in the world is going on?" Vanessa's brows furrowed. "Xavi—" she called.

"No-o. Don't!" Her mother put her hand over her daughter's mouth. "You see that car that man is walking toward?" Jackie asked, darting her gaze to the right of the hotel. "That's the car the bogus tour company used. And I think that's one of the men sitting inside of it."

"Do you recognize the guy getting in the car?" Vanessa asked. Her heart felt as if it were in her throat as she looked back inside the lobby and saw Xavier disappear around the corner.

"No."

Vanessa's mind was in a spin. "Then that must be the other one with Xavier. What's going on here? Why is Xavier with him?" Then it dawned on her. "Xavier must be in trouble."

"We've got to get the police," Jackie said, her voice panicked.

"I don't think there's time." Vanessa looked up and down the street trying to figure out what to do. She ran into the lobby. Her heart bolted with relief when she spotted a security guard coming down the hall with the clerk.

"Mr. Dalton, remember Vanessa Bradley?" the clerk began amiably. "I told you—"

Vanessa stopped him. "Not now. Something horrible is happening. One of the men who attempted to hurt my mother is in the hotel. He's got Xavier. I don't know if he's holding a gun on him or what."

"Where are they?" the security guard asked as Jackie joined them.

"They just went up the elevator. I don't know where they're going. We checked out of our rooms more than an hour ago." Vanessa pulled him toward the elevator. "We've got to hurry."

Vanessa pressed the Up button. "Mama, stay here with the hotel clerk."

"Maybe Xavier wants him to think he still has his room," the security guard said as the elevator arrived and he and Vanessa dashed inside. "What floor?"

"Three," Vanessa said quickly.

When the elevator opened on the third floor, Xavier and the man were standing outside his old hotel room door.

"What's going on down there?" the security guard yelled.

It was the distraction Xavier needed. He knocked the knife from the man's hand. Scared and cornered, the culprit ran for the exit.

Jackie and the hotel clerk waited in the lobby after calling the police. Nothing could have prepared them for the would-be criminal bursting through the stairwell door.

"That's him!" Jackie shouted as the man headed for them, his target the main entrance.

"He-ey!" the hotel clerk yelled.

"He's trying to get away!" Jackie shouted again. She grabbed a vase from the counter. "I'll teach you to leave me in some desert." Jackie hit him in the head. He fell out cold just as Xavier, Vanessa, and the security guard reached the lobby. Mr. Dalton ran over and pulled the criminal's arms on top of his back.

"I bet he won't be leaving anybody else out there," Jackie said as the commotion picked up outside the hotel entrance. Several police cars were blocking in the phony tour car.

"Are you okay?" Vanessa asked her mother.

"I am. But I'm glad to say he's not feeling too good." She looked at the groggy young man.

The clerk launched into telling how Jackie clobbered the criminal with the vase, and it was difficult for everyone not to burst into laughter. A while later the young criminal was led out with handcuffs around his wrists.

The lead officer shook his head as he scribbled down some information. "Some young people these days. It's this whole cultural thing. Trying to be Aborigine and trying to live in this society is tough. But it's no excuse for committing crimes."

They all watched as Kaapa and his two friends were handcuffed and put in vehicles.

"So you've had some problems like this before," Vanessa said.

"Not this serious," the officer answered. He turned to Xavier. "From what you've told me, I think these young mates got a whiff of big money and got really crazy and reckless. Some vandalism, a little bit of burglary, we've dealt with that." He tapped his pen against his clipboard. "But nothing as serious as attempted murder."

"And you will look into what I told you about World Import and Exports?"

"Absolutely," the officer replied. "There is protection now for the Aboriginal community. Mainly land rights, but we take all kinds of cultural theft real serious around here. For many Aboriginal communities their art and music are their economic backbones. And it goes without saying, embezzlement of any kind is strictly against the law."

"And thanks for leaning on Kaapa and getting me the name of the man involved in this at the museum in the U.S.," Xavier said.

"No problem. We'll get the rest of the information to you once it's ready. I've got your fax number right here. We'll get the crime report typed up, along with Kaapa's statement, and fax it to you."

"I believe that will work wonders," Xavier replied.

There was a moment of silence.

Vanessa stuck her hand out. "We best be on our way. We need to get to the airport early if we're going to fly standby."

The policeman put his pen in his pocket. "I'll get out of your way, then. And it was really a pleasure seeing you, Mrs. Bradley." His eyes twinkled. "We always like it when a missing persons case turns out positively."

"No one is more pleased than I am about that," Jackie replied.

Minutes later, Xavier, Vanessa, and Jackie were in a cab and on their way to the airport.

On their way home.

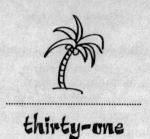

thirty-one

Jackie entered the house and stopped just inside the door. Vanessa stepped up behind her. "I thought I'd never see this house again," Jackie said softly.

Vanessa put her hand on her shoulder. "Welcome home, Mama."

Despite her recovering strength, Jackie broke down and cried.

"Why don't you sit down and let me put the suitcases in our rooms," Vanessa suggested.

Jackie made her way to the couch as Vanessa pulled the suitcases toward the bedrooms. Slowly, she looked around the familiar living-dining room. When Jackie looked through the screen door again, Miss Bea was standing there.

"Jackie! Lord, is that you?"

"It's me, Bea. It's me."

When Vanessa reentered the room, the two old friends were hugging and crying.

"I had almost given you up, Jackie. I had almost given you up," Miss Bea repeated herself. "But I went to church yesterday and I prayed for you, and the whole congregation prayed too. And when I left church I said, if it's meant to be, Loord, it's meant to be, and I bend, God, to your will. I submitted, Jackie, and because of that, God has brought my friend back." They hugged again before Miss Bea let go and stood back.

"What they been feeding you over there? Nothing?" She squeezed Jackie's thin arm, which was almost as slim as her own.

"Woman, you wait till you hear what happened to me." Jackie gave her one of those looks.

"Well, let's sit down first." Miss Bea tugged on Jackie's arm as she sat down on the couch. "I feel weak enough from seeing you standing here. So I know what you're about to tell me is going to take my breath away."

"Well, I'm going to let you two talk while I take a shower," Vanessa said. She walked down the hall with her mother announcing, "Two men left me in the desert to die." When Vanessa returned thirty minutes later, Miss Bea's voice was the first she heard.

"You get out of here." Miss Bea slapped her leg. "So what were they giving you to drink?"

"I don't know, child. It smell real bad and it taste awful. But whenever I would drink it, this calm would come over me, and all my fears about being there would just kind of melt away. Then I'd go back to sleep."

"That was some powerful stuff." Miss Bea's lips pursed.

"Yes, it was."

Miss Bea leaned toward her friend. "What were the Aborigines like, Jackie?"

"People with good hearts. Just like you and me, and anybody else. Sure they got their own ways, but for them to take me in and care for me so well, they had to be good people."

"So when did you find your mother, Nessa?" Miss Bea turned in her seat.

"We'd been there about three days before we found her."

"You and Xavier?"

Vanessa looked down and smiled. "Yep."

"Now that's a story," Jackie said, nudging Miss Bea.

"I bet it is."

"Mama, why don't you continue to tell your story. I didn't come in here for you two to start talking about me."

Miss Bea's eyebrows went up. "Well, can I ask you this?"

Vanessa tilted her head. "What?"

"How did you two know where to find Jackie?"

"We stayed in this little cabin off of the main road and we met this man named Joseph. He's an Aborigine who knew that part of Australia really well. He was sort of the area nomad, and he eventually offered to help us."

"So Xavier Johnson was with you the entire time while you were there?"

"Yes. He most certainly was," Vanessa said softly.

"Now that's love." Miss Bea settled back on the couch. "I wish I had met a man who would have stuck with me through thick and thin like that. He'd be mine today."

"I can tell things haven't changed around here." Vanessa smiled.

"And you should have seen them together, Bea." Jackie stuck her two fingers together.

"They were like that, huh?"

"M-m huh," Jackie replied.

"And I'm so glad you're back. We're going to have to celebrate," Miss Bea said as the telephone rang.

"That's a great idea," Vanessa said as she answered the phone. "Hello." Then she added in a much more intimate voice, "I'm fine. How are you?"

"That's him," Jackie and Miss Bea said to one another.

"Tell him we're going to have a dinner tomorrow night to celebrate, and we want him to come," Miss Bea said as Vanessa took the cordless phone and started for the side door to the yard.

"Did you hear that?" Vanessa asked.

"What?" Xavier replied.

"Miss Bea told me to tell you you're invited to a celebration dinner tomorrow night." She sat beneath her favorite tree.

"I remember Miss Bea, she's the woman who, from the very beginning, was trying to get me interested in you."

"No she wasn't," Vanessa chuckled.

"Yes, she was. If she had said just a little bit more I would have sworn she was your agent."

"You need to quit," Vanessa replied.

"But baby, you didn't need an agent." His voice turned serious. "I was very aware of you from the start." He waited in silence before saying, "How's your mother?"

"When she got in the house she started to cry," Vanessa said. "But once she saw Miss Bea, it was instantly like old times again."

"Good for her."

They listened to one another breathe.

"I wish you were here," Xavier finally said.

"Me too, but it's already rather late and I'm going to spend the rest of the evening settling in and spending a little more time with Mama."

"That sounds like a good idea. But be fore-warned, after dinner tomorrow we're going for a ride. At least that's what we'll tell everybody. And it will somewhat be true. By then I'll be ready to take you for the ride of your life."

"Well you can't do it now, so stop talking about it," Vanessa said softly.

"Haven't you ever heard of phone sex before?"

She leaned her head back and closed her eyes.

"Of course I have. But after waiting all this time I want you to be front and center when I expend this energy."

"When you put it that way, you'll get no argument from me." Xavier paused. "Do you go back to work tomorrow?"

"No, I still have the rest of the week off. What about you?"

"I plan to go in. I hope to have a few choice words with one of my coworkers after I make a very important phone call."

"Boy, the Marshall Art Museum is going to be rocking and rolling tomorrow."

"I sure hope so." Xavier paused. "Well, good night, my love."

Vanessa's eyes closed. "Good night. . . . *my* love."

thirty-two

Xavier pushed the old revolving door and entered the Marshall Art Museum. As usual at this time of morning, his footsteps echoed in the large, hollow hall. When he entered the business office, Sand was on the telephone. She smiled a big, silent smile and waved as he walked by. He had barely made it around his desk when she popped her head in the door to his office.

"How'd it go?" she asked.

Xavier gave the thumbs-up sign.

Sand gave him a silent applause, then looked up and down the hall before whispering, "Curtis is already acting like he's won."

"Is he here now?" Xavier inquired.

"Yes. He's in Mr. Marshall's office." The phone rang at her desk. "Got to go." She reciprocated the thumbs-up sign, then dashed away.

Xavier took a file folder out of his satchel and headed out of his office. Mr. Marshall's door was partially open when he arrived. He tapped it with his knuckle.

"Come in, Sand." Mr. Marshall's Southern accent was as present as ever.

Xavier opened the door. "It's not Sand, Mr. Marshall."

"Xavier. You're back," Mr. Marshall said.

"That was a quick trip," Curtis noted. "You must have gotten over there and saw you were wasting your time."

Xavier gave Curtis a meaningful look. "That's not what happened at all, Curtis."

Mr. Marshall's eyebrows went up. "It's not?"

"Not by a long shot."

"Why don't you pull up a chair and tell us about it." Mr. Marshall gestured toward an old leather chair. "I was just telling Curtis that the Aboriginal art exhibit would have added something different to what we normally offer down here. Our attendance numbers haven't been all that great for quite a while, and I firmly believed that exhibit would have brought people from neighboring cities, mainly Atlanta."

"Well, you know I couldn't agree with you more," Xavier replied. "And it looks like we're back in the seat again."

"Really?" Mr. Marshall looked pleasantly surprised. "You mean to tell me the paintings will be coming?"

"After more money is put on the table."

Curtis reared back. "I *knew* there was some kind of hook to this. I couldn't imagine how Xavier could have gotten the deal without *more* money. But it goes to show he hasn't been listening too well. There is *no* more money for this project, Xavier. The board members and our special committee said they have offered all they are going to offer before you left here."

Mr. Marshall sat back. "I'm afraid Curtis is right. And honestly speaking, I felt our offer was more than generous. Secondly, it was my understanding the Pintupi had changed their minds for religious reasons."

Curtis snickered. "Yours and everybody else's, Uncle. Except for Mr. Johnson here."

Xavier looked down at the folder in his lap. "Basically, Mr. Marshall, what you've said is true." He ignored Curtis. "But I actually spoke to the medicine man, or *mekigar*, as they call him, who is the spokesman for the Pintupi group. He was a very wise man, and after a simple heart-to-heart talk he agreed to allow the paintings to come to the museum. He believed that I would make sure they were honored in the spirit in which they were created."

"Well . . ." Curtis cleared his throat. "Getting the Pintupi to see beyond their limited cultural mores was only a small part of the problem. Money is the real issue here."

"Ye-es . . ." Xavier hesitated meaningfully. "Money has been a big issue. It appears there were some people involved with this deal who turned money into a bigger issue than it should have been. So big, they decided to take quite a bit of it for themselves and offer the Aborigines the leftovers. That's why the Pintupi agreed at first, then later changed their minds."

Mr. Marshall sat forward again. "Are you saying somebody stole some of the money?"

Xavier's gaze never wavered. "I certainly am."

Curtis crossed his arms. "This is ridiculous."

"Xavier, you know that is a serious charge," Mr. Marshall warned. "Do you have any proof of this?"

"Plenty." Xavier placed the folder on Mr. Marshall's desk. "Some young hoods who were being used as go-betweens for the deal got a little upset because they didn't receive as much money as they thought they would. After that, they decided to take matters into their own hands. Things didn't work out too great, and they were caught. One of them, a guy by the name of Kaapa, confessed everything in his statement to the police."

Curtis looked back and forth nervously. "You said they were 'hoods.' How can you trust what they told the police?"

Xavier eyed Curtis. "Yes, they are young men who got off on the wrong foot, but the one named Kaapa knew the names of the people at World Import and Exports who were involved in the deal."

"But that—"

"And he also mentioned your name, Curtis."

Mr. Marshall never looked up; he continued to read the typed report in silence.

Curtis pointed to his chest. "My name?"

"Yes. Your name," Xavier repeated.

"I never received any money from anybody," Curtis swore. "You can check my banking accounts."

"It seemed you had a larger interest in keeping the exhibit in Australia," Xavier said. "You didn't want it to come here. You may not have known everything that was happening down there, but you didn't want to know," Xavier explained. "What you did was make it easier for them to steal by okaying a stipulation that a large fee could be kept by World Import and Exports if any partner in the deal dropped out. But you knew that if you offered the Pintupi a pittance of the original dollar figure they would not hand over the paintings."

"I have never heard such crap in my life," Curtis argued. "You're just trying to cover your ass. You don't have any more money to put down on this deal, so regardless, the deal is dead and you're out of here."

"Actually, I do have more money," Xavier said. "Some members of the Atlanta, Georgia, Boulé— it's the most prestigious African American fraternity in the nation—have made a substantial donation toward ensuring the Pintupi art reaches our shores."

"Wha-wha-wha—" Curtis stammered.

"May I make a copy of this?" Mr. Marshall asked quietly.

"Sure you can," Xavier replied.

Mr. Marshall intercommed Sand. She hurried into the office.

"Make a copy of this for me, Sand," Mr. Marshall instructed.

"Yes, Mr. Marshall." She looked questioningly at everyone, then hurried out.

Mr. Marshall kept his gaze focused on Xavier. "And you say you have secured enough money from this Black fraternity to make good on this deal?"

"That's right," Xavier replied.

Mr. Marshall stood up and extended his hand. "Congratulations, Xavier, you did a fine job and you are an asset to this museum. I'm going to make sure we make more use of your talents in the future."

Xavier shook his hand. "Thank you, Mr. Marshall." He started out the door just as Sand was returning with the copy.

"Give the original to Xavier on your way out," Mr. Marshall said.

Sand gave Mr. Marshall the copy and passed the original to Xavier. But before the door closed, Xavier and Sand could hear Mr. Marshall say with a mighty force, "What in the hell did you think you were doing? If you weren't my only sister's son I would fire you today."

thirty-three

Vanessa took one last look in the mirror. A daring image looked back. Daring for Vanessa, that is. A rather generous amount of cleavage showed at the top of the short dress, and plenty of leg streamed down from the bottom. This would be the first time Xavier had seen her really made up since. . . . Vanessa took a deep breath. Just the thought of making love to Xavier affected her every time.

She walked out of the hall bathroom and bumped into Miss Bea.

"Ooo-we. You look absolutely great." Miss Bea placed her boney hands around Vanessa's upper arms. "There will be fireworks tonight." She smiled knowingly.

Vanessa laughed. "You are never going to change."

"To change is to die, honey. And I feel like I've got plenty of life in me."

"Well I'm glad." She placed a kiss on Miss Bea's papery cheek.

"And I hope you know, we are all living through you vicariously."

"Oh, I know you are."

"No, seriously, Nessa. We are. And it's the most exciting thing," she said conspiratorially. "Never again will I have the experience you are having now. To love a man the way you love this one."

"How do you know I love him, Miss Bea?" Vanessa asked softly.

"Have you looked into your own eyes lately?"

Vanessa smiled and nodded.

"Ooo, to have a man love me like that." She closed her eyes. "To love every inch, every curve." Miss Bea sniggled like a little girl. "When a man loves you that way, it is a celebration of your womanhood." Her gaze seemed to be looking into the past.

"How beautiful," Vanessa said softly. "You are a treasure."

"I'd prefer to be young and attractive again," Miss Bea replied.

"Really?"

Miss Bea thought for a moment. "In some ways, but not in others. I don't know if I could take the intensity of the emotional ups and downs of being in love. There is no high like that one, and Lord knows, there certainly is no low that compares to it. Broken heart pains are like heart attacks . . . you never forget them, and you try to avoid them afterwards at all costs."

"Gosh, that's kind of scary," Vanessa said.

"Ye-es. It's one of those chances you have to take when you join your life with another person. But when it works the benefits are worth every moment." Miss Bea raised her gray eyebrows. "At least that's what I hear." She laughed.

"So you don't know of anyone who has really done it?" Vanessa looked disappointed, then apprehensive.

"Why, sure I do. And you do too. Your mother and father. They did it."

"Mmm," Vanessa murmured. "I think you're right."

"I know I am. So we'll be watching you tonight. Getting our kicks off of you and that gorgeous young man of yours." A sensual twinkle entered her gray-rimmed eyes. "Now let me get in here before I embarrass every one of us."

Vanessa smiled and stepped away from the bathroom door. "See you at the table."

"Wouldn't miss it for the world," Miss Bea replied.

The doorbell rang.

"Got it," Vanessa called. "I feel like I've got an entire butterfly garden in my stomach," she added to herself before she opened the door.

It was Lillie, holding a foil-covered pan. "Well hello-o. How are you?"

Vanessa touched her cheek against the taller one. "I'm fine, Lillie. How about you?"

"I'll be okay once I hurry up and get this in there. This macaroni and cheese is starting to burn my hands it's so fresh and hot."

"You want me to take it?" Vanessa offered.

"No-no, I'll do it," Lillie replied, dancing a slight jig. Then Vanessa understood it was her way of announcing what she had brought for dinner.

"I can't wait to taste it," Vanessa cooed, plumping Lillie's feathers as she squeezed by. "You know how I love your macaroni and cheese. I've been eating it practically all my life."

"You just hush," Lillie said, smiling as she made her way to the kitchen.

Vanessa was about to close the door when a familiar voice said, "And I thought you'd be glad to see me." Xavier had turned onto the walkway in the midst of the commotion.

"Xavier."

"At least you remember my name." He stood close, looking down at her from his heightened advantage. The most exquisite smell of male cologne Vanessa had ever known wafted around him.

"How could I forget?" she said softly as she looked into his eyes.

"Don't I get a kiss?" His voice was husky as he lowered his lips. The kiss was so sweet, so tantalizing, it was hard for Vanessa to break away.

"We better step inside or the neighbors won't have to rent that R-rated movie they planned for tonight." She took his hand and closed the door.

Vanessa led Xavier to the kitchen. Jackie, Mrs. Bertha, and Lillie were busy inside.

Jackie was the first to spot them. "Xavier, you made it." Both Lillie and Mrs. Bertha turned around.

"Wouldn't have missed it for anything, Mrs. Bradley."

"Why don't you introduce him, Ne-Vanessa," Jackie said proudly.

Vanessa smiled. "Lillie, Mrs. Bertha, this is Xavier Johnson."

"We've heard so much about you," Mrs. Bertha chimed.

"We certainly have, and it's been all good," Lillie added.

Xavier smiled charmingly. "I've heard about you too, and it's a pleasure meeting you."

"Where's Bea?" Jackie asked.

"She's in the bathroom. I'm sure she'll be out in a moment," Vanessa informed them.

"I hope you won't mind being the only man tonight," Jackie continued. "We've been sort of an all-female club."

"That's the best kind," Xavier replied.

Appreciatively, all the women smiled.

"So why don't you and Vanessa have a seat at the table," Jackie said, herding them in that direction. "Everything's ready. We just need to serve it."

"You sure you don't want me to do anything?" Vanessa asked.

"You just keep Xavier company while we put everything on the table," her mother insisted.

Vanessa complied. Minutes later, several hot, steaming platters of food were placed on the table, which was set with Jackie's best china.

"I don't know how well all of this is going to sit on my stomach after a few days' fare of emu and lizard, but I'm definitely going to find out," Xavier commented, inhaling the aroma of turkey, roast beef, collards, corn, and macaroni and cheese.

"Lord knows, if we ate like this every day"— Vanessa looked toward the kitchen because she knew there was more to come—"we'd all be as big as this table."

"And I like you just as you are," Xavier said.

Vanessa felt the heat rise to her face appropriately. "Do you ever run out of them?"

"Run out of what?"

"These perfect things to say," she replied.

"I guess I will when I feel so moved. But right now those perfect things are all I know."

"Bea hasn't come out of that bathroom yet?" Mrs. Bertha asked when she set the rolls on the table.

"I guess she hasn't. I better go check on her." Vanessa got up. "Excuse me, Xavier."

Vanessa was halfway down the hall when Miss Bea emerged.

"I was coming to get you," Vanessa said. "We thought perhaps you had fallen in," she joked.

"Not quite." Miss Bea wiped her forehead with a tissue.

"You all right?"

"I'm fine." Miss Bea took a deep breath. "Just felt a little nauseated for a moment. But I feel much better now."

"Well, come on. All the food is practically on the table. I'm simply waiting for you to bring out your incomparable pineapple upside-down cake."

Miss Bea gave a little smile. "Coming right up."

thirty-four

"And you should have seen the look on Vanessa's face when she popped that grub worm in her mouth." Jackie continued to laugh as tears spilled down her cheeks.

Vanessa balked at being the brunt of the joke. "Well you and Xavier didn't look too pleased either."

Lillie laughed. "I'm sure they didn't. But it's hard to picture the little girl who hated getting dirt on her overalls eating a grub worm."

Xavier squeezed Vanessa's hand under the table. Finally, the laughter died down.

"That's my girl, Nessa," Miss Bea defended her. "You showed them you could hang with the best of them." It was one of few comments she'd made all evening.

"Thank you, Miss Bea."

Forks and plates began to clink again.

Jackie cut another piece of roast beef. "Xavier, what did you make of that note I sent you with my poem? It was signed by an interesting name."

"I was very curious about it," Xavier replied. "It was one of the main things on my mind when I headed for Australia."

Surprised, Vanessa's brow furrowed. *How could something be so important to Xavier, but he never mentioned it to me?*

"It was interesting, wasn't it?" Jackie continued. "I got it at the street festival from a man who was sitting on the bench next to me. The festival where we first met."

"Yes, I remember," Xavier said.

"You mean the homeless man?" Vanessa asked.

Xavier stopped with his utensils in midair before he looked at the table.

"You remember him too," Jackie replied. "He was talking to himself about family and some other things that I couldn't quite make out. It was almost as if he was having lucid moments and then they would just slip away."

"How old was he?" Xavier asked quietly.

"I'd say around sixty," Jackie calculated. "Quite handsome despite the hat and all." She paused. "And then, at what seemed like a clearer moment, I heard him say, 'We should be proud of our young men,' and he was looking at you. That's how I spotted you in the first place." She paused as she thought about it. "Then he passed me that note, and what he had written was so beautiful. I just never would have thought."

"What did he write?" Vanessa asked.

Jackie squinted as she tried to remember. "Something about you are not your father's son." She looked at Xavier for assistance.

"Yes. It was something like that," he said quietly.

"When I found the paper in my pocket a couple of days later I got this feeling that he wanted you to have it. He may have said as much, if my memory serves me right." She made a face. "Of course I wouldn't have bothered if what he had written wasn't so beautiful." Jackie paused. "And the name that was signed beneath it . . . I don't know if it was his name or the author's name, but it was quite exotic," Jackie added.

"It was Xenophon," Xavier said with a strange lack of emotion.

Miss Bea put her elbow on the table and leaned her forehead into her hand. "I hate to be a party pooper, but I'm just not feeling like myself this evening."

"I noticed you weren't saying very much," Jackie replied. "Do you want to go lay down on my bed for a little while?"

"No-o," Miss Bea said in a tired voice. "I think I need to go home. Maybe all the excitement with you coming back and everything has taken more out of me than I realized."

"Do you need me to drop you off?" Xavier offered.

"No, young man. You stay here and enjoy yourself. My house is right in back of here. As a matter of fact, our backyards touch." Miss Bea took a deep breath.

"Maybe Xavier can walk you to your door, Miss Bea," Vanessa offered. "I think we have all eaten our fill, and although I was thinking about eating another slice of your pineapple upside-down cake, I don't think my stomach would allow it."

"If it isn't any trouble," Miss Bea said softly.

Jackie's eyebrows furrowed with concern as she looked at her lifelong friend, who never accepted help.

"No trouble at all," Xavier replied.

"And we'll save you some of the leftovers," Jackie assured her.

"You better," Miss Bea said with some of her old spunk.

"Do you want to go for a ride after I get back?" Xavier gave the signal.

"Sure," Vanessa smiled, but suddenly looked away. "I'll help clear the table while you walk Miss Bea home."

Xavier ended up helping Miss Bea, because she was having difficulty getting up. Vanessa stood by her side. "Okay now. I want you feeling better than this when I see you tomorrow."

"You're such a sweetheart." Miss Bea touched Vanessa's cheek, then gave her a hug. "Always remember what I told you in the hall," she said with her arms still around her. "We all live vicariously through you. Be thankful for that young man of yours. He's the treasure."

Vanessa didn't know what to make of Miss Bea's departing words. "And you remember what I just told you. Better by tomorrow." She kissed Miss Bea's cheek for the second time that evening.

Miss Bea hugged all her old friends, holding on to Jackie the longest before she and Xavier walked out the door.

thirty-five

Xavier unlocked the door to his house and waited for Vanessa to step inside. Then he locked it behind them, put the keys down, and, without turning on the light, pulled her into his arms. All the questions that had been forming in Vanessa's head on the way over vanished with his heated kiss. He pressed her body against the wall with a hint of roughness, kissing her and calling her name. Vanessa had never known Xavier's desire to be so volatile. For a moment it frightened her, but the heat from his body ignited her own, and Vanessa writhed against him. Noises she didn't know she was capable of began to escape her lips.

"Xavier, what has gotten into you?" she rasped, and her desire increased. "You have no idea how you make me feel."

"Tell me," he replied huskily as he made wise

use of her short dress. "Tell me what I do to you, Nessa."

She tried to form the words, but they wouldn't come out. What words could adequately express the pleasurable feelings? "You start this fire inside of me." The words trembled. "And every time I feel it can't get any hotter, any more powerful, it does. My legs are so weak, and where you're touching me now is pulsating with pleasure, expanding until . . ." Vanessa could barely talk.

"Until I make you forget everything but me. Every other man. Every other moment." Xavier directed her body down to the couch beside the door. "I even want you to forget to think about the fire. Forget to think how powerful it is and simply feel me inside of you."

Vanessa's back arched with his entry, and with every part of her she obeyed Xavier's command. He moved within her with a fury that Vanessa had not known. She tried to hold on, but the onslaught was relentless. The sensations building so fast. "Oh, Xavier. I can't—I can't take this." Her words were broken.

"Take me, Vanessa. Take all of me," he rasped in her ear, his tongue tracing out the meaning of his words. "Every way I come to you, I want you to take me. With every move I make. With every part of me." His thrusts heightened, and Vanessa cried out from the intensity of it all.

"My God, Xavier. My God."

When they were done, every part of Vanessa's

body tingled. She didn't know if she could open her eyes. She was aware of Xavier lying heavily upon her. His heart racing. His breaths fast.

Slowly, Vanessa lifted her eyelids. "My God, Xavier," she repeated, as if they were the only words she knew.

His body stilled, a little. His breaths became more normal. His heartbeats, slower.

Vanessa's eyes adjusted to the moonlit room, and she touched his hair. Xavier raised his head and looked at her.

"That was like the devil possessed you," she said softly, looking at how their bodies hung off the couch.

He didn't say a word, but his eyes burned.

"What is it?" Vanessa asked.

He rolled away. "Nothing."

"Nothing?" Vanessa squinted with disbelief. "We haven't known each other long, but I know there is something." She tried to laugh. "Perhaps you just don't want to tell me."

Xavier remained on his knees next to the couch. He turned his face toward the lighted window.

Vanessa was beginning to feel blocked out. "Xavier, say something."

"I'll tell you when I'm ready," he finally said. "It has nothing to do with you."

"It does have something to do with me. You take me like some wild thing and afterwards you act like this? But you tell me there's nothing wrong. I don't believe you."

"Leave it alone, Vanessa," he said cryptically.

"What?" She couldn't believe he'd said that. "This has something to do with that man in the park, and the note my mother sent to you. The one that you never told me about. Yet you said it was one of the main things on your mind when you went to Australia."

"Maybe it was."

"Then why didn't you tell me?"

"You had enough on your mind, Vanessa, and frankly," he paused, "I didn't think it was any of your affair."

Vanessa was stunned. "None of my affair. But I thought . . . you made me feel, at least while we were in Australia—" She stopped abruptly. "And I thought you were helping me out of the goodness of your heart. Now I think you had a hidden agenda."

Xavier shook his head. "That's not true."

"What is true, Xavier?" Vanessa sat up. She was suddenly aware of the position of her dress. Self-conscious, she pulled it down.

"It was something that was on my mind. But there never seemed to be a time that was right for me to bring it up. Once, I tried, but . . . other more pressing issues took precedent, so I didn't pursue it until we got here."

"You didn't pursue it at all," Vanessa threw back at him. "My mother brought it up at the dinner table." She folded her arms. "Perhaps you were waiting for a time when the two of you could talk about it. It's obvious this was something that was *really* important to you, and you didn't want to discuss it with me."

"You are twisting this, Vanessa," he said in a tired fashion, but there was an underlying harshness.

"Then tell me what's going on and I won't have anything to twist."

Xavier got up and flipped on the light. He stood by the switch. "Do you really want to know?" His mouth was firm.

"Yes, I do." Vanessa shrank from his sudden movement.

"I think that man is my father."

"Your father," she repeated slowly.

"Yes. The 'homeless man,' as you referred to him, my father."

"You lied about your father being dead?" Her eyes filled with abhorrence.

He shook his head again. "No."

"Yes, you did. You told me he was dead." Vanessa looked at him with disbelief.

"It was sort of an agreement, a game that my mother and I played."

Now it was Vanessa's turn to shake her head.

"Now look at how you're looking at me," he snarled. "As soon as your perfect picture wasn't perfect any more."

"I simply don't understand what kind of cruel joke—" She glanced down.

"You want to hear cruel." Xavier walked over to her. "I'll tell you cruel. Cruel is seeing your father slip away from you, but he's still there. Cruel is being a little boy of five and running up to your dad and he doesn't recognize you. Cruel is having people say your dad is crazy and you're going to turn out just like your old man. That's cruel, Vanessa."

She got up from the couch. "Oh-h, Xavier."

"No. I don't need your pity now. Maybe a little while ago. But not now." His eyes turned to onyx.

"But you didn't explain it to me." She tried to touch his face. He walked away.

"I told you it was something my mother and I shared." His eyes were hard as he looked at her. "She found out early on it was easier to say my father was dead. And he *was* dead to us. He didn't even know us." Xavier looked away. "So my mother found a way to lessen the pain. After that I didn't have to explain the situation every time I went into a new class or neighborhood. Or when I met new people in junior high and high school. And especially not the folks in college. A lot of them like you coming from perfect little backgrounds, trying to make life and themselves perfect."

"I don't deserve that," Vanessa replied.

"And I didn't deserve that look you gave me."

"I know that now." Vanessa wanted to take it back.

"But you should have *known* it then. Known that there was a good reason, especially after all we've been through together."

"I'm sorry," she said softly.

"Well I'm sorry too."

Vanessa had never heard sorry sound so harsh.

"Maybe I gave you too much credit. Maybe I put you too high up on a pedestal. I'll never do it again."

Their eyes met before Vanessa looked away. An intense pressure formed in her chest. She had never been stabbed before, but now she believed she knew how it would feel. When Vanessa tried to look Xavier in the eyes again, she couldn't. "I need to use your bathroom and then I'll be ready to go."

"It's straight down the hall, on your left," Xavier said without offering to show her.

Vanessa managed to keep her head high until she closed the bathroom door. After that she cried as if she had been beaten. When she finally pulled herself together, enough to walk out again, she was grateful Xavier had turned off the lights and was standing in the open door. In silence he locked up. In silence he drove her home.

thirty-six

"Vanessa." Jackie tapped lightly on the bedroom door. "Are you still asleep?"

"I guess I was," she replied, feeling groggy.

"I'm about to go over and check on Bea. I didn't want you to find me gone this morning, and not know why."

"Okay." Vanessa tried to open her eyes, but they felt so puffy from crying that it was difficult. "Mama?"

"Yes." Jackie's voice sounded a little further away. "What time is it?"

"It's almost ten." There was a moment of silence. "Are you okay?"

Vanessa turned her face into the pillow as the tears started to flow again. She swallowed before she spoke. "I'm fine." She could visualize her mother standing in the hall weighing her response.

"I'll be back in a minute," Jackie finally said.

"All right."

Vanessa let her eyelids go back to where they wanted to be, closed. She felt weak, as if she had been through a major illness. Every time she thought of the words she and Xavier had shared, hot tears squeezed out of the corners of her eyes. They formed a stream across the bridge of her nose and puddled together on her already damp pillow. She touched the wet material with a shaky hand. Was it possible she could have been crying in her sleep? From the way she felt anything was possible. But on the other hand she hadn't slept much.

Vanessa was lying there feeling her own pain when she heard her mother scream.

"Nessa! Nessa!"

Vanessa ran out of her bedroom and met her mother in the dining area. "What is it?"

"It's Bea." Jackie's eyes filled with tears. "She's dead."

Vanessa clutched her chest. "Oh-h Mama."

With tears streaming down both their faces they reached out and held on, truly for dear life. At that moment Vanessa wasn't so sure life was dear or kind; maybe it was just a series of painful events.

Sniffing, Jackie was the first to pull away. "I've got to call . . ." She started turning from side to side. "I've got to call . . ."

Seeing her mother's distress, Vanessa gathered her strength. "I'll call the ambulance, Mama."

"Would you?" Bleak eyes met her own. "I got to get back to Bea. She wouldn't want those ambulance people seeing her like she is now. She'd want to look her best. That was so important to Bea. To always look her best."

"Yes it was." Vanessa tried to stop the tears from falling with her hands.

But Jackie just stood there as if she didn't know what to do next. Didn't realize what she had determined to do.

"You go back to Miss Bea," Vanessa prodded. "And I'll make the necessary phone calls."

"Yes. That's what I'll do." Jackie turned to walk toward the door, but she stopped and looked back. "I've known Bea since I was in high school, and you know what?" Her resigned gaze connected with Vanessa.

"What?"

"It seems like only yesterday." Jackie turned slowly and continued on her way.

Now Vanessa knew what people meant when they said you can keep going long after you can't. The pain of how she and Xavier had parted was still with her, but she could not let it get in the way. Hurriedly, she got dressed and called an ambulance. Next she went into the kitchen and put on some coffee and made preparations to cook, if the need arose.

The emergency vehicle was there in a matter of minutes, and before Vanessa knew it, she and her mother were standing with Lillie, Mrs. Bertha, and some other neighbors, watching it pull out with lights blazing.

"Would you all like some coffee and hot biscuits?" Vanessa offered the group of women, who were minus a very important part of them. They glanced at each other, shrugged, and mumbled. "Please come inside and let me fix you something. If only a cup of coffee," she insisted.

They did come inside, and coffee was a silent time with tears, endearing looks of friendship, and loss. When Lillie and Mrs. Bertha left, Jackie sat on the couch. She didn't turn on the television. She didn't pick up a book. She just sat there. Vanessa came and sat beside her.

"Why don't you go lay down, Mama."

"I don't want to lay down. Bea laid down last night and that was it. She died in her sleep."

"Just because it happened to her doesn't mean it's going to happen to you." She touched her mother's hand. "But it will happen to all of us one day." Vanessa hesitated. "You've recently said we shouldn't be afraid of something so natural. That death is a part of the life cycle."

"I'm not afraid of dying, Nessa." Jackie's eyes reassured Vanessa that she spoke the truth. "I'm more afraid of leaving you alone. I guess because it's been one of your biggest fears. The one you always tried to hide. But I knew it was there, born out of all the travelling your father and I did." Then Jackie's eyes brightened a tad. "But now of course Xavier is in your life, and I truly believe he is the one."

Vanessa looked away. She cursed the tear that couldn't wait to fall.

Jackie leaned to see her face. "Nessa. What's wrong, honey?"

Vanessa couldn't speak. She simply shook her head.

"Did something happen between you and Xavier when you left here last night?"

Vanessa sighed loudly. "Yes. We had a fight."

"About what?" Jackie became all mother.

"He thinks that man we saw on the bench is his father."

"I knew there was something going on there," Jackie said. "I knew it."

"Well, you may have known it, but there is no way that I could have because Xavier told me his father was dead. So you can imagine how shocked I was to hear he thought that man was his father." Vanessa wanted her mother to understand. "Later he explained he grew up being told that by his mother. He said he and his mother found it simpler to say his father was dead because of his dad's mental state. It just made things easier." She made a gesture to show her inability to understand. "I guess he felt I should have understood and that I betrayed him at the moment he needed me most." She closed her eyes. "And basically he said I would never get the opportunity to do it again. He would never trust me that much." Vanessa covered her face. "I'm sorry. You've got enough on your shoulders right now."

"No-o." Jackie placed her arm around her daughter. "This is what family is about. What friendship is about. Providing strength and love whenever it's needed." She squeezed Vanessa's shoulders. "Goodness, that must be hard," Jackie added softly.

"What?" Vanessa asked.

"Having someone as important as a parent so near but yet so far away."

"I don't know." Vanessa shook her head again. "It seems rather cruel that his mother decided to cope with his father's illness that way. To tell her child he was dead. To teach him to do the same."

"Don't judge her too harshly, Vanessa. You don't know what was going on between them at that time. What she had been through. What had colored her life for her to handle it that way. Sometimes it's easy to see the mistakes others have made, while our own are far more difficult to see."

Vanessa nodded. "It sure is a painful place for Xavier."

"And that's what you have to remember. When he said those things to you in anger that hurt you so bad, you've got to remember there was real pain beneath them." Jackie wiped her daughter's eyes with a crumpled piece of tissue she'd been holding in her hand. "I think men have more difficulty dealing with emotional hurts. We'll cry and find some release, but what they seem to do is lash out." Jackie sighed. "And to think Xavier's hurt has been building up since he was a little boy."

"Me of all people, I should be able to understand that," Vanessa replied. "But you know something good?" A tiny smile touched Vanessa's lips. "I think I have finally put my issues with you and Dad to rest."

"Truly?" Hope found a corner in Jackie's sad eyes.

"Yes. Seeing you go to Australia like you did and knowing your reason, I really understood you two loved each other. You weren't trying to hurt me when you left me behind. You were keeping the love you had together alive. For some couples that means sticking together and gathering the children around them. For others, holding the children in between. I know you did the best you could for me, Mama." Vanessa's teeth encased her bottom lip. "And you know who really brought it together for me?"

"Who?"

"Miss Bea." The name trembled when she said it. "Last night we had a little chat in the hall and she made me realize you and Dad were a great example of two people who loved one another."

"Bea." Jackie repeated the name softly. "She used to call your father and me her dream couple. When we first got together she said all we had to do was come around and everybody near us could feel our love. So whenever we did all that travelling . . ."

Vanessa nodded.

"She said I was following a dream. The dream of love. The man that had made my life so complete. I guess that's why the Australian Aboriginal Dreamtime called to me so. I thought if I followed that dream I would see your father again. And I did."

Vanessa looked down at her lap. "I guess the best thing I could do for Miss Bea is follow my dream, huh?"

"I think so. Keeping love alive is like the Dreaming. You have to sing about it. Dance about it. Speak wonderful, kind words . . ." Jackie's voice faded as she looked at a young portrait of Vanessa's father. When she looked at Vanessa again she said, "Search in your heart, Vanessa, and you'll find a way."

Afterward they sat on the couch and held hands in silence.

thirty-seven

Vanessa sat in her car, exhausted. For two days she had run in and out of Atlanta homeless shelters and crisis facilities, trying to find Xavier's father. Her search had turned up absolutely nothing. It was time for her to drive back to Columbus, but a pouring rain had just begun, and Vanessa decided to wait it out.

The rain wasn't the only reason she sat in front of the small building. Xavier was teaching a class for illiterate adults inside. A part of her wanted to wait until his class was over. Tell him what she had attempted to do. Tell him that she had secretly watched him through the window as he patiently, with care, tutored the men and women in need. But the rain had driven Vanessa inside her car. So she waited, her head back, her eyes closed, trying to make up her mind what to do.

When the sound and feel of the raindrops lessened, Vanessa prepared to drive away. She had decided it was no use to come to Xavier empty-handed. She wanted to do something for him like he had done for her when he'd helped her find her mother.

Vanessa released a resigned breath and reached for the car keys that were still in the ignition when a dark shadow next to the building caught her eye.

She tried to see through the rain. On closer examination, Vanessa realized the shadow was a man. He too was peering through the window, his body positioned not to see the class but to see Xavier.

Vanessa sat and watched him. He was impervious to the weather as he remained standing near the building. This was a man with a purpose, she thought. A man with clear intent. Vanessa's heart beat faster as she watched, and with each passing moment her conviction grew. No one would go to such lengths except one who loved another.

Vanessa got out of the car and walked rapidly toward him. So engrossed was he in his vigil that he did not realize Vanessa was approaching until she was at his side.

"Xenophon Johnson."

"Yes," he answered in that intuitive fashion that only a person responding to his own name will do. His eyes were a little too bright, but they were Xavier's eyes, and that was all that mattered to Vanessa.

"I'm so glad to meet you." She stuck out her hand with rain dripping down her face.

He smiled slightly and reached out a gloved hand with fingers escaping through several of the tips. "Me too."

They watched together as the class was dismissed, and Xavier was left in the building alone.

"I know he'd be so happy to see you," Vanessa said softly.

Xenophon began to shake his head in protest.

"I know he would because I love him too," Vanessa said. Xenophon's uncertain eyes searched her trusting ones. "Come inside with me, and let's say hello."

He looked unsure, then looked back through the window.

"He's waited for you a long time," Vanessa coaxed. "I'm sure you two could help one another."

"I could help him?" Hope blending with years of disbelief emanated from Xenophon's face.

Vanessa took his arm and started forward. "By just going up to him and saying his name."

Xenophon offered no further protest, and when they entered the building Xavier had his back to the door. He turned when he heard their footsteps, and his face became a mask. His eyes, though, were intense. Halfway down the aisle, Vanessa stopped. Xenophon looked at her.

"Go ahead, Mr. Johnson. Help your son," she said softly.

Xenophon continued alone until he stood in

front of his child. "Xavier," Vanessa heard him
say.

"Father?" Xavier took a few steps. There was a
tender youthfulness in his voice.

Xenophon Johnson moved his arms as if he
wanted to reach out to his son but didn't know
how. So it was Xavier who made the move.
Vanessa watched as Xavier first embraced his father's face with his eyes. Then, right before her
eyes, he reached out and pulled his father into his
arms. Again, Vanessa's tears began to flow. But
this time it was from pure satisfaction. She took a
couple of steps back. Vanessa had done what
she'd set out to do. She turned and left.

The next morning Vanessa helped her mother,
Lillie, and Mrs. Bertha prepare Miss Bea's house
for the reception after the funeral. None of Miss
Bea's family ever came forward, but no one was
surprised. Through the years everyone had as-
sumed she was an orphan because she'd never
spoken of any kin.

Despite the sad circumstances, Vanessa's heart
felt lightened by the events of the night before. If
she never gave Xavier anything else, Vanessa believed she had given him the greatest gift she
could ever give . . . except for a child. She chided
herself for such extreme thoughts. He wasn't
even speaking to her. A child would be a gift they
would give to one another, and under the current
circumstances the chances for that were very
slim.

Vanessa drove her mother to the funeral. As she sat behind the wheel she couldn't help but wonder why black was the chosen color for a funeral. How much more uplifting orange or yellow would have been. Miss Bea, for one, surely would have thought so. Vanessa knew that for a fact, for in Miss Bea's closet, totally encased in cleaner's plastic, was a red dress, accessories, and shoes. "My Funeral Attire" was pinned to it on a yellowed piece of paper. They had all wondered how long ago Miss Bea had made her choice.

Vanessa looked at her mother. "You ready?"

"I'm ready," Jackie replied.

They got out of the car and went inside. It was a small church that wouldn't hold many people, but those that would come would be there out of the purest sincerity.

Vanessa and Jackie took a seat on a pew with several other people.

"We were almost late," Jackie whispered.

"But we made it," Vanessa replied. She looked around the church. "Miss Bea would have loved these flowers."

"I'm sure she *is* enjoying them," her mother said.

This time it never crossed Vanessa's mind to dispute her.

She watched as one last standing floral arrangement was added. It was totally made of white roses except for a red rose heart in the center. Vanessa stared at the easel.

"I wonder who gave her that?" she said to her mother. "Isn't it beautiful?"

"It sure is. Whoever did it gave it a lot of thought," Jackie replied.

"Do you think Miss Bea had a male admirer?" Vanessa asked.

"She sure did." Xavier leaned forward from the pew behind them. "I admired her for her love of life, and how she didn't hold back when she spoke up for you the day we met."

Vanessa turned. "How did you know?" was all she said.

"Your mother told me." Xavier placed his hand on Jackie's shoulder.

Jackie and Vanessa's eyes met, and they shared a moment of true understanding.

"I'm glad you came," Jackie said.

"And so am I," Vanessa seconded. She placed her hand on top of his.

"And so am I," Xavier added.

The music began, and, with it, the ceremony.

thirty-eight

The funeral was over, and everyone began to file out of the pews. Xavier waited for Vanessa and Jackie. His eyes met Vanessa's watery ones, but no words were spoken.

"We're having food at Miss Bea's house. You're invited to come." Jackie wiped her eyes as she walked between them.

"Thank you. I'd like that," Xavier said.

They shuffled within the crowd.

"Will you be going to Miss Bea's house right away?" Xavier's eyes never left Vanessa's face.

"Right after we leave here. I've got to let everybody in," Jackie told him. "We don't want to make anybody wait."

When they were outside the church several people stopped to talk. Xavier stood beside Vanessa and secretly slipped her hand into his.

"We need to hurry, Vanessa," Jackie urged. "We want to be ready when the people come. Bea hated for people to be late."

"I'm ready, Mama." Vanessa squeezed Xavier's hand. "I'll meet you there," she told him.

He allowed her hand to drift through his fingers as she walked away. "Yes" was his only reply.

About ten minutes later Jackie unlocked Miss Bea's door and let several people inside the house. Lillie and Mrs. Bertha had also arrived. They busied themselves uncovering food dishes and removing others from the refrigerator, but overall things were well in hand. Several other offerings were brought by guests, and it was obvious that during her lifetime, Miss Bea had been loved.

Vanessa watched everything with a strange kind of detached feeling. It was surreal to be in Miss Bea's home without her there. It would be difficult to live life without her. Vanessa looked at her mother. She was standing over the table with a perplexed expression on her face. Vanessa went to her side. "What is it, Mama?"

"Something's missing." Jackie looked at the table. "I just don't know what it is." She swiped at a tear before she exclaimed, "I kno-ow. This table needs my African violets sitting right in the middle. Bea would get a kick out of that."

Vanessa kissed her mother on the cheek.

"What's that for?" Jackie's sad eyes were full of determination.

"For being a strong woman, a loving woman

who has never failed me even when I didn't know it."

Jackie gently leaned against her daughter.

"I'll go get the African violets," Vanessa volunteered. She looked around the adjoining room, then out the window for Xavier. But he was nowhere to be seen.

Disappointed, she cut through the backyard and unlocked her kitchen door. Vanessa went to her bedroom and placed the black hat she was wearing on her bed. When she returned, Xavier was standing in the kitchen.

"Xavier."

"Your mother told me I'd find you here." His gaze soaked in her face. "I hope you didn't mind my coming in like this. I know I'm not incapable of making mistakes. I made a big one the other night."

"Oh-h it's okay," she said quickly. The tenderness in his eyes was so raw that Vanessa couldn't stand to look in them.

"I want to thank you for giving my father back to me," he said softly.

Vanessa's smile was small and nervous. "He had come on his own, Xavier. I only encouraged him to let you know that he was there."

"I believe your encouragement made all the difference. He told me he'd watched me like that many, many times before." Xavier reached out and took her hand.

Vanessa looked down. Her hand was so small in his. "How is he?"

"Better," Xavier replied. "I took him to a mental health facility this morning. They say with medication he can lead a somewhat normal life, but it will have to be in an assisted care facility. I'm going to take care of that, and I'll be able to know where he is . . . to see him." Then he added, "Develop some kind of relationship."

"I'm glad for you, Xavier."

At that moment Vanessa thought of Dellia. The palm reader had been right about Xavier coming into her life, and their coming together at a time when they could help each other. But only time would tell if their childhood wounds were really healed.

Silence filled the kitchen, and the energy between them was so intense that Vanessa couldn't stand it.

"I came to get the African violets," she said, filling the space with nervous chatter. "Miss Bea always coveted these old plants. I don't know why." She let go of his hand and reached for the plants.

"It's easy to covet a thing of beauty," Xavier said softly as he pulled her to him. "And you are beautiful, Vanessa, inside and out."

"There you go saying the perfect thing again." She looked into his eyes. Vanessa loved the love she saw there.

Xavier held her close and placed his head on top of hers. "Let's enjoy our perfect moment. Because if we stay together long enough, I'm sure

these moments will come and go. But I intend to
stay as long as you'll have me," he ended softly.

Vanessa paused. "I will have you for this lifetime, Xavier, and if God's willing, many, many
more."

She thought of her father and Miss Bea.
Vanessa thought of the children that were to
come, and their ancestors, and their children, and
at that moment it all was one continuous circle.
One Dreaming that would last for eternity.

MAYBE BABY

by

ELAINE FOX

Dr. Delaney Poole thinks Harp Cove, Maine, will be
the perfect place to settle down and raise her infant
daughter . . . but this single mom feels duty bound to
keep the gossips at bay and invent a husband. But
what happens when sexy Jack Shepard, her baby's
father, walks unsuspectingly back into her life? And
what will happen to their budding romance when the
truth comes out?

ACA 0701